I Owe My Soul

The Black Diamond Covenant

Diane Mechem Kinser

PublishAmerica
Baltimore

First printing

ISBN: 1-60563-239-2 (softcover)
ISBN: 978-1-4489-0854-7 (hardcover)
PUBLISHED BY PUBLISHAMERICA, LLLP
www.publishamerica.com
Baltimore

Printed in the United States of America

This work is dedicated first to my grandchildren Alicia and Taylor Harris, who cheerfully went with me on many research trips, stomping through old coal mines, seeking out the ghost town of San Toy, and visiting stops on the Underground Railroad, some of them haunted. Only Alicia could see the ghosts, but she convinced me! Carrying chunks of coal around in their pockets was simply "above and beyond." They are my heart.

Second, I dedicate this to the memory of my wonderful grandparents, Mary and Walter Mechem, the prototypes for Mary Rose and Billy Blake Markham. It was their unconditional love which brought me to Nelsonville in the first place, their business acumen which allowed me to write of those early days of merchandising, their inspiration which allowed me to get inside the hearts and souls of those whose lives were bound to the whims of the coal-mining industry.

"St. Peter, don't you call me 'cause I can't go. I owe my soul to the company store."

–"Sixteen Tons"
written by Merle Travis in 1947
performed by Tennessee Ernie Ford

PART 1—MARY ROSE

Chapter 1 – Encounter

[September 1903]

She rode like an Indian, confidently, with her hair streaming behind her and her face raised to the wind. There the similarity stopped, however. This young woman was as blond as the silks of the corn peeping from the field as she passed, and her eyes reflected the sky. In spite of the bonnets she usually wore, the summer sun had tanned her arms and her cheeks enough that the glow made her even more stunning than normal. She seemed unaware of her beauty and that fact added even more to her appeal.

It was always an amusing sight to see Mary Rose Knight galloping her chestnut across hill and dale; she looked so fragile, like a butterfly atop a wooly mammoth—but there was nothing fragile about the young woman. She loved to ride, anytime, anywhere.

On this Saturday morning, the young schoolteacher was enjoying her time off from school. She had volunteered to do the family marketing in nearby Caldwell, mainly for the excuse to ride her beloved mare Sylvia seven miles in the glorious Ohio late September sunshine. When she rode willy-nilly across the hills, she felt free and powerful.

As she rode, she thought of her students, what kind of lives they had outside the classroom, if they had enough to eat, proper clothing to wear. Times were tough for many of them with the problems the mines were having. The families depended totally on the mines for their survival, and on their patch gardens. Mary Rose had volunteered for this trip, planning to keep her eye out for any bargains she could find which might help children like the Middletons. Don and Ann Middleton were struggling to feed their five children; more so since Don had been laid off from the mine.

Not that her parents would object to her generosity, but it embarrassed Mary Rose sometimes for them to know she was feeding and clothing a few children as well as tending to their education. Schoolteachers didn't make a lot of money...but Mary Rose stretched every dollar, made it seem like two.

The traveler had already made one stop, at a tiny roadside market which displayed knit sweaters made by an elderly lady who brought them in to sell. As if the accident in the mine hadn't been enough of a hardship for the miners' children, now an epidemic of measles had reduced the work force of one mine by another ten men, desperately sick as adults can be with measles. Two breaker boys had died of this disease; three trappers were now sick, so the mine, which had just reopened from the accident was now closed again until the sickness passed.

It was so easy to pass disease in the closed, stifling atmosphere of a coal mine; if one man was sick, most would become sick soon. Mines closed to prevent the rampant spread of a deadly disease, but miners so hated to miss work that they often camouflaged their illness as long as they could, spreading the disease anyway.

Although it was still in the eighties that late September morning, Mary Rose remembered that Ohio temperatures can drop overnight by thirty degrees. Several of her charges would be in dire straits for warmer clothing, since the miners' budgets were already stretched past the breaking point. Mary Rose bought three sweaters, stuffed them into the huge saddle bags she carried when taking Sylvia instead of the more practical family buggy for her shopping adventures. Now she was cantering at top speed again as the business district of Caldwell came into view.

* * *

Billy Blake Markham just happened to be sweeping in front of the general store which he ran with his father on this fateful late September morning in 1903. Hearing the thunderous clopping of hooves, he looked up with a touch of fright just as Mary Rose Knight pulled hard on the reins, bringing her horse to a sudden stop amid a cloud of dust. The graceful horse virtually slid to the rail in front of Billy, alarming him that he just might have a horse as part of his window dressing! Annoyed, Billy Blake wiped dust from his eyes and turned around to see who had perpetrated such silliness.

As the dust cleared, and the rider alighted, his eyes fell upon her face, flushed and happy, and he felt his heart lurch, and not just from the scare he had just had. She had been in the store before, this spirited creature, with her mother or her sisters, but somehow she had escaped his notice. He couldn't imagine now how that had been possible. This time her entrance was too much to miss…and so was she. Slightly disheveled by the wind in her curls, her bonnet flapping against her back, Mary Rose Knight was simply the most heart-stopping vision the young man had ever seen. Not often distracted from his work by lovely young women who found him attractive and fussed and flirted to capture his attention, this moment was different: he was distracted indeed! He recognized to his embarrassment that he was standing gaping, with his mouth open when she spoke to him: "Good morning, Mr. Markham. May I tie Sylvia here? I won't be long…"

"Um…yes…um…it's all right…uh…" he stammered out, his mouth dry. Summoning extra effort, he continued, "Yes, ma'am, that will be just fine…" and then stopped, red-faced and totally without vocabulary. With an exaggerated effort, he put his broom back in motion, dramatically sweeping the small avalanche of dust from her equally dramatic entrance back into the street, then purposefully leaned the broom against the outer wall.

Amused, Mary Rose smiled, nodded to him, reattached her bonnet covering the cascade of golden curls, and passing close to the stone-struck young man, entered Markham's General Store. Realizing that he had been staring open-mouthed at her again, Billy Blake shook his head to restore his senses, snapped his jaws shut and entered his father's store just behind the object of his fascination.

"Is there something I can help you with? I mean, can I give you something…I mean…" the usually quiet but eloquent 22-year-old attempted. "Drat!" he thought, "I'm never this stupid around girls…"

"Oh, indeed. You may assist me with several things," she replied. She had just discovered the effect she was having on the man's concentration and was enjoying her own part of this little game they seemed to have been drawn into. Mischievously, the tiny woman stepped closer to the young man who towered over her by at least a foot, raised her eyes to meet his, discovering to her shock that she was looking into eyes the mirror image of hers, achingly blue, intelligent and playful. And she stared. At that moment, time began to spin out of control, as their eyes locked for the first time, and he found himself engulfed in her scent, lilac, sunshine, and woman. It is possible that both of them knew the significance of this moment; nevertheless, Billy Blake Markham was the first to break the connection between them, as he asked hoarsely, "What did you need, Miss Knight?" hoping her shopping list was outrageously long.

Drawn back to reality, Mary Rose pulled her list from her riding skirt pocket, moved away with difficulty—from Billy Blake toward the counter; he, with concentrated effort, stepped behind the very same counter. Efficiently, she moved through her list as if it were a school assignment—flour, salt, soda, blue thread, needles… Efficiently, he filled her order, in the mechanical way he was able to do from years of practice. Goods piled up on the counter. The shopping was getting done, little by little, with brief interruptions for a quick stolen glance, first hers toward his strong back, then his toward her amazing hair. They both pretended that they were transacting business as normal. It was clear, nonetheless, that something in the atmosphere remained charged, as if a lightning storm had just ravaged the store.

Packaging her groceries and dry goods for her, accepting her payment, giving back her change…all were routine actions. There was nothing routine, however, about the strangely oppressive feeling in his chest, which was making it difficult for him to breathe. Thinking of ways to prolong her visit, he cleared his throat of its hoarseness and said, "Miss Knight, have you seen the new book corner I created? Since you're a teacher…you are a teacher, aren't you?…you might enjoy spending a moment there. You could give me your opinion of the department…" Stepping from behind the counter, he motioned for her to follow him, silent pleading in his eyes.

Grateful for an excuse to continue this encounter, Mary Rose followed, replying, "What a clever thing to do, Mr. Markham! I had no idea…" A misty place was beginning to form in her mind, one of which she was as yet unaware, but the thoughts tumbled willy-nilly: "He likes books! Who would ever have thought? He knows I am a teacher. He knows I would like his books. He…He is amazing. He…"

The book corner was a delightful surprise, the second one she had today, cozy and inviting, with two comfortable rocking chairs placed on a small rug. It had a wooden table covered with magazines, and bookshelves filled with an array of wonderful books, classics, mostly, on both walls of the corner. A tiny pot-bellied stove in the precise corner of the nook was just the perfect finishing touch. The area had ambience, the feel of a safe haven, comforting, warm, very nurturing, like a place one could return to after a hard day at work to share a peaceful moment with a loved one. Mary Rose Knight smiled one of her dazzling smiles, looked up into those amazing eyes and said softly and sincerely, "It's wonderful, Mr. Markham. You seem to have thought of everything. May I sit for a moment?"

He thought, "For a moment? How about for a year? Or forever…" but he said, "Please, I would be honored…" and motioned for her to take one of the chairs. She crossed to the first bookshelf, quietly running the tip of her finger over the gold letters on the spines of the books, nodding as she recognized and approved of the selections he had made. She caressed the beautifully sanded and polished wood of the shelf Billy Blake had crafted himself, and finally settled with a contented sigh into the nearest rocker. Watching her, his heart wasn't working quite right...his mind, not at all...

Giving in to his need to prolong this moment with her in any way he could, in an unprecedented move, he took the other rocker, thankful that no other customers were in need of his attention. He picked up a copy of *Tale of Two Cities* and began to leaf through it, enjoying the quiet, the innocent intimacy of their tableau. It felt so natural, so right, so pre-ordained, there in their two matched chairs, wordlessly rocking and reveling in each other's presence, surrounded by books.

As she reached for an exquisite leather-bound edition of *Wuthering Heights*, Mary Rose, a woman who rarely sat still, noticed too how right it felt to be sharing this corner, these twin chairs, this silence...this moment with this man. She had always loved silence but men, she noted, always seemed to have to be doing, just doing anything, busy stuff. A man one could be silent with...what an unexpected blessing! Her fingers turned the pages, but her mind was lost to blue eyes, a quiet power, a comforting strength...and she knew, beyond any doubt, her heart was lost as well.

Chapter 2 – Post-Encounter

[September 1903]

Sometimes when a person meets the individual who is to be his destiny, it takes a while to know it. Not this time! Mary Rose Knight headed home after her "encounter" with Billy Blake Markham a very different woman than she was when she slid to a dramatic stop in front of his store. Instead of galloping Sylvia in her usual breakneck manner, the 12-mile trip back home was leisurely, more trot than gallop—but her mind was galloping indeed! Sylvia, puzzled by the gentle touch from her usually aggressive rider, snorted more than once, looked over her shoulder, signaled "Let's go" in her equine way—but to no avail. Her rider was there in body only; the normally self-possessed Mary Rose Knight was somewhere else, a very special somewhere else.

At the fork of Duck Creek, two branches break off east and west, not far from the beginning of one of the most popular routes of the Underground Railroad a half-century earlier. Mary Rose, her head in the clouds, reined Sylvia in, letting her drink from the creek while she, Mary Rose, perched on a large, flat-topped rock, slipped off her shoes and dangled her toes in the chilly creek. Her mind raced: "That man, that beautiful man…He really saw me…he wasn't flirting at all…he just SAW me, and listened to me…books! A man who likes books…and being quiet…should I go back? Could it be… Am I being a silly girl?"

But Mary Rose was rarely a "silly girl" and she sensed that the unexplainable connection she had felt with Billy Blake Markham was meant as a signal. The non-verbal aspect of communication was the most intensely exhilarating in this new and exciting experience, the silent closeness, the enjoyment of sharing space and air, the recognition of something charged and vibrant which had enveloped her during the brief encounter with this charismatic man. It wasn't like violins playing; there were no cymbals crashing. What there was instead was a sense of harmony and balance which overrode the electrical magnetism which she had felt in his presence.

Looking wistfully about her, noticing her surroundings as if they had miraculously just appeared, Mary Rose raised her face to the late September sun. She closed her eyes and breathed in the scents of early fall, the faintest hint of drying leaves, pine needles underfoot, the slightly fishy but not unpleasant smell of the creek which emptied into the Ohio River a few dozen miles south, and pictured playful blue eyes. The creek murmured a greeting to her as she settled in, a hypnotic, rhythmic whisper which, had she been less emotionally charged, could easily have lulled her to sleep.

The sky, at its bluest in September with the most perfect clouds and a radiant sun to warm the air just enough, this time of year, Indian summer, was always her favorite. Even as a child, Mary Rose had loved to run barefoot through the leaves, inhale the woodsy, slightly musky scents of autumn and revel in the radiance of the sun whose rays were no less energizing for being lower in the sky. As she absent-mindedly tossed a pebble into the dark water and watched the ripples echo out, out, out, she allowed her mind free rein.

"This place has so much history," she thought to herself, imagining for a moment the huge wooden boats with cargo holds filled, not with goods for market, but with human cargo, men, women, children seeking a new life of freedom. She could almost feel their presence, smell their fear, these brave adventurers who had forged a path for others to follow, a path which cost many their lives but offered hope to others. Freedom, man's most precious gift, what America means…and it was their gift to their children. Those thoughts always humbled Mary Rose.

She thought too, as she always did in this pristine location, about the Indians who had paddled birchbark canoes up this same creek in earlier centuries, who had shared the land comfortably with the deer, the beaver, the other of God's creatures, knowing as no man had recognized since that the land and the water were only theirs to borrow, never to own or to plunder. She imagined a strong, silent man with weathered red skin, hair black and silky blowing in the breeze off the creek, standing where she now sat, gazing north, head held high testing the wind, deciding where to make camp…or perhaps, where to call home. This peaceful spot must have been used by many before her, to think, to make decisions, just to clear the cobwebs from the brain. The image of the red man faded; black hair changed to light brown; brown eyes changed to crystal blue…and there he was again, just behind her eyes. She closed her eyes to cherish a moment longer the unbidden vision…

Above her a golden hawk circled, eyeing her, deciding she was not prey, and moving on to a more advantageous hunting spot. To her left she could see, when she opened her emotion-laden eyes, an avalanche of rocks which led down further into the creek and sunning itself on one of them, a tiny green lizard, who also eyed her but found her no threat, and thus continued its nap. Beside Mary Rose, Sylvia snorted in the unexpected pleasure of a respite by the creek, shaking her head, water droplets flying everywhere, startling the lizard who disappeared in an instant; the gentle chestnut mare lowered her head to drink again, moving closer to Mary Rose, who reached out her hand, caressing the mare's ankle, whispering, "Soon, girl, just a few moments more…"

As the sun reached its zenith, the sojourner recognized that more time had passed than she had intended to spend. With great effort, Mary Rose roped in her unruly mind which had jumped fence, and recaptured her shoes, choosing to put them in the saddle bag and continue her journey barefoot, a guilty pleasure, one not enjoyed since she had become a teacher. "Sometimes being a grownup is no fun at all," the teacher on holiday mused. Grasping the reins and saddle horn, she mounted Sylvia, took one last appreciative look at the wooded haven she was leaving, sighed and resumed her journey, more peaceful, perhaps, but certainly not more decided about her next step. Billy Blake Markham…yes, he is part of the next step, she acknowledged with a dreamy smile.

* * *

The afternoon shadows had just begun to reach Markham's General Store, cooling the air quickly as happened in early fall. Pulling his grandfather's watch from his pocket, Billy Blake noted that it was time to begin the Saturday afternoon closing process…and wondered where the last two hours had gone! His usual sharp focus was lost in a fog, a fog with golden curls, a musical laugh, a gentle touch. Discovering that he had just cleaned and polished the same panel of door glass for the second time, the young storekeeper focused with great effort on his chores, usually enjoyable, but this time, requiring an amazing effort of concentration.

He worked efficiently for awhile, but every so often, caught himself standing totally still, staring off into space…remembering the scent of her, of spring lilac mingled with fresh air, and his breath caught in his chest. Moving on to the next task with lightning speed and over-focused effort, he caught up for awhile and then…off he went again on a journey in his mind. Not an unpleasant place to journey, nevertheless, this sentimental type of thing was not at all characteristic of the efficient, focused Billy Blake Markham, shopkeeper. "Billy, get your head back on business," he thought to himself, "this will never do. We have things to do here."

But his cleaning tasks had brought him from the front of the store to the rear, circling ever closer to the reading corner and there he stopped, mesmerized by the image, by the sense, of the two of them, rocking side by side, silent but filling each other's air space…and he felt an unfamiliar but very pleasant thrill beginning in his chest and traveling up and down his spine, as the reading center pulled him in and back in time. With no consciousness of motion, his hand reached out to caress the shelf her hand had caressed and he imagined that he could feel her there, her presence, her aura. His fingers followed the route hers had taken earlier, over the spines of the classic books, outlining the gold printing, smoothing the supple, aged leather and finally they found their way to the back of the chair which had held her. Holding her… He stopped there, allowing himself to imagine what it would feel like if he were to hold her, to touch her hair, her face…and he was jolted by the power of that image. She appeared before him as if by magic; he remembered the lilt of her laughter, the way her voice got all husky when she met his eyes and found him, strangely misty, following her every move.

So mesmerized was he by this amazing, mystifying visual memory, so real he felt he could reach out and her golden curls would be at his fingertips…that he didn't hear his father come in the back door, didn't notice Edward staring at his eldest son in puzzlement until his voice startled the young man out of his reverie: "Are you all right, son? You look…I don't know, pale or something…" This was so totally unlike the solid, efficient, focused Billy Blake that Edward was downright alarmed. Edward was an exceptionally intuitive father, and he felt that he was in the presence of a profound moment.

Embarrassed, Billy met his father's questioning eyes, allowed a whimsical smile to grace his lips, and nodded, just nodded silently.

"Billy, what's wrong? You are acting really odd…" the concerned father queried, moving closer to his son and reaching out to grasp his upper arm.

"No, Dad, I'm fine. Really. Fine. Just fine…"

"Are you sure? Do you want to talk about anything?" the astute elder Markham offered.

"Not much to say, Dad. I just…well, I just met the woman I'm going to marry."

* * *

Mary Rose decided to trot the rest of the way home, enjoying the breeze in her face, letting her bonnet flap against her back, unconcerned about the tanning effect of the sun and in no hurry at all. Her smile felt funny; she imagined what someone would say, seeing her smiling like that, at nothing at all. "They would think I have totally lost my mind," she mused, and made up her mind to stop smiling like an idiot. That resolve lasted about thirty seconds and she felt the corners of her mouth pulling upward as if they had a mind of their own. That struck her as really funny and she giggled, then laughed, and then whooped, startling Sylvia into a canter. Letting Sylvia take her head, the skilled rider galloped over the rolling foothills of the Appalachian Mountains, the grateful horse enjoying the exercise but puzzling over the peculiar behavior of her owner.

Coming within sight of the farm on which Mary Rose had been raised, she slowed Sylvia to a trot, smoothed down her wild batch of curls, reattached her bonnet, and debated about the wisdom of riding in helter-skelter, and barefoot at that...and decided, "Oh, fiddle, anyway. They know I'm crazy sometimes..." and left her shoes tied across her saddle bags. Dismounting just inside the log gate and walking Sylvia toward the barn, Mary Rose made concentrated effort to discipline her unruly thoughts, to focus on removing the saddle bags loaded with groceries...oh, from Markham's! leapt into her thoughts...brushing and wiping down her favorite horse, putting Sylvia in her stall to feed and giving her a carrot to enjoy, but her mind kept drifting back to eyes which seemed to see into her soul, the quiet presence which nevertheless filled all the space and energized all the air in his radius...and finally, she gave up acting normal, knowing she would never be "normal" again. That recognition, although it frightened her with its enormity, at the same time, calmed her, brought her a feeling of inevitability, and the certainty that something terribly profound had taken place today in her life, in her heart.

Grabbing the heavy grocery sacks out of the saddle bags and tossing her shoes, tied together, over her shoulder, she strode barefoot through the back porch door and into the Knight family's large, airy kitchen, letting the screen door bang, startling the cat which had been dozing, as cats do, in a patch of sunlight.

As she put the food away in the cabinets, her younger sister Sue, who had been working at her needlepoint until the slamming door alerted her that her best friend and sister had reappeared, came into the kitchen, chattering away in her usual cheerful and distracted manner: "Hi, Sis. I see you're back. Is it warm out? Oh, did you remember my blue thread? Mary, you have to see this new pattern I am working on! It is so pretty, but a little hard, it makes my eyes water with the tiny stitches. It's a waterfall...Come see it when you are finished here, will you..."

And stopped talking as rapidly as she had begun, her mouth hanging open, shocked as Mary Rose slowly turned to acknowledge her sister... "Mary, what's wrong? You look like you saw a ghost, or a vision, or...what's wrong?"

Mary Rose realized she must be wearing that involuntary, sappy smile which had attached itself to her with no will of her own a few hours ago, and she met Sue's eyes, turning the smile into one more like what her sister would expect. "Nothing's wrong, sweetie. Everything's right, really right with the world!"

Considering that strange response, Sue stepped in closer, studied her beloved sister's face, her own face scrunching up in bewilderment, and felt reassured that Mary wasn't sick or anything, but she was totally baffled at the distant and misty expression in her eyes, on her lips. "Okay, if you're okay, what's going on? Come on, put that flour down and tell me what's going on."

Mary Rose turned back to the flour canister, and began busying herself with emptying her new purchase into it, as she answered her sister's question: "What's going on? Well, not much. Just that this afternoon, I met the man I am going to marry, that's all."

Chapter 3 – They Came to Nelsonville

[August 1907]

They rode into Nelsonville just after six in the evening, over dusty roads of clay, packed tight after the March flood. Billy Blake Markham looked at his wife's tired face, the strain of the journey taking its toll, but still she smiled up at him, her eyes filled with love, and he felt humble. She never complained, his wonderful, tough wife. They were all tired, even the horses. Myrtle was the horse chosen from the stable to pull the wagon, and Sylvia, Mary Rose's beloved saddle horse was tethered in the rear. On they had plodded, none of them wanting to stop until they reached their new home.

"Papa. Papa," came from the rear of the wagon. Two-year-old Frankie awoke as the cadence of the horses' hooves changed, clopping noisily on the packed clay of the road leading into Nelsonville, the town which was destined to be their new home. "Hungwy, Papa…"

"Hello, son. You didn't sleep very long," Billy Blake called to his boy. "Come on up, squirt. We'll be stopping soon."

Mary Rose smiled and kissed Frank's sweaty cheek as he scrambled to the front of the wagon bed and over into the seat between his parents. "Mama's hungry too, Frankie. We'll find a place to stop. Just sit here with Mama for a few minutes." He snuggled, still sleepy, against her side. She looked around to get her bearings.

Billy Blake watched her face go through a gamut of emotions as she viewed the messy-looking dried clumps of mud adhering strangely to the trunks of trees, broken branches still mixed with the mud, remnants of a raging flood which had stolen homes, businesses and barns and destroyed lives. "What are you seeing, dear?" Billy asked gently.

"…such a tragedy. Those poor people." She needed to say no more. Billy understood.

He had a nearly psychic connection with this bright, sensitive woman, his wife of three years. "Indeed. I know. Over a hundred, wasn't it?"

This was the road, Billy Blake knew, the one which ran along the well-traveled Hocking Canal, which had been six feet under water only five months earlier. His father had written, telling how the Hocking River had rejected its restrictive banks and run amok, swollen to twelve feet above flood stage by the melting of the biggest February snowfall on record, followed by five days of torrential rains. Even opening all the locks between Logan and Cincinnati to their fullest extent hadn't warded off the devastation of ravaging flood waters.

As Mary Rose looked around, her face clouded, she saw lives lost in the raging torrent—children, cattle, dogs, bloated in death. "More than that. Nearly two hundred." Shaking off, with effort, the grisly image, Mary Rose put her arm around Frank, who was playing quietly with the wooden wagon his uncle Stewart had made for him. The baby Elizabeth began to fuss, from her cradle. "Well, that's everyone heard from. Can we stop for just awhile? The children are hungry…I need to feed the babies…I know you want to find the house, but…"

"Yes, just let me pull over by those maples. You'll have some shade there and I can water Myrtle and Sylvia. They're good old girls, aren't you, ladies?" And the weary father guided their horses off the road to a clearing near the canal, helped his wife down from the dusty wagon and turned back to reach for Frank.

"Papa, Papa, doggie…"An unappetizing shaggy-looking mongrel had come up to greet Myrtle and then, bored, moved off to scratch at his fleas languidly in the late summer heat. In his father's arms, Frank wiggled, trying to get loose to go to the dog, but Billy Blake held on. Frank could find an animal wherever they went. His mother wasn't always thrilled with the menagerie her son proudly presented to her, snakes, half-dead birds, chipmunks. Fortunately, the unhealthy-looking dog had lost interest in them and moved on, saving Billy an argument.

"See, son, he needs to be by himself. Let's help Mama get the blanket spread out so she can feed you and Betsy. There, that's Papa's big boy!" And Frank, disappointed, but obedient, tugged on the red blanket which had crept out of the wagon's trunk.

It was 1907, late August, and very hot, as Ohio usually is that time of year, even at that time of evening. It was much like the September day in 1903 when Mary Rose had slid into his life, changing it forever. In spite of the heat and his fatigue, the memory brought a sly smile to Billy Blake's lips as he wiped his brow with a stained and drenched handkerchief. He helped Mary Rose, who still had one arm full of whimpering, wiggling baby, to spread the blanket under the trees, Frankie pulling ineffectively at one corner. She settled against a tree trunk with a sigh. He knew his wife was worn out; the baby was only six months old and Mary Rose had had a rough time bringing their Betsy into the world. Her strength was not back to normal, but she rarely complained. He felt guilty about this journey…so long, so hot, so unwanted by her. She had always been spirited…defiant, almost, but these last six months had sapped her strength and her spirit. She just wasn't her usual playful, teasing self; it seemed to be all she could do to make it through her daily chores without tears of exhaustion or frustration. Billy Blake's heart ached when he thought these thoughts…his little spit-fire Mary Rose. Lord willing, she would be back…

Shaking off the melancholy, Billy Blake searched his overall's pocket, finding the well-drawn, detailed map his father had sent to him to help them find their way to the house he had located for them. It would be their temporary home while their permanent house, their dream house, across town was being built. Edward had told his son that the house wasn't elegant, but was "sound," with plenty of room for the growing family. As a bonus, it had a shed for Myrtle and Sylvia, the only horses the Markhams were bringing along. The others were being boarded in Caldwell at the home of a kind church elder with extra stalls, much to Mary Rose's dismay…she loved her horses. Billy knew this separation made the move even harder for Mary Rose.

* * *

Mary Rose Markham fought hard to hide the fatigue which had her fighting tears. As she looked at her husband's worried face, she knew she was the source of his worry. "This can't be," she thought to herself, forcing her back to straighten and her face to form something resembling a smile. "I'm okay, Billy. Really I am. I just need to get a second wind…"

He looked at her doubtfully, bending over to capture a blond curl which always managed to escape from any bonnet or headdress she was wearing. She grabbed his hand and pulled it to her lips, holding it there in a wordless gesture. He relaxed slightly and walked toward the canal to check on the horses. Relieved, Mary Rose allowed herself to slump against the tree. "It's time for some serious self-talk, Mrs. Markham," she told herself. "This move is important to all of us…"

She hated leaving Caldwell and their first home. She hated leaving her mother and father, her two sisters, her horses. She hated leaving Duck Creek and the rich farmland she had grown up on.

She remembered, though, how much she had also hated leaving her school and her students three years earlier, yet from that fateful moment when she had looked into Billy Blake Markham's eyes, she knew her teaching days were numbered. She had finished out that, her first and last year, and bid her charges a tearful goodbye. The memory rushed back: packing her meager desk items into her father's wagon that misty day in May of 1904 with seventeen disappointed students and a handful of parents gathered around. The sun had glinted off her engagement ring; she dried her tears as she looked ahead to her much-anticipated future with her Billy. She had never regretted her choice, not for one instant. Her husband was indeed her soul mate. So, Mary Rose Knight Markham had learned to trust that things happen for a reason, and for now, the horses stayed behind but the junior Markhams must move on.

Nevertheless, until she and her family determined that the Nelsonville move was a permanent one, Mary Rose was reluctant to sell even one of the four additional horses...she knew that was the only humane alternative in the long run, though, and that she was just postponing the inevitable.

* * *

Approaching their new residence, Billy Blake knew instinctively that the house would be more than just "sound." He trusted his father's judgment in all things, business and personal. They thought alike, father and son; their business partnership flourished because of common values and mutual trust. Father and son were also a rare entity: true friends as well.

Turning to Mary Rose, Billy Blake asked, "Do you need to stop at the market for anything? It's right up ahead. We should be at the house in a half-hour or so...see, there's the market Dad told us about..."

"No, dear, we can do that tomorrow—I have enough for now. I just want to get to our home and get the children settled for the night. Do you know where to go?" Looking around warily at her unfamiliar surroundings, Mary Rose looked fearful.

"Why, Mary Rose Markham, have I ever gotten us lost?" he joked. His sense of direction was nearly uncanny, and her father-in-law gave very clear directions.

"No, dear, pardon the momentary insecurity." She squeezed his hand.

Nelsonville had become the home of the senior Markhams, Edward and Elizabeth, six months earlier while they established the new dry goods store. Finding the town both profitable and much to their liking, they felt confident asking their son to bring his young family to make a new start. Billy Blake knew that the dry goods store was too much work for his father alone—long, tedious hours of retail merchandising—and he felt no hesitation coming to assist. It was Mary Rose whom he worried about, her health, her state of mind. Her discomfort at the thought of leaving behind all they had known since they had met four years earlier was evident in her strained expression every time they discussed the upcoming venture. But even his concern for her and his bone-aching fatigue couldn't eclipse the excitement he felt to know that this store would soon be his! It was the day he had waited for for years, the one for which he had prepared with long hours and many headaches, back in Caldwell.

* * *

As the horse and wagon plodded on, Mary Rose dozed fitfully. She was determined to keep looking ahead to their new adventure instead of looking back with sorrow.

True, Mary Rose hadn't wanted to come. She was settled in their first home in Caldwell, the tiny four-room cottage Billy Blake had taken her to as a bride. Nevertheless, she too knew it had been rough on Edward running the new store with only Stewart to help. Stewart was enthusiastic, but Edward was used to having Billy Blake's quiet strength and unflagging energy to draw on. Mary Rose loved and respected Edward. She knew he would never ask for Billy's help if he didn't really need it and if he didn't think it would be good for Billy Blake and his family, in the long run.

Elizabeth had never liked working in the store, Mary Rose knew; a shy and quiet woman, she did it only rarely, when Edward was too exhausted from the ten-hour days managing the store alone, and she was relieved when Edward hired spinster sisters Audrey and Lillian to help wait on customers.

Two children were still at home with Elizabeth, Stewart and Charley; Stewart had been helpful, smart with the inventory and friendly with customers—he seemed to have the Markham instinct. But after all, he was only sixteen, although his height made him look older, and school would be starting in two weeks. Thus, Billy Blake's young family was making the journey in the oppressive August heat, to relieve Stewart from his store duties and let him return to the role of school boy. Mary Rose's compassion for her in-laws made her determined not to make too much of a fuss about moving; she knew it was the right thing to do. She also knew intuitively that this was the chance Billy had been waiting for, and she wanted it for him.

Thinking out loud, she said, "It's too bad Harry doesn't like the business. He is so smart…but that's book smart, not people smart."

"I know. He's going to be a famous lawyer. Maybe he can be the lawyer for the future Markham Enterprises, what do you think? My brother, Harry Joseph Markham, Esquire…has a nice ring, doesn't it?" Billy responded.

"Maybe so. That will be good."

Harry, the brother between Billy Blake and Stewart, hadn't made the move with Edward and Elizabeth, but had instead traveled to Boston to stay with cousins before heading off to Harvard Law School. The family was shamelessly proud of Harry's determination; it had gotten him a scholarship to Ohio State for his pre-law classes. He was never cut out for shopkeeping. Harry had let Edward know early that his destiny was a courtroom. Billy Blake was required to take on more hours since Harry had gone to college, but he didn't mind. Not school smart himself—he did only average work there—he was nonetheless shrewd with people and merchandising, and was determined to let Harry, only one year younger, pursue his dream.

Now, in Nelsonville on this sweltering early evening, Mary Rose noticed that the baby had finished eating and was drifting off to sleep in her mother's arms while Frank threw pebbles from the back of the wagon, laughing at the duck he startled with his missile.

"Son, we're almost home. Won't that be nice, Frank? Our new home?" Mary Rose called to her adventurous boy, who was perched precariously on the back rung of the wagon. When his mother called, he crawled on his skinny little legs to climb back into the front of the wagon. Stroking her two-year-old's hair, she bent over to tuck the baby into her box behind the seat, then settled in for the last leg of the journey.

Following the course of the canal, Billy Blake passed the market Edward had described, pointed out with interest a hardware store, a blacksmith shop, and an assortment of small homes with businesses connected—a doctor, a barber, and one of the business offices of Sunday Creek Coal and mentally noted that the town did indeed look to be thriving—before he turned the buggy east for a short quarter-mile trek to Fayette Street, which he found easily.

"Look, Mary, we will be there in no time!" Billy Blake exclaimed, pointing at the street sign which did indeed read "Fayette Street," excited enough to throw off the fatigue which an hour ago seemed suffocating. Mary Rose would be more comfortable in their house, surrounded by her own things, he knew. She had bravely given up most of the furnishings from their first home, but Billy Blake had insisted on making room in the wagon for her rocking chair and the small chest of drawers he and Stewart had made for her as a wedding gift, with the darker wooden inlays in the shape of an M, the Markham store trademark.

It was a work of art and she loved that they had made it special for her. The sturdy wagon was indeed crowded, but it was enough to ask her to make this move and leaving behind those two treasures would have been unthinkable.

At his excited exclamation, she craned her neck to look. Beyond the large brick church on the corner which dwarfed the homes near it, Mary Rose spotted the light cream frame two-story trimmed in brick red, which Edward had described in his letter—and was astonished to see a delightful, cheery inviting haven, surrounded by mature oaks trees and complete with covered porch across the front and around the left side with a porch swing gracing the front, just outside the graceful parlor window—all this where she had expected dreary!

She squealed with delight, "Oh, Billy, look, look at it! It looks like a cottage from a fairy tale—only bigger!" Billy Blake saw at that moment the exuberant 18-year-old he had fallen in love with four years earlier, before two children and an eight-hour trip had worn her out. Her exhaustion was momentarily eclipsed by her excitement, and his heart swelled with love and pride…and relief, as well.

Approaching their house, Billy Blake had to admit the reality was much better than the anticipation, and that his faith in Edward's decision-making had been justified. He turned into a narrow gravel lane which led alongside a covered porch to the back of the property and a sturdy shed. Stopping near the side of their inviting house, and temporarily tethering Sylvia to an iron pole, the young man admired the solid windows. Someone, probably his dad, had opened them to allow any breeze which may have survived the heat to circulate through the house. Billy admitted to himself, with a huge sigh of relief, that this was indeed a fine home.

Frank was already trying to scramble down from the wagon when it came to a halt, before his parents could alight and help him, but Billy Blake noticed that Mary Rose had done the same thing, excited now at the sight of her house. Instead of needing to help his family down, he discovered they had found their own way and were already on the front porch, both beaming with anticipation. Momentarily amused, Billy Blake called to his wife, "Dear, did you forget something?"

"Oh, my, the baby! Bring her, Billy, bring her in, let's go in and look around." Mary Rose bubbled, reminding him again of that teenager her hadn't seen for awhile. As Billy Blake turned to take Elizabeth, his Betsy, from her cradle without waking her, he heard more laughter. His wife and son found their way through the front door to the entry hall. Following them, he first took a moment to admire the handsome porch which shaded the entire front of the house, and the sturdy columns, also painted brick red, holding up a sound roof. "Hmm. Very nice," Billy declared to no one in particular.

The young father entered the house to discover that his wife and son were already making their way from a small rose-toned comfortable parlor with a bay window front and side, across the hall to a warm and cozy dining room-playroom combination, complete with elegant fireplace nearly six feet high and graced by an ornate walnut mantle. The fireplace stopped him in his tracks.

Billy Blake momentarily pictured four Christmas stockings hanging from that marvelous mantle and a peaceful smile graced his face. His family seemed to have forgotten their fatigue, he noticed. Mary Rose, with the excitement of a home maker, was enjoying her new nest and Frank with just the typical exuberance of a two-year-old, had discovered a fairyland of a play area. Frankie's enthusiastic whooping, amused at the echo his voice made in the cavernous room, made his father laugh as well.

Billy Blake stepped back into the parlor, moved to the inner wall, calling, "Mary, come here and look how nice these lamps are, and low enough that you should be able to reach them to light them easily." She joined him as he reached out, lifting the delicate frosted and etched globe to show her the knob which brought a soft glow of gaslight into the room, just beginning to fill with shadows. Watching him intently, she then moved to the next lamp, lighting it herself with no difficulty, relieved that her five-foot frame would not require an assist from her six-foot husband just to light a lamp.

"Those are beautiful. I love the color they give the room, like an early sunset! Come, Billy, let's look at the kitchen. I hope it is big!" They moved together to the rear of the first floor, listening to Frank's feet thundering overhead as he explored the second-story bedrooms on his own. "Frankie, come down carefully and see our kitchen," Mary Rose called up the graceful staircase to her son. In no time, he galloped to join them in the kitchen, running ahead to poke his nose into the deep and spacious lower cabinets. Mary Rose made a mental note to find a way to lock those cabinets…it might be a bit too inviting as a hiding place for mischievous toddlers.

Dusk had begun to fall and shadows played with the imagination. Moving further into the room, Billy lit a huge, overly ornate brass kerosene lamp on the wall. The dusky light allowed them both to recognize the familiar rough table Edward had brought with him from Caldwell. "Oh, Billy! It's their table," Mary Rose cried.

"Well, so it is! Dad said he bought a new one, but I had no idea! That's just dandy!" It leant a homey air, the kerosene light and the old homestead table, and provided a touch of the familiar.

As she looked around the huge, very workable kitchen, Mary Rose's eyes again fell on the table, and she exclaimed, "Oh, look, Billy, they left some flowers on the table. Isn't that sweet? It's amazing that Elizabeth had time to do that...oh! and the curtains, too, with the store and the other children..." Reaching for the blue glass vase filled with roses and daisies from her mother-in-law's garden, the young woman lifted the bouquet to her nose.

Raising her eyes to her husband, he noticed tears in her crystal blue eyes, but knew the tears weren't sadness but, instead, relief that the dreaded move had been made more bearable by her in-laws' homey touches. Elizabeth Markham, the second, Billy Blake's mother, was a woman of few words but a loving and sensitive nature, and she had sensed just what young Mary Rose would need to feel at home. It was obvious that the senior Markhams had worked magic.

The young couple continued their examination of the large, airy kitchen, admiring its excellent cross-ventilation, thanks to windows on three sides and yet another small covered porch, on the back protecting the room from becoming overly hot. That porch was graced with a small round table and two chairs. The heavy black coal stove was old but looked workable, and the ice box was large and well insulated, complete with a fresh block of ice provided by Edward, evidently. Running water gushed from an ugly but functional spigot attached to a cast iron sink, slightly rusty—both sink and water—but otherwise fine, cold, even. She was excited that the house had running water, as she had anticipated having to pump instead.

Her inspection continued: the petite Mary Rose chuckled to see the tall upper cabinets, painted white with beveled glass panels. She stretched up on tiptoe to just barely reach the bottom of the upper cabinet, and she teased, "Well, husband, you will just have to be here to help me with meals, since I can't reach above the bottom shelf."

In response, he smiled, replying, "Well, let's see about that. What if we put all the dishes in the lower cabinets, then you won't need me after all, will you?"

After a gentle laugh, Mary Rose's eyes softened even more and she whispered, "That day will never come, love, when I don't need you." She put her arms around his waist and her head on his chest, careful not to waken Betsy.

Even after three years of marriage and two children, she made his heart flutter. This was a love match, no doubt about it, and Billy Blake breathed a silent sigh of relief that his lovely bride seemed fine about the move, now that her house was passing inspection. He thought, "I must tell Mother and Dad that they have outdone themselves, finding this wonderful house. They knew just what we needed…"

Just at that moment, Betsy startled awake, her eyes darting around looking for a familiar face, lip and chin beginning to quiver, before seeing her father who had been holding her somewhat like a sack of potatoes. He now turned her around to face him and her mother.

He proclaimed softly, "It's all right, little one. We are home."

And he knew that those words were true.

Chapter 4 – Winter's Worries

[December 1907]

"As if 1907 hasn't offered enough weather challenges, what is this winter?" exclaimed Billy Blake Markham. "Blizzard. Snowstorm. Ice storm. Blizzard! When will it end?" he grumbled. He buttoned up his good wool topcoat, wrapped the green muffler his mother had knit for him over his head and around his neck, pulled his good leather cap with earmuffs over the whole bundle. His jaw set in determination, he prepared himself to step onto the porch.

"Bye, all. Nanook of the North is off to his sled." Frankie and Mary Rose giggled as the man of the house opened the door with effort. Snow blasted him, taking his breath away, making his eyes tear.

It had snowed fourteen inches in the first two weeks of December alone. Temperatures rarely rose above freezing, snow accumulated in huge drifts and in dirty piles along the tree route behind the junior Markhams' home. Each new snowfall changed the drifts to white again. Billy Blake narrowly missed being blown into one especially treacherous drift, shifting his footing at the last minute to avoid a spill.

This day had dawned with very little sun to grace it. Billy Blake, a man of perpetual good humor, had grumbled uncharacteristically to his assembled family that the day wasn't fit for man or beast...but Frankie disagreed heartily. As soon as his father left for work, trudging his way through drifts and fighting brutal wind gusts for the half-mile walk to the dry goods store, Frankie began his morning onslaught: "Outside, Mama! Go outside and play! Peeze?" hopping up and down, shaking his tiny hands in excitement. In spite of the gray gloom of the day, Frankie saw only fresh snow blanketing the yard and longed to make the first tracks in it.

Two-and-a-half-year-old Frankie rejoiced at each new snowfall, finding endless adventure in a world made of ice and snow. Given half a chance, he would adopt every tiny cold animal, bring it inside in his pocket; fortunately, he never succeeded in his amusing efforts to catch squirrels and birds. He whined relentlessly to go out to play in the back yard. "Bunnies, Mama! See bunnies…"

Amused at his excitement, Mary Rose nevertheless groaned. Obviously, Frankie had forgotten that each time, after five minutes or so, he then would be whining to go in. Mary Rose, like all mothers since the beginning of time, dreaded the battle of dressing her offspring for five minutes of play, but she equally dreaded the battle of keeping him inside when there was so much to explore. "There are no bunnies, Frankie! The bunnies are sleeping in their warm beds," she reasoned.

Her son's face fell and he seemed to be considering her words. Peering out the side window, Mary Rose hoped Frankie couldn't see the birds, trying hard to find food. Their feet left only the faintest tracks in the crisp white covering as they foraged wherever they could. Yet even those tiny creatures seemed to be energized as they fought the winds which whipped through their habitat, causing them to hold their heads high in order to maintain their balance. Mary Rose smiled as she watched their brave plight.

Although she dreaded the bundling and unbundling which accompanied Frankie's snow play, Mary Rose found his excitement contagious, the sun glistening off the snow exhilarating. She often bundled herself and Betsy to join him in his fantasy village, teaching him to build a lopsided snowman or make snow angels. But not today. This was indeed a day not fit for man or beast and Mary Rose steeled herself for an argument.

* * *

Usually, Billy Blake loved winter just as the rest of his family did. The trees along the canal looked ghostly when they stood bare, but then when they were miraculously tipped with delicate ice crystals, Ohio winter created a fairyland.

Comfortably settled in their rented home in Nelsonville, the Markhams, both generations, loved the way the snow magically washed the world clean, the way the wind stole their breath but made their senses work overtime. Fighting the onslaught of blinding snow, Billy's mind conjured up his wife's face, smiling, happy. Her exuberance had returned with rest and her new home, to his relief. Mary Rose, who loved all seasons, found something to revel over even in the most extreme of conditions, such as today. "I'll bet that youngster of mine has her bundling him up to play! The kid's tougher than his old man." The image of Frankie in his snowsuit looking like a bear made him smile in spite of the frigid air. "Ouch. That hurt," he mumbled as his face tingled.

Billy Blake loved his son's adventurous spirit. He loved Frankie's compassion for animals. When a wayward rabbit appeared in the yard, Frankie carried on a jabbered conversation with the creature, who was, no doubt, oblivious to his charm as it searched the snow for a wayward blade of grass.

Trudging through the snow, Billy Blake's thoughts traveled backward to his home, where he wished he could still be. The squirrels did well in that yard—walnuts were everywhere. The walnut trees behind the house, sickly when the young family moved in late that summer, flourished under Billy Blake's excellent care. He was indecently proud of the large messy walnuts, which had fallen from the tree in the summer to be stored in airtight containers for use during the winter. Mary Rose loved to make cookies and apple salad using the nuts grown in her own yard. But a few stray nuts remained on the ground under the snow near the shed, and somehow, the squirrels knew they were there and managed to ferret them out.

* * *

As hard as she found it to refuse Frankie's exuberant requests, this day Mary Rose insisted, "Frank, it is freezing out there, and the wind would freeze your little cheeks to ice! Let's make some cookies and build a fire in the parlor. Won't that be fun? Then if you are very, very good, you can help me make a bird feeder with corn cobs. What do you say?" Initially, his face clouded over and his lip began to quiver. After a moment of thinking about cookies and playing on the soft rug in the parlor, where normally children weren't allowed to play, he seemed to have reconsidered. His sunny disposition came back…the temptation of the bird feeder just cinched the deal.

His clear blue eyes, inherited from both parents, twinkled as he exclaimed, "Cookies! Me help, Mama? Me help?" and the bouncing began anew, bringing a hearty laugh to his mother. Mary Rose felt a rush of love for this high-spirited, happy child with her golden curls and optimistic nature and his father's good looks. He never met a stranger, this youngster, and when visiting his father at work, he loved to charge maniacally up the long aisle at the dry goods store to greet each customer with his alluring grin. Today he was dazzling his mother.

"Yes, son, how could I make a single cookie without you to stir the dough for me?" she replied, and picking up Betsy, who was now crawling quite competently, she led her little foraging party into the large, friendly kitchen.

* * *

Billy Blake began to step into the snow-filled gutter to cross the last street approaching his store when he was startled back onto the walk by a lorry. It careened around the corner, slipping slightly on the ice, throwing dirty, crusted snow in Billy's face. "Hey! Idiot…" Rarely cross, Billy Blake uttered an epithet quite unlike his usual vocabulary, and began to brush the filthy residue from his navy wool coat. Peering through his muffler to see who the reckless idiot was, he was surprised to recognize that it was Albert Garrett. Albert often did deliveries for Billy Blake when he was available on Saturdays. Home delivery was a courtesy only Markham's offered, and customers liked both the service and Albert. Owning one of the first motorized vehicles in Nelsonville (Billy's father Edward owned a Buick), Garrett's lorry was still a curiosity.

Puzzled, Billy Blake thought, "Why, that's not like Albert at all…I hope everything is all right…" The lorry shrieked around the corner onto Hocking Street, still slipping and sliding at speeds much too fast for the weather. Billy Blake's concern continued. He peered after Albert until he could no long see the lorry, then, shaking his head in bewilderment, continued the final chilly leg of his journey to the store.

As he entered Markham's, his Markham's, the warm and cheery feeling always prevailed. Breathing deeply of the scents of wood, fabric, floral cosmetics and cleaning oil, Billy Blake cheered instantly and he forgot about the puzzling Albert Garrett. The store was dark and deserted; he was the first one in. "Not too surprising," he thought to himself, "given the storm and all…Dad will undoubtedly be here soon."

He began the morning ritual of opening his dry goods store for the day's business: Raise the blinds on the twin front entrance doors; light the twelve electric lamps along the side walls; stoke the furnace with the morning's allotment of coal; remove the fabric dust covers from the clothing racks; clean the massive front windows and the heavy display cases with ammonia water; unlock the cash register; sweep the long narrow aisles until their dark wood patina gleams, even though they were swept at the close of business last night; and finally, light the tiny gas stove in the storage room to make his coffee. Finally, with pride, march confidently forward to throw open the doors which proudly proclaimed "Markham's" to the world at large.

This was Billy Blake's second favorite place to be, next to the home he shared with his family. This place showcased his love of and concern for the people of Nelsonville and his ability to anticipate their needs. He unlocked the doors this morning…but no one entered. The blizzard reigned supreme.

Just as he had done in Caldwell, Billy Blake had added a gentle, caring touch to the business established by his very wise father. One of his first projects was to add the book corner, which had been so popular in Caldwell and had brought his beautiful bride into his life. In this store, Billy had also followed Mary Rose's counsel. She suggested he provide a comfortable nook across from the reading corner so that women could look at pattern books, reach out and feel fabric, sip a cup of tea, and visualize their sewing projects completed.

When he followed his wife's counsel, he was always glad he did. Markham's had acquired several customers who had previously shopped elsewhere, just for the coziness and sense of family which Billy Blake and his wife had brought to the establishment. Mary Rose could knit, crochet, and embroider very well, and she had insisted that her husband order yarns of all kinds for the local ladies to select from as well. She occasionally displayed one of her finished projects as an example of what could be done with just a needle, yarn, and some imagination. The two younger Markhams had contributed excitement and imagination to this establishment, and the residents of this coal-mining capital loved what they found at Markham's, and couldn't wait to spend their paychecks there!

When time permitted, Mary Rose now joined him in the store. She was a wizard with bookkeeping, and contributed many positive suggestions to his marketing efforts as well. She also had a knack of knowing how to arrange and display merchandise, better than Edward or Billy's tendency to just "put stuff out." She showcased. He missed her when she stayed home, but today was too raw to take the children to his mother's so Mary Rose opted to allow him to go on by himself.

An hour later, Edward still hadn't arrived. Billy Blake felt a mild concern, but as he knew the store traffic would be light due to the storm, he imagined that his mother Elizabeth had persuaded her stubborn husband that his eldest son was perfectly capable of running the store, for Heaven's sake, no need to catch a chill and wind up with pneumonia, and so on and so on. Smiling to himself, he thought, "Yes, Mother, I can do it alone and yes, Mother, he is getting on in years…but don't you ever tell him that if you want a happy home!" Billy Blake Markham knew his father so well…proud, independent, stubborn.

Half an hour later, he was still alone. He really didn't mind. The coffee was brewed, its fragrance permeating the entire rear section of the store. Billy Blake, following his nose, poured himself a large cup, lit his first cigar of the day, and perched on the table which was used for cutting blinds…thankful for the solitude. A friendly man, he nevertheless enjoyed moments to himself; he didn't get very many, not with a thriving business, an energetic wife and two small children. He was able, this morning, to open a box in his mind which stayed closed during busy times, to take out the mental blueprint of Markham's stores of the future, to examine them, make alterations, adjust the timetable. He privately called this compartment of his brain the "fantasy empire," and he really loved to go there!

He examined the Markhams' holdings, currently consisting of three stores, the dry goods establishment in which he was sitting, a shoe store in Athens, and the general store in Caldwell. "Mighty fine," he thought to himself, "yes, indeed." All three were doing well. His father Edward had hired a competent manager for the general store and it seemed to be running itself, with only occasional visits from Edward or Billy Blake. The manager was a good hire, focused on the needs of Caldwell's citizens. He had learned to anticipate and project well enough to keep his inventory current and well stocked.

Why, just last month, that manager, Gerald Kingsley, had asked permission to expand Billy Blake's book corner to include a section of children's books…"Good idea," Billy Blake thought to himself. "Wonder why I didn't think of that." Word traveled fast in the small town of Caldwell, so it wasn't any time at all until the children's book orders matched the volume of the classics and adventures. "Good man, Gerald…" Billy Blake muttered to himself.

George, Edward's cousin, was currently running the shoe store in Athens, and although it was in its first year as was the dry goods store, George was already showing a profit. He seemed to be able to predict what college students would need, in spite of his being well past middle age. He looked—and thought—years younger than his calendar age, fortunately. The local residents of Athens kept George busy as well. "Not bad, not bad at all!" Billy was glad that Edward, who had thought about opening this dry goods store in a Columbus location, had decided on the booming coal town of Nelsonville. Yes, it was a better market…nonetheless, Billy thought, the time might be right to try a small store, perhaps just shoes, or just women's clothing, in the metropolis of Columbus.

Interrupting Billy Blake's reverie, a fire whistle shrilled through the silence, sending the young man loping to the front of the store to peer out, trying to see the direction the fire truck was going. Thinking, "How awful, fighting a fire in this dreadful cold," Billy didn't make the connection with his near escape earlier that morning.

Or with Albert Garrett, for that matter…

* * *

The fire wagon ripped down Columbus Street in front of Markham's, heading at breakneck speed back the way Billy Blake Markham had traveled on his morning walk. It peeled around the corner, following the same path that Albert Garrett had taken ninety minutes earlier. Coming to a halt just two blocks from the younger Markhams' home, the five volunteer firemen leaped from the truck, grabbing the huge hose as they went. The fire was already through the roof of the house on Griggs Street, its residents huddled in a horse blanket fifty feet away, watching in horror as their home went up in flames. A large crowd had gathered to watch, as was the way of human beings: curious, sympathetic, and secretly thinking how glad they were that it was not their home being destroyed that morning.

A police officer arrived on horseback, huddled against the biting storm. Senior Officer Terry Prentice arrived just as the first firemen reached the home, and then a second officer, rookie Jerry Matheny, came from the opposite direction, finding it somewhat difficult to maneuver through the growing crowd of onlookers. Officer Prentice, the older and more veteran of the two called to the scene, climbed down and strode over to the huddled family and, with his notebook and a pencil in hand, began to try to find out what had transpired to bring about this sequence of events.

He was afraid he already knew, however; the home's owner was Gordon Brooks, the business manager of Sunday Creek Mine, the man who had refused to negotiate with the union. Turning his back on his striking employees, Brooks had instead hired scab laborers to keep the mine working. Albert Garrett, whose two sons were both miners involved in the strike of Sunday Creek #4, had threatened Brooks publicly. There wasn't much doubt that this was his handiwork. Nonetheless, it was Officer Terry Prentice's job to ask the questions; ask he did, going through the motions of an investigation.

One of the bystanders began to sidle closer to the second policeman, a ragged-looking man of around thirty years who introduced himself as John Squire. Finally gaining the attention of the officer, he stammered, "I seen that man, that Garrett, I seen him…he…uh…he throwed a torch or somethin'…" and his words dried up. Several dozen pairs of eyes were upon Squire, and he found the attention discomforting; attempting to turn away from the crowd, he continued, "I dunno who was with 'im, but I knowed it was Garrett and two other men in the truck, 'n' he stuck aroun' jist long enough to make sure the house went up…man, it went up real fast!"

The young officer was definitely listening now, and as he made notes, a middle-aged woman in galoshes and a bathrobe added, "Yep, that was him, all right, I saw him too! He jumped out of the truck, ran real low like, up to the side of the porch, throwed something in the window, then ran back…why would he do something like that, huh?" She began to weep. "I ran over and pounded on the door so Mrs. Brooks would hear and I yelled to her to get the children…and then the side of the house just went up and I ran…" Weeping uncontrollably now, the Good Samaritan sought out the Brooks family with her eyes, breathed a ragged sigh of relief to find all five children huddled with their mother, and began to hurry toward them, as the wind intensified, blowing ashes into her already stinging eyes.

The young officer joined his superior, and shared the information he had just been given; Officer Prentice just nodded, patted the young man's shoulder, and said, "Good job, Jerry. That's a good job. Now get their names and addresses for me, would you?" and walked back to the crowd still watching as the Brooks' home was consumed by fire.

Locked in a personal moral dilemma, Terry Prentice knew his job would soon take an ugly turn as he arrested Albert Garrett for arson. Garrett was well supported in his opposition to Brooks and his tactics. He also had friends in city government, friends who could ruin Prentice's career. But on the other hand, Prentice's respect for the law and his personal integrity couldn't allow the law to be taken into the hands of angry, vindictive citizens. That would be a giant step backward, Western frontier justice in a progressive Midwest town. With a heavy heart and a great deal of trepidation, Officer Prentice put his notebook away and mounted, not looking forward to his next duty, bringing Albert Garrett in for questioning.

What efforts the fire fighters made were lost; the blaze—not the firefighters—was in control, so the frustrated firemen began to wet the sides and roofs of the adjacent homes, hoping at least to save them, not freeze them into igloos. Looking like a scene from Dante's inferno, the sinister orange flames lapped higher and higher into the gray sky, devouring any sun which dared to penetrate the gloom, filling the air with soot and cinders. In spite of the extreme cold of the day, the area surrounding the fire was warm as August, melting the snow which ran in rivulets, joining the runoff from the hoses, which then froze again far from the blaze, causing the firefighters to slip and slide, making for alternating patches of ice and slush. A gruesome tableau, indeed, of fire and ice…

* * *

Just after ten in the morning, Billy Blake greeted his first customer of the day. The middle-aged matron Betty Culson and her rather simple-minded daughter arrived in search of a Christmas gift, but were bubbling over with news of the fire. Listening attentively, Billy Blake was startled when Albert Garrett's name was mentioned as a possible arsonist…but as his mind flashed back two hours, he remembered nearly being run over by the very same man. His eyes narrowed in sadness; Albert was a decent person. How could he have done such a thing? Billy Blake Markham was never quick to judge another person, and he automatically looked for ways to excuse his casual friend Albert, to find reasons for bizarre behavior.

Listening to Mrs. Culson rattle on, he hoped that a mistake had been made…but he feared it hadn't. He knew the mantra "as goes the mine, so goes the town." That had been his experience in Caldwell: when the Belmont mines had gone on strike, not only had his business fallen off drastically, but also the attitude of the entire town seemed to be one of apprehension and suspicion. It worried Billy Blake when an entire family was dependent on a mine for its survival and even more when an entire town was so dependent. "What if," he kept wondering, "what if something happens to the mining industry? It's possible. Anything is possible. Who knows? Someone might find a better way to heat homes. Or to run a train or ship…or even another way to make steel…then what happens to the coal mines? Without the coal mines, what happens to Nelsonville?" The thought stuck…and a seed was planted: "Should I take the business to an area not dependent on just one industry? Would that be more prudent?"

As the snow continued to pelt the front windows, business inside persisted, warm and comforting. Another customer had stopped, fighting against the blizzard to examine closely the winter coats and scarves displayed in the middle window, and then she too entered the store, brushing tiny drifts off her shoulders with a laugh. Shaking off the slightly sick feeling of premonition he had experienced since learning of the fire, Billy Blake forced a smile back to his face, waved to the new customer and herded Mrs. Culson and her daughter over to the jewelry counter, suggesting, "What about a silver chain for your sister? We have lovely charms which could be added to any of these chains…" As his mind went into automatic mode…always the merchant, always the salesman…the feeling of foreboding continued.

Chapter 5 – Expanding the Family

[Fall 1908]

The air was refreshingly chilly that morning, the kind of day Mary Rose always looked forward to when she was a girl. Fall was nearly over, she mused, noting that most of the leaves were gone from the friendly walnuts back by the shed and the massive oak in the front yard. Late afternoon sun now brightened the parlor this time of year, unhampered by the shading branches. That same sun found its way in the morning, along with the aroma of freshly brewed coffee, to her kitchen table, now that the walnuts were denuded of leaves. As much as she loved those gnarled trees in full foliage, she loved even more the feel of winter sunshine on her face as she enjoyed her morning coffee and fed her young family. This morning, after kissing her husband goodbye, Mary Rose paused on the porch, raising her face to the brisk wind, sniffing the air like a wild deer, loving the scent of clean, peppered only slightly by the drift of coal dust from nearby fires. This was the posture, face to the wind, which had inspired her father to nickname her "Steamboat Annie," for her love of wind in her face acquired by an early trip aboard a steamwheeler out of Marietta. That was an affectionate memory and a nickname which followed her into her adulthood.

As Billy Blake had already left for the store and Frankie and Betsy were still sleeping, Mary Rose was blessed with a rare quiet moment to commune with nature before the hectic day with two toddlers commenced. When the new baby came in the spring, she knew she would have to get some help if she was to have enough energy left to help with the two new stores her husband and his dad were acquiring and planning to open in the year to come. She loved the grand openings of Markham's stores and hadn't really planned to have a baby at this time…but God had another plan, so she knew they would all adapt. They always had…

Inhaling the crisp morning air always cleared her head and, at the present, helped to calm the nausea; she was grateful for a brief respite this morning. Taking advantage of the moment, pulling her shawl more tightly around her shoulders, Mary Rose Markham sank into the deeply cushioned rocker, which sat in a sunbeam beside the parlor window.

It was common for Mary Rose to be reflective; all her life, she had enjoyed trips into the recesses of her mind, into her past, into even less joyful moments; it was settling to her to reflect on some of her life's journeys and bumps in the road. She was rarely regretful, but it helped her keep her life in perspective to replay some of its more poignant moments, to find added meaning, or perhaps to come to grips with difficult memories.

This morning, inspired by fall's briskness, and feeling sentimental as the baby turned gently within her, her mind turned to another brisk fall day. Billy Blake Markham had swallowed his obvious terror, evidenced by his white, pinched face, and dropped awkwardly to one knee, his bloodless face shining as brightly as the emerald and diamond ring he placed upon the ring finger of her left hand as he haltingly, pleadingly, asked her to become his wife. She chuckled as she remembered his stammered proposal, one which, nevertheless, did the job well and made them an officially engaged couple.

"No" was never an option, as she had decided she was going to be his wife after their first encounter earlier that year, but she still let him believe that he had convinced her. She remembered how the sun had shone on his face, how his love for her glowed in his eyes…and how right it all felt. That was a special memory for her, one which served to remind her, when days got too hectic or married life too predictable, of their love and their beginnings. Never once regretting that moment, Mary Rose was still, nearly five years later, madly in love with her husband and she didn't care who knew it.

Leaning her head back on the cushion to absorb a bit more of the sun's warmth, the young mother remembered one decision she had reached last night, after mulling over an approaching dilemma as Billy lay asleep beside her. She now took it out and gave it some free rein in her mind: the new baby would be arriving not long before the opening of the two new stores, and if she was to be of any help to Billy and Edward, she would have to find someone she could trust to help out with the children. This choice couldn't be put off much longer. Who could fill that bill? Frankie, while a good and obedient child, was nevertheless boisterous and a typical all-boy three-year-old specimen. Betsy was walking now, grabbing at everything within her reach to pull it into her curious mouth. Even the dog, a patient beagle new to the family last Christmas, had experienced Betsy's teeth and had learned to face her instead of allowing her to creep up behind him!

Both children required constant watching; who could do that? Would the elder Elizabeth be able to handle them and a new baby, with Charley still at home and of the age which could be the most challenging, pre-teen? Besides, Elizabeth had raised her own family. It was time for her to slow down somewhat and enjoy the fruits of her and Edward's labors. No, as an emergency caregiver, Elizabeth would do, but not for a more regular nanny. A professional nanny was the best option…but where to find one?

As an inventory of possible caregivers paraded itself through her mind, Mary Rose heard her daughter's early morning cry, more of an "I'm awake, come get me" siren than a true cry. With a last reluctant deep breath of invigorating air, she rose and entered her home to rescue the energetic 18-month-old from her confinement known as a crib, climbing the stairs just in time to greet Frankie, also awakened by Betsy's good lungs. Scooping Betsy up in one arm and Frankie in the other, Mary Rose sank carefully to the floor of the upper hall, hugging and nuzzling her youngsters with all her might, making them both giggle hysterically.

She let them go, began to stand up with an effort, thinking, "I had better stop doing that or one day soon, if I get as big as a house like I did with Betsy, I won't be able to get up," and using the wall as an aid, righted herself. Frankie had already scrambled down the stairs as Mary Rose returned her wriggling daughter, jabbering wordlessly, to her bedroom to have a clean diaper before bringing her down to join Frank at the cozy kitchen table.

This was the life Mary Rose loved, this life and this family she had created with the man she loved. The fact that they had also been fortunate enough to afford a few luxuries was a plus, but certainly not a necessity. Their new house, being built at the end of Fort Street, would have not only running water but also electricity, one of the first homes in Nelsonville with that new convenience. It would have four large bedrooms, a bath in the center of the upper floor, and fabulous windows in all rooms so that wherever the sun was, it would be captured by at least one of the Markhams' bedrooms. Her favorite room in the new house, she suspected, would be the sunporch, a room totally enclosed by glass but with carpeted floors and good heat so that the children could have the feeling of playing outside even on the coldest of winter days, and many years later, when the children were grown and gone, Mary Rose could picture herself rocking, doing her needlework, basking in the pleasure of her beloved sunshine.

Thinking about her new house was exciting, but she had to admit that she had come to love this house, too, this graceful story-and-a-half which they had rented now for just over a year. Its massive porch which protected the exterior on two and a half sides made the cream-colored home inviting; the porch swing which

Edward had installed for her often found her rocking one or both of her children after dark had set in and both were dozing peacefully in her arms.

Change was surprisingly difficult for Mary Rose, a fact which Billy Blake found incongruous with her personality. It wasn't that she didn't enjoy new developments, or that she was in any way sorry that the Markham store complex was doing so very well. No, those were sources of great pride to her. It was just that there was, buried deep but nevertheless asserting itself vigorously, the urge to "nest." She honestly hoped that this wonderful house on Fort Street would be the house in which she would watch her children grow up, graduate from school, meet and marry their beloveds…and that it would cradle her when her final days came. Those were thoughts which others might have found morbid; on the contrary, they gave Mary Rose Markham a sense of solidity.

* * *

Billy Blake knew how his wife felt, and he had spared no expense to provide everything she could possibly want in a home…now and as far into the future as he could foresee.

But the business was another story. Here there would be no status quo. Now, in the fall of 1908 and always, here Billy Blake Markham was a dreamer, a schemer, an experimenter and a pioneer. His father had instilled in him a sense of hunger, hunger for achievement and prosperity, not just for money but for prestige and reputation. Fortunately, both men were innately honest and would not find any achievements gained from dishonest means to be of any satisfaction; no, instead, both knew that pleasing others was the only way, the ultimate way to please themselves. And so the empire began to grow, one customer at a time, one new store at a time.

As Mary Rose began her day with her young brood, Billy Blake and Edward Markham met with their lawyer, James Clavenger, to pore over the financial records of a shoe and luggage store, Napson's, in Lancaster, which was going under quickly and whose owner wanted to sell out to avoid bankruptcy. As the examination went on, it became evident that the collapse of the present store was not due to shady dealings, nor to a problem economy. Instead, the poor man Napson was just terribly undercapitalized and lacking in business acumen. Had he been better schooled in marketing to the existing public and backed with adequate operating capital, he could have been raking in the profits. It occurred to Edward that he could benefit both by purchasing this floundering store and by retaining Napson as manager…as long as Billy Blake would train him to reach his customer base more efficiently. Whispering this idea to Billy, his son's eyes lit up and he nodded vigorously; including the attorney in the conversation, it was evident to the worried Napson that some sort of agreement had been reached and his stomach lurched.

It was indeed a good day for the Markham men! As Mr. Riley Napson squirmed and sweated silently, the Markhams and their attorney frowned, read, frowned some more, pointed out things, frowned and read some more, saying little, seeming to read one another's minds…and nearly simultaneously breaking into excited smiles, meeting one another's eyes with a raised eyebrow…obviously having reached a decision. Napson held his breath as the three huddled with their heads together a few more minutes, looking his way occasionally, and exhaled in an explosion as the elder Markham exclaimed, "Done, Mr. Napson! Your offer is fair! How soon can we take possession?"

With their relieved beneficiary now weak in his seat, Edward painted for Napson the vision he and Billy had just developed, with occasional input from the attorney, describing the managerial authority Napson would have, without the financial headache he had been experiencing. Weak with gratitude, Riley Napson, who had hoped at best to be out from under his huge debt but was very sad at the prospect of leaving a business he had grown to love, now found himself manager of the newest Markham's. Ecstatic, he exited the room on wobbly legs.

Satisfied that they had indeed pulled off a very wise business arrangement, Billy and Edward hugged one another in a gesture other attorneys would have found awkward and unprofessional, but Clavenger, who had handled the Markhams' legal matters for three years now, knew as a vote of confidence for a job well done. He too beamed, clapped both Markhams on the back, and sat back down, saying, "Well done, gentlemen! Now, let's look at our list of inventory again…"

PART 2—JANE

Chapter 6 – The San Toy Saga

Just a single-lane rugged asphalt road leads to it now, to the town of San Toy, once a Mecca of prosperity. In the early decades of the twentieth century, it had a school, a church, a real downtown, many houses…and even the only hospital in Perry County, Ohio. At the foot of the hill, maybe a half-mile from the county road, lies the entrance to Sunday Creek #2 mine, completely covered by foliage in the summer and fall. A phenomenon known only to coal mining, this town, along with the nearby towns of Moxahala and Congo, sprung up within a decade of 1900, were "planted" like crops for the miners and their families, existed in their glory days for twenty-five years or so…and then simply vanished.

One has to work hard to visualize where the San Toy flagpole once stood, where the downtown area bustled with foot traffic, where the children of the area scrambled up the hill to attend their school. Even before the school was built, high on the hill, there was school—held in one of the three local taverns! Where there were miners, there were taverns. Gunfights broke out at night in the taverns; school children were distracted the next morning by bullet holes in the walls of their "classroom," and they waggled their fingers through those holes until called back to attention by their teachers.

The town of San Toy even had a street light, one of the first in Ohio, brick streets, and a sturdily constructed jail, part of which is still standing. Ironic that the only buildings still standing are the jail and the church…representing both the evil and the good men do, and oddly representative of the town of San Toy, crude, blasphemous, violent at times and united, at other times, almost eerily so, in fellowship quite unlike that found in other towns outside of the "Little Cities of Black Diamonds" region.

Many legends surround the naming of San Toy. No one seems to know for sure its origin. One of the legends suggests that a local boxer by the name of Sam Troy was the inspiration for the town's moniker but that the ink smeared when the charter was registered, resulting in San Toy. Another legend holds that as Chinese names were popular around 1900, the founders just liked the Asian sound of the two syllables. Yet a third legend says that the backers of the town of San Toy had, just the previous year, backed a stage play by the name of "San Toy" which had been a miserable flop; when they collected for the chartering of the new coal-mining town, one of the backers is quoted as saying, "Let's just hope this isn't another San Toy!"

What is so amazing, no matter how the boom town got its name, is that it didn't exist in 1890, and was at one of its two peaks of glory in1904, courtesy of Sunday Creek Mining Company which had expanded its holdings into Perry County and created a town—actually, a whole community—for its employees. It peaked again in the early 1920s but by 1929 was no more than a ghost town. When the mine closed, so did San Toy; the buildings were literally folded up and carted away by rail, as were the stores, the hospital, and all other peripheral businesses except the church and a handful of houses. Like the mythical Brigadoon, the town simply ceased to exist, disappearing into the mists of Perry County.

* * *

Frederick Hunt was born in nearby New Lexington in 1868, over thirty years before San Toy appeared. He grew up there, attended school and church in New Lexington and began working in the construction industry, one of many industries which boomed because the coal industry and the iron furnaces boomed. Fred played baseball, went to the local secondary school, and made hordes of friends, with whom he skated on the creek in the winter and rode horses over the steep hills surrounding the town he loved, the hills of Perry County which are adorned with elegant foliage April through October and take on a pristine, ethereal beauty in their stark nakedness the remaining months.

Fred loved to hunt in the woods and fish in the creek as well, alone or with friends, the lazy water relaxing him to the point where he often snoozed along the bank, his cap tipped over his eyes and his fishing pole wedged between two rocks; he worked hard on the days he had jobs and was tired, but his exceptional health allowed him to keep up a pace which would stop a boy of normal stamina. Nevertheless, he found it quite easy to fall asleep on the creek bank, and his friends often played pranks on their dozing friend, filling his boots with sand, placing a tiny lizard or snake on his chest to crawl around, or hooking a can or tree trunk to his fishing line—and the good-natured Fred would take it all in stride. He often got even, though it was always in the form of a prank, never maliciousness. Life was good for the teenager from New Lexington.

Secure in the love of his family, Fred's home consisted of loving, hard-working parents whose marriage seemed to be a model of wedded bliss, and two younger sisters, both bright, talkative, and inquisitive, who worshipped their big brother. Although it was just too tempting to fall into the typical "big brother" trap of teasing, goading, and annoying his sisters, the pranks were all harmless, no spiders in the bedclothes, for instance. Brotherly pranks aside, he instinctively protected them and was always glad to have them around to talk with. All three of the Hunt children were chatty from their infancy, and the house buzzed with conversation morning through evening.

His mother Dorothy came from a coal-mining family, so she knew hard work; she rarely complained, even when the paychecks were a little short, and she had to make meals out of the barest of leftovers. Although she could be crusty at times, she was usually pleasant to be around and her children often congregated at the kitchen table while she was completing chores, just to listen to her tell stories of her ancestors' journey from England to Ohio by way of Canada. She made the tales take on the splendor of a melodrama with her gift for description and her mesmerizing way of spinning out the saga, which held the children wide-eyed for hours on end. Fred and his sisters inherited their mother's skill with language. All three of them were wordsmiths, creative with stories and poetry, and had vocabularies which astounded their teachers and classmates.

* * *

"Hey, Freddie, what's a bronco-saurus?" the taller blonde asks.

"What, Henny-Penny?" Fred responds, flipping her pigtail up in the air.

"A bronco-saurus. What is it?" she insists, yanking her pigtail away. "My teacher said it was real big, like a house."

"Oh, a brontosaurus. It's a…giant Henny-Penny!"

Penny giggles. "No, silly. You don't know, do ya, huh, do ya?"

"Of course I know. I just don't want to tell you!" He grabs the other pigtail and attempts to tie them in a knot.

"Mother! Tell Fred to quit pulling my hair," she squeals.

Dorothy peeks into the dining room where her three children are supposedly working on their lessons, and determining the squeal is just her over-dramatic middle child's way of besting her older brother, she smiles and returns to her dinner preparations. This is just a typical exchange in the Hunt household, the two older children scrapping, the "baby" Mary Kate sitting in her chair, chewing on her pencil and watching her siblings, wide eyes moving from face to face as the exchange heats up.

"Homework, children…" Dorothy calls from the kitchen.

"Mother, I know something Fred doesn't know, na na," Penny chides.

"Do not. You're just a silly little Henny-Penny," Fred says. "A brontosaurus is a dinosaur, silly willy."

"Quit calling me Henny-Penny, you silly willy you." She giggles, putting her arms around her big brother's neck. His arm absent-mindedly goes around her waist.

"Shhush now. I have geography to learn. Go read your lessons," Fred instructs her with a kiss to the top of her head. She returns to her chair.

* * *

The family owes much of their unity to a strong religious base, attending church as a group on Sundays and Wednesdays, sharing prayer before meals and bedtime. The children never miss Sunday school classes. Often Dorothy and the children study the Bible at the kitchen table at least one evening during the week. All of the Hunts believe the Ten Commandments are to be practiced, not just acknowledged, yet they never act too "holy" for their friends to enjoy. Never missing catechism class, the Hunts study, learn and internalize the teachings. They believe in acting out their faith rather than talking about it.

The Hunt children rejoice through song as well; all three have excellent singing voices and are mainstays in the church choirs, Fred singing in the adult choir, Penny in the junior choir, and Mary Kate in the children's choir.

When he was ten, Fred began working to help out his family, doing odd jobs at the general store, cleaning up after barn raisings, feeding and caring for livestock when their owners had to be away. He found, quite young, that there was satisfaction in doing a job well, in seeing that his labors had produced a concrete result. Recognizing that it wasn't just the result which mattered but also the "doing," his skills with tools grew in direct proportion to the number and complexity of jobs he attempted. Even though the money he earned at these jobs was minimal, it did help out with expenses at home; he began to look for jobs he could do even if money wasn't an object, just for the thrill of the accomplishment.

The finished project was sufficient reward for Fred. It didn't take long for the neighbors to learn that if one had a task which needed to be completed in a tidy manner, Fred Hunt was the boy to do it. Work became as gratifying to Fred as did his youthful avocations, and he would frequently take on projects which provided greater and greater challenge.

As a teenager, Fred's tanned, muscular body and angular face make him look years older than he is, and he has recently noticed the young ladies of New Lexington admiring him as he works to build a barn or a shed for a family in the area. Fred finds it amusing to be the object of feminine attention; he finds it even more amusing when he realizes how much it annoys his sisters, though, that they are constantly answering questions about their older brother: "No, he's not married. Yes, he really is always smiling. No, he doesn't have a sweetheart. He's only sixteen, all right? Yes, he is as nice as he looks..." and so on until the brother they adore becomes, by virtue of his charm and attraction, an irritation. At night, they list for him the comments made and who made them and under what circumstances...and Fred just rocks back in the chair, an ear-to-ear grin on his wholesome face and takes it all in.

Fred knows they are proud of him, and that their complaints are really teasing. He also knows their time is coming soon. They are getting prettier each day. He expects to be fighting off some suitors in the near future.

As the girls list the day's comments, Fred mentally stores all the names in his directory; he definitely has an eye for the ladies. In his rare free time, between school, baseball, church, and his jobs, he has discovered that meandering about near the Methodist church can provide a never-ending source of feminine companionship. A substantial group of young ladies belong to a girls' youth group which meets at the Methodist church, and before long, Fred Hunt knows all their names, what grade they are in, what their hopes and dreams are—and has captured more than one heart. The girls have seen him in school but when he revealed his personality more fully, flashing his charismatic smile, his warm caramel-brown eyes sparkling, they were star-struck.

Captivating them with stories he tells, seemingly without having to think about them, his gift with words is coming in handy in yet another venue! Fred Hunt, ladies' man.

* * *

Sara Brown was the first to own Fred's heart. He knew from the moment he met her that he wanted to marry her. Not an outgoing girl, Sara was nonetheless warm and witty. When Fred first met her in front of the Methodist church, he was uncharacteristically tongue-tied. She wasn't a radiant beauty, not at all, but there was a magic about her which told him to make the effort to know her. As she smiled shyly into his eyes, hanging on his words, Fred found himself suddenly in love for the first time. Eyes met, hearts locked.

As their romance blossomed, it became apparent in no time to the disappointed throng at the Methodist church that Fred Hunt was no longer on the market. Faithful and attentive to her first passion, Sara adored him as well and the two courted through high school, exploring love and its pain and ecstasy…until she moved, against her wishes, to West Virginia with her family, leaving Fred broken-hearted. He thought of following her…but his family persuaded him that would be unwise, so he stayed behind, throwing himself into his work, saddened by the first heartache of love.

Although word traveled fast that the desirable Fred was now without a sweetheart, he took his time to heal before turning his eye back to the young lovelies who had figuratively lined up to compete for the opportunity to heal Fred's wounded heart. He prayed often, asking God to take care of Sara since he wouldn't be around to do it. The girls found him even more attractive because of his willingness to allow his feelings to be seen, his love for Sara, and his loss of her. They found it enigmatic that this devout boy was so devastatingly attractive. Other young men might not consider it "manly" to grieve; Fred didn't care what was "manly." He was then and always would be intense, passionate, devoted, and honest—he was what he was and if that didn't suit others, that was a problem for them, not for him.

Eventually, other young ladies found themselves in the company of the charismatic Fred Hunt; he enjoyed their charms, loved to exchange ideas with them, courted a few for short periods of time, but didn't allow himself the luxury of the emotional intimacy he had shared with Sara.

* * *

Fred is twenty. It is 1888. "Dad, I have something to tell you."

Looking over his newspaper, Raymond Hunt sees his son looking very intense. "What, son?"

"Dad…I was offered a job today," Fred begins.

"Okay. What kind of job?"

"A building job."

"Okay. That's good…so…is there a problem?" Ray asks.

"Not…well, maybe you might think so. I don't, but…"

"Let's hear it." Ray is listening intently, his intelligent brown eyes investigating his son's face.

Fred slowly and carefully tells his story. His eyes sparkle as he tells his father he has been offered the opportunity to travel with his construction crew to the site of a cozy community nestled in the hills, eighteen miles from New Lexington. A coal entrepreneur who already employs over two thousand men, Colonel William Rend, discovered the village, at that time a lumber town with the busiest sawmill in the area, and anticipating that the coal vein running through the area would bring profit, sunk a mine shaft and purchased much of the town. He leased land from the Ohio Central Coal Company and underwrote the construction of a company store, rooming houses and a hotel. When the mine shaft proved lucrative, Colonel Rend hired the construction crew Fred had been working with to aid the expansion. He personally had asked Fred to come along to do the finish work inside.

Ray listens carefully, nodding and frowning as he begins to understand: Fred is going away. After a silence, during which Fred finds his mouth dry and his heart racing, Ray asks quietly, "Have you told your mother?"

"No, not yet. I wanted to tell you first. It's a great job, Dad. This man, this Colonel Rend, has a lot of pretty exciting plans."

"Go on, son."

Fred continues his story.

Rendville, as it began to be called, was building permanent homes for the immigrants who were coming in to work one of the seven mines in a ten-mile radius of Rendville's center. That seemed like a good plan to Fred, an exciting new venture in which he could participate, be involved in the future. A town adjacent to the Rendville site by the name of Corning sprung up practically overnight, and was overflowing with people, as miners sent for their wives and children, or went seeking wives to share their lives.

Convinced that his oldest child had really considered all the necessary factors, Raymond consented to Fred's joining the crew to build Rendville. Ray paved the way, but Fred's hardest challenge was Dorothy, who wept, protested, then acquiesced when she was reassured that there was a Catholic Church already in the works.

As Fred packed, Dorothy puttered in and out of his room, asking if he had enough socks, had he packed his razor, would he find enough to eat, would he write every week…finally handing him a white leather-bound Bible she had intended to save for Fred's wedding. He answered all her worried questions patiently, accepted the Bible with tears in his eyes, enfolded his mother in his arms, promising to come home for all holidays that he possibly could.

He left by train that very day, his first train ride in a year of many firsts.

* * *

As Fred stepped from his room in the new and already overflowing boarding house his first evening in Rendville, he was immediately struck by the difference between the idyllic life he had known in New Lexington and the treacherous, brutal streets of Rendville. Always up for a good time, Fred Hunt found himself ill-prepared for having to dive for his life as a fight in one of the taverns spilled out into the street, amid curses, thrown bricks and bottles, swinging fists and even bullets. Always a quick learner, he vowed to develop eyes in the back of his head, a sixth sense to warn him when danger was near—and to learn quickly to be part of the fun but not of the violence, a wise choice for one so young and innocent of the world of coal miners.

Miners were by nature a rowdy bunch when they were single, but the married ones were homebodies, grounded by family and saved from frittering away their money in saloons and their lives in the rough, bullet-ridden streets. The most prosperous businesses in Corning, next to the mines, were the saloons. Bored miners, lacking female companionship, drank too much, started fights which often spilled out into the streets and frequently ended in gunfire, one or more miner lying in a pool of blood.

Rendville followed suit, of course, building one saloon for every twenty-five miners, Saturday night fights driving God-fearing folks into their homes before dark. Churches built as well, competing with the saloons and brothels for the souls of the "godless."

A unique blend of ethnic backgrounds, Rendville was, in the 1880s, an almost equal balance of white Americans, black Americans recruited from Alabama, and white immigrants lured by the prosperity that could be found in the mines…or so they had heard. So many black sharecroppers migrated from Alabama, as a matter of fact, that one housing area began to be known as "Alabama Ridge," a name which stuck permanently. Very few racial problems ever occurred in Rendville, surprisingly. The problems were more likely to be over a woman or a stolen horse or a spilled drink…any excuse for a fight was a good excuse. Since women were an endangered species in this coal-mining town, even an unattractive lass could find herself at the center of a scuffle!

As Rendville continued to develop, train loads of southern sharecroppers arrived daily, frustrated by the farming life in the Deep South, an area still riddled with Jim Crow laws and with hatred, not always well hidden. Fred's construction crew could barely keep ahead of the need for bachelors' quarters and tiny, two-room houses for the married miners. Mine foremen hired local farmers and working men to travel by train south to Alabama to recruit black workers and accompany them back to Ohio; they found an abundance of willing and ready labor.

Hard-working black men saved their hard-earned money and sent for their families as well and the town of Rendville rapidly grew to over two thousand people, the majority of them now black. The race issue didn't seem to be much of an issue in Rendville. As the population became more and more black, the town embraced the descendants of slaves and initiated a celebration called "Emancipation Day," a day more meaningful to black Americans than Independence Day. September 22 marked the anniversary of the Emancipation Proclamation; that day became an official holiday in Rendville, to be celebrated forevermore.

Fred's tenure in Rendville was brief; much of the available space to build had already been used by houses, boarding houses, barracks-style dwellings for bachelor miners. It was a quick education for the naïve youngster, both about building and about wild living. After a six-month stay to complete small, two-room homes for married miners, Fred's crew moved on to expand Moxahala, to create Congo, to a handful of other dots on the map of Perry County, developing town after town to accommodate the ever-growing mine industry.

There seemed to be no limit to new coal strikes; it was easy for speculators to assume the affluence would go on forever, so the expansion went on unchecked, glutting the coffers of the coal barons, and providing quick profit for shopkeepers, saloonkeepers, and other peripheral mine businesses. If only they could have seen into the future…

* * *

Spending the next ten years building every type of building required by coal towns—theaters, jails, barracks, rooming houses, restaurants, blacksmith shops, churches, and of course, saloons—Fred became a noted expert on "build it fast, make it last," and his reputation and work ethic grew until he was much in demand by builders.

Dreaming of having his own construction company, in 1898, Fred followed the boom to a picturesque oasis in a region of steep hills—loaded with coal, ore, and clay. The town to be developed was named San Toy. Three mine shafts were already in operation, with the majority of the miners traveling the five or more miles from Rendville and Congo, costing valuable travel time which could be better spent in the mines.

City planners, resting on their laurels after successful builds in Corning, Moxahala, Rendville, and Congo, planned the entire town at once: business district with bricked streets, row after row of company homes built on brick foundations, nearly close enough to touch, utilizing the space between hills as efficiently as possible. The specter of profit often clouds the judgment of city planners. Those who visualized the money to be made in San Toy were no exception. Having neighbors two feet from one's door may not be in the best interest of the resident, but it crowds ten or twelve more homes—which the coal company would own and rent out, making yet more profit—into a small space. San Toy expanded to fill any available space in the small niche between coal-laden hills.

Dozens and dozens of identical three-room dwellings were on the agenda, easy work for skilled builders like Fred Hunt and his crew. Fred's expertise in building these inexpensive dwellings and his innovative work techniques allowed him to build faster without additional cost to the mine company. Since mine companies are all about profit, Fred Hunt became the man of the hour, and the construction company he had worked with for well over ten years received praise, recognition, and even bonuses, which ingratiated him so much with the owners that the partners Cable and Rowen, after a brief strategic discussion, offered the young man a partnership in the company.

The thirty-year-old builder didn't hesitate to accept the offer; his lack of personal finances never once daunted him. He had saved well and, although he hadn't amassed sufficient fortune to purchase the partnership outright, he believed, as he always had, that anything was possible if the strategy was sound. Accordingly he prepared an energetic, forward-looking presentation for the First National Bank of Nelsonville, and walked out of the brick building with a loan for three thousand dollars, with which he bought the partnership and a huge chunk of the future he had already envisioned.

Thanking God first, and then celebrating in the Whitefront Saloon with his new partners and finally in the bed of a local girl named Jenny who lived above the newly completed Lyric Theater, Fred believed his future sparkled like the surfaces of a chunk of Sunday Creek coal, coal already earning the nickname "black diamonds."

Cable, Rowen, and Hunt finished the San Toy housing in less than eight months, added three more buildings to the downtown, and completed the school high on the hill overlooking the company homes, allowing the children finally to have their own place to learn, unencumbered by the distractions of gaining an education in a saloon…and returning the saloon to its original purpose during the daytime hours as well as nighttime hours. The fights went on; bullets found their way into the walls as before, but the children of San Toy were now safe and sound and away from the aftermath of melees. Less exciting perhaps, but more conducive to learning.

Last to be completed was the hospital, which Perry County had long needed. Speculators, believing that this strike of coal was unlimited, encouraged the further development of San Toy, anticipating another wealthy metropolis the likes of Columbus or Cleveland, and the hospital became the first—and only—in Perry County. Surprisingly, the hospital had no trouble recruiting physicians; many lived in the area and had been spending more hours in their buggies commuting to Athens or Lancaster than they could spend with patients, and consequently, were delighted to apply their skills with miners, shopkeepers, and others who followed the mines to this part of the county.

By late 1900, San Toy was complete, booming, overflowing with humanity packed cheek by jowl, cranking out trainloads of coal, seemingly limitless trainloads. Proud of their accomplishment, Fred and the other partners of Cable, Rowen, and Hunt accepted their final payments, shook hands all around, got drunk with their crew and the off-duty miners, and, hang-overs firmly in place, packed up their equipment and personal items the next day and moved on to further develop a budding coal Mecca named Buchtel.

Chapter 7 – Breaker Boy

Patrick "Bud" Neeley started working in a Pennsylvania mine as a breaker boy in 1895. He was twelve years old. The minimum "legal age" for breaker boys was fourteen, but if a boy was tall and looked strong, he soon found himself in the breath-stealing damp of the mine. Bud's da Aiden had been a miner; his grandda Clancy had been a miner. Undoubtedly, Bud Neeley knew, his sons would be miners.

It was hard to ignore the fact that his da had died at 32 of miner's asthma, a common, deadly fate of anthracite coal miners. Bud had been only eight but he remembered well hiding under his blanket at night, trying not to hear Aiden's racking cough. He tried hard not to see how the man he worshipped weakened, his frame becoming shriveled as his weight dropped and dropped. At the end, it was hard to tell his da from his grandda, as both showed the effects of a lifetime breathing coal dust. Clancy, strong as a bull, sat, his Irish green eyes clouded with grief, silent tears creasing his weathered, face, watching his first-born son pass from this life. Clancy held Aiden's hand as if he were a child and rocked forward and backward in the anguish known only to a parent whose child is preceding him in death, upsetting the natural order.

For twelve hours, sometimes fourteen hours, like his da and grandda had done, Bud ruined his back on the same hard wooden bench in the breaker, high above the colliery, bending over the bins. He broke his knuckles and his nails to a bloody mess picking chunks of slate and rock from the valuable coal, learning to ignore the agonizing pain in his back and the raw wounds on his hands as they scraped against the bins. He was a breaker boy, starting a lifelong cycle which would progress through trapper boy to driver to laborer to miner…and then, as old age took its toll, back to the breaker.

It hadn't occurred to Bud that there might be another sort of life for him, a life of education, wearing clean clothing, breathing fresh air. He was blessed with good looks, the classic wavy black hair and blue eyes of Irish legend. His quick mind could have taken him out of the mines to some vocation much less taxing and more rewarding. Of this fact, Bud was oblivious. Mining coal was all he knew, all he had seen since infancy, save for the few men who ran businesses which also relied on the mines for their existence.

Indeed, Bud could have been a lawyer or a teacher. He loved to learn and to help others to improve their minds. The other breaker boys called him "professor" when they saw him stash a book in his pack and pull it out to read just a page or two as he waited for the doors of the breaker to open. Yes, he would have made a fine teacher. Instead, he learned very young to accept constant fatigue, the incessant din of the machinery in the shafts and the gangways, the danger of succumbing to one or more of the poisonous gasses which insidiously overtook miners, the stench of coal and mule droppings which clung to his nostrils even after washing them away. This was the way of life. He knew no other; therefore, he desired no other. Born in the shadows of the colliery outside Pittsburgh, Bud figured he would die the same way his da had...yet, it didn't make him sad, just resigned.

With a deep and abiding belief in God, faith that He would not send more Bud's way than he could handle, Bud began and ended each day in prayer. Sunday was Bud's favorite day, even when he was a small child, because he was able to spend most of it in church. Listening to the hypnotic lull of mass being said in Latin, talking with his God, healing his spirit for another week of hard labor; he would then spend the remainder of the day reading quietly with his mother and sisters.

Bud believed miners who labored hard, lived clean, blessed their savior and did His work were favored in the hereafter by God. He believed that miners lived a good life. It was what his mother had taught him, what his da and grandda had believed, and even when the end came much too early for Aiden, leaving his family to grieve and carry on, Aiden died struggling to find the breath to praise the Lord. This fact spoke volumes to Aiden Neeley's boy, and from that day on, Bud never questioned God's will.

As the starting whistle blew at 7 each morning, Bud and the other breaker boys were in place and ready for their day. Relentlessly the belts brought the coal down from the drift mine. The bent and blackened miners and laborers battled in their ongoing war against nature in the western Pennsylvania mountainside. Maple trees grew in abundance on the mine property, yet they wore black leaves, thick with the coal dust which escaped the breaker. Even the stream which bordered the mine ran with black water, rendering it unsafe to drink. All in all, for a non-miner, it was a grisly scene. The miners saw it every day and didn't notice.

Working as a breaker boy was punishing work, yet the boys hollered jokes and curses back and forth among themselves in language more fitting for a grown man and during their too-rare work breaks, scuffled and chased one another in jollity over the culm piles. Eventually a superintendent or foreman would put an end to their boyish behavior, sending them back to work in the breaker. Bud shared in the jokes and the frolicking but never in the curses...his ma would wash his mouth with lye soap if she heard him curse.

Breaker boys learned quickly not to make mistakes in the breakers; mistakes cost money. Their meager wages, usually 60 cents a day, wouldn't support a family but they helped, when added to the wages of their fathers who were drivers, laborers, and the most-prized position of all, miners. Some prize. Miners took their lives into their hands every day, carefully drilling into a breast of coal, placing blasting caps into holes they had bored and detonating them, always with a muttered prayer that the vein would open up to reveal its riches without bringing the timbers down to crush the lives from all of them.

It was true that the miners labored shorter hours, being paid by the car load; when the breast was exploited sufficiently to fill the allotted cars, the miners were free to go home, leaving in the capable hands of their laborers the backbreaking work of loading the coal onto the cars and turning it over to the drivers. It was this shorter day which generated the fiction that miners had a special job and why breaker boys, trapper boys and laborers alike all looked forward to that glorious day when they could be certified as miners. The young men learned to overlook the statistic which proved "miner" to be the most dangerous of all occupations, inside and outside the mine.

It was also true that laborers worked physically much harder, loading the cars, a task which took many hours and paid only half what the miner made. But the laborers knew that it was only through years of conscientiously serving their miner "butty" that they would qualify to take the legendary certification test for the prized job of miner. Consequently, they slaved over the piles of loosened coal, picking it up, placing it in cars and helping the drivers to direct the mules up the dangerous slopes.

Many unfortunate laborers, who turning their backs too soon, found themselves minus a limb or crushed to death beneath the wheels of the car which wasn't properly hooked to the preceding one by laborers. Teamwork wasn't a luxury in the mines; it was a matter of survival.

Some breaker and trapper boys, wise beyond their years or benefiting from good guidance from a former breaker boy, took advantage of an opportunity to lay aside a small portion of their pay through the company, secretly, before the pay rolls were signed, squirreling away 50 cents or a dollar a week for their own futures. Usually, their mothers were none the wiser, and whatever the breaker boy brought home was accepted gratefully. It was only in the homes which were all miners, even the women, that the savings plans of the boys were discovered, to the dismay of mother and son alike. Women and smaller children, on occasion, worked on the culm pile, searching for the small bits of coal which may have been missed in the breaker; they were allowed, in some mines, to pick those tiny pellets of coal for their home use.

* * *

For three years, Bud worked the breaker quickly and efficiently, earning the notice of the breaker boss. All breaker boys worked hard but few did their jobs silently and as diligently as Bud did. Still only fifteen, Bud's diligence paid off and the breaker boss recommended he be moved to the position of trapper, a job which paid much more and caused less physical pain.

In the fall of 1898, Bud Neeley moved from a social job, albeit a physically agonizing job, to a mentally agonizing one. Now his day was spent standing or sitting in the dark bowels of the mine for hours on end with only his tin cap lamp and a book for company, working the ventilator shaft door, waiting as the cars, pulled by stupid but hardworking mules, approached the door to the shaft, opening and closing the doors so as to lose no time and sparing the precious life-saving air which was blown in by massive fans placed in vertical shafts overhead.

As a trapper, Bud rarely saw his old friends from the breaker, rarely exchanged words with another human. The older drivers were often broken-spirited, and even the younger drivers, not much older than Bud, knew it was in their best interests to appear to be all business, so they passed by him with only a brief nod. It was a solitary life but a safer one than the ones which awaited him on the other side of the doors.

Many trapper boys, unable to read, out of sheer boredom, drew amazing murals on the walls of the shaft, telling tales in pictures for future trapper boys to see—unless the breast was exhausted, and then the shaft was sealed, sealing in the artistic endeavor of as much as a year's work. An avid reader, Bud learned to be content with his own company and his books, a trait which would serve him well the remainder of his life.

For the two years he served as trapper boy, Bud learned to find solace and stimulation in books. Even though his eyes watered and his head ached from attempting to read in the near dark with only the flickering flame of a miner's cap light, his mind expanded with each book he finished. Although neither his da nor his grandda could read, his gentle mother loved to read aloud, read the Bible, read anything she could get her hands on and she taught Bud and his two sisters to read and enjoy books.

By lantern light after their weary and ailing da had fallen into a deep stupor, the three Neeley children traveled in their imaginations to faraway ports, embarking on adventure after adventure—Bible stories, Irish folk tales, fairy tales—first mesmerized by the soft, hypnotic sound of their mother's voice as she read the enchanting tales to them, then later, as Aiden grew sicker and their worried mother cared for him, the children took turns reading aloud as best they could until sleep overtook them.

Years later, alone in the dark, squinting at the tiny pinpoint of light from his cap light, Bud thanked God and his mother for the gifts he had been given, the ability to read and the gift of desire to know more about life than the walls and pillars of the damp and moldy mines could ever provide. He thanked his da for the faith in God which helped him get through the long, lonely days, never feeling totally alone but, rather, comfortably in God's presence.

For two years, Bud passed his time at the doors, jumping to attention when the rumble of the returning coal cars approached, then returning to his private world. When Bud was seventeen, as a new century dawned, a rumor traveled quickly through the mines of a second large coal discovery in southeastern Ohio, in a town named Buchtel. These mines were run by a man, one John R. Buchtel, who was, legend had it, quite unlike other mine owners, a kind man who had made tremendous efforts to create safer mines and better working conditions.

John Buchtel had opened a store, even, which was operated at a minimal profit, offering prices to the miners and their families equal to or even below what they would pay in the nearby towns. This was unheard of; the "company store" was notorious for robbing the miners, even though such exploitation was now illegal.

As the story of this new mine and its owner traveled by word of mouth, the reputation of this owner took on the proportion of a Santa Claus or perhaps even a disciple of Jesus Christ himself. A smart man, Bud knew the way of folklore in and around the mines—unreliable; nevertheless, during the miners' strike of 1897, many older miners and laborers had migrated to Ohio looking for work, and the news of their success and prosperity had trickled back to the mines in Pennsylvania.

The prospect of travel had always fascinated Bud and he discovered that day that, God willing, he would like to head west. Man of the family, though, from the age of eight, Bud knew he could never leave his family with no source of support. Yet again, God had a plan for Bud: in 1902, Bud's mother Elaine married a widowed farmer she had met in church. A taciturn man, his new step-father, Bud found it awkward when his mother and sisters moved to the farm. This seemed to be a message to him that he was released, somewhat, at least, from his role of sole provider. He had saved well for two years to accumulate enough money to go—and the dream had never left his mind.

* * *

Packing everything he owned into two large satchels that sunny day in early autumn 1902, extracting promises from his sisters to be good for their mother and not to cry at his leaving, he kissed them goodbye. Bud shook hands with his somber step-father, wished his weeping mother farewell with a promise to write when he was settled. With intense misgivings but also great exhilaration, Bud picked up his last paycheck and bought a ticket on the Chesapeake and Ohio Railroad heading west into Ohio. He had never before been farther than five miles from the company home in which he was born.

As the train rattled through the Allegheny Mountains just turning vivid with fall's paintbrush, the young miner's eyes were wide with the wonder of the world outside a coal mine. He was going away from the only home he had ever known, and although his heart occasionally caught in trepidation, it beat faster at the life he was to make.

As the mountains gave way to a rolling landscape, still resplendent with foliage, the train passed several huge mining companies, the tipples towering above the wheel houses, train tracks making circular patterns very familiar to Bud. The busy scenes were familiar to the traveler; he saw scores of men with horses and mules laboring outside the mines who turned their heads his way and waved as the train passed, as if somehow they knew he was one of them.

Night fell before the hypnotic clackety-clackety-clack of the train's wheels began to slow a bit, then a bit more, until, with a hearty blast of the whistle, the C. and O. came to a clumsy stop in front of the long, low station house in Nelsonville, Ohio. Standing and gratefully stretching his cramped legs, Bud grabbed his smaller satchel from the overhead bin and moved to the door, peering right and left, up and down the track, trying to see in the typical Southeastern Ohio warm-weather evening fog, and finally, with his larger satchel over his shoulder, he realized for the first time the enormity of the step he had taken: he was completely alone, on his own, for the first time in his life, in a strange place.

He squinted to see the walls of the mighty Hocking Valley Canal, which ran parallel to the tracks, sitting idle now at midnight, but one of the busiest canals in Ohio during the day, or so Bud had heard. The fog made him strangely claustrophobic. Trees looked like they were advancing and retreating, a ghostly sight, and the air felt sparse, stifling. Crossing himself as he stepped away from the station, he realized he had no idea where he was going. Turning back to the stationmaster, he asked in his lilting Irish way, "Yo, mister, would ye be knowin' a place I could get a room for the night?"

Nodding over his shoulder, the master replied, "Yep, over yonder, see that light? That's the Dew House. It's about a half mile up that there road. They've got some single rooms that don't go too dear, I heard," and went back to his magazine.

Looking the way the master had nodded, Bud's eyes could barely make out a light shimmering eerily in the fog. Used to fog in Pennsylvania, still, this fog seemed almost thick enough to slice; it was disconcerting. "Thank ye, sir," Bud said, with a tip of his cap, and ignoring the sense of apprehension caused both by the fog and the unfamiliarity of his surrounding, the young man set off walking toward the light. "Lord, help me find this hotel before I fall in the canal and drown," he prayed, hoping he wasn't drawing his last breaths.

Through the grace of God and his own determination, after about fifteen minutes, Bud nearly walked smack into the columns of the Dew House porch before he realized he had arrived at his destination, just putting one foot in front of the other and looking ahead at nothing but soggy gray and an occasional flicker of yellow light. Sighing with relief, and wiping the moisture—part fog and part sweat—from his face, Bud entered the cheery hotel, the first one he had ever been in in his short life, and made his way to the desk where the desk clerk was dozing, fitful snores escaping from under his huge moustache.

The lobby, with its cherry furnishings and cut crystal gaslight lamps, looked so elegant to Bud that he was momentarily afraid that he couldn't afford to stay there—but fatigue won out and he woke the clerk to inquire about a single room. Giving fifty cents for a sleeping room for just one night, a dear price, the adventurer realized that he would have to make his way to Buchtel and find cheaper lodging really soon or he would be sleeping on the ground!

The young miner from Pennsylvania couldn't resist looking around this grand place, despite his fatigue, and he wandered up and down the upper hall, his eyes wide. He ran his fingertips over flocked wallpaper, peering out over the balcony at the lobby below, thinking to himself how much he wished his mother and sisters could be seeing this incredible place...that thought suddenly making him very homesick. Not fond of his mother's new husband, Bud had to acknowledge that he had mixed feelings about this adventure. Elaine appeared happy, however, and the girls were treated well...so his worries seemed pointless. Besides, his room was cozy, the bed was comfortable, and after washing up at the washstand, nibbling on a bit of beef jerky and saying his prayers, young Bud Neeley, in his new surroundings, slept the sleep of the innocent of heart, knowing, somehow, his God would provide.

Chapter 8 – A Carpenter, a Miner, and a Lady

[Winter 1903]

Bud Neeley didn't behave like a miner outside the mine. The young man didn't drink alcohol. He didn't chase women. He didn't even own a gun. An Irish Catholic, religion was something he practiced, standards he lived by, not just words to say in church on Sunday. These convictions set him apart from the hard-drinking, rough-talking, pistol-packing crew of Sunday Creek #4 mine operating in Buchtel. Maintaining his own priorities, he located the Catholic church before he even found a place to live, a single room in Minnie Claire's Rooming House.

Bud had a difficult time reconciling the behavior of his fellow workers with the religion they all claimed to have…on Sunday mornings. To Bud Neeley, religion meant living a clean and decent life, doing God's work, working hard, praying hard, not drinking yourself into a frenzy, picking a fight, laying with the loose women who hung around the saloons near the mine. For Bud, relaxation meant going home, washing off, preparing a humble but nourishing meal, reading quietly until bedtime, then restoring his spirits in sleep.

But one day when he was least expecting it, Bud realized that he had found the woman who added a different dimension to his life, the woman who was the one he wanted by his side, and he quickly recognized that going home alone no longer satisfied him. The fact that he had to compete with another man to win her hand made her even more a prize to be treasured.

She had her sights set on Fred Hunt, it was clear, the day in 1903 when then twenty-year-old Bud was first captivated by the charms of a green-eyed seventeen-year-old minx, Jane Moore, as she came into the company store in Buchtel. But that made her all the more intriguing to Bud. Quiet by nature, and inexperienced with women, Bud kept an eye out for her any time he was near the store her father ran for the mine company. Jane's father Peter Moore was a well-respected and fair man, the only type of man the late John Buchtel would hire to serve his miners.

Moore, as general manager and junior partner, kept the mark-up on goods at 10%, usually less than that charged by the independent merchants in Athens and Nelsonville, and he granted credit extensions readily, knowing the fickle nature of the mines.

The object of Jane's affection, Fred Hunt, occasionally helped out his old friend, Jane's father, on busy Saturdays in the store. His daytime hours during the week were spent building houses and cabins with his own building company in nearby Modoc to be rented to the miners with families. Bud had known Fred for several months. They were members of the same parish, and Bud had seen Fred work relentlessly with the crews hired to create housing for the ever-growing swarm of miners lured to southeastern Ohio by the rapid expansion of the mining industry. A hard worker himself, Bud respected a man with a strong work ethic.

The man destined to be Bud's rival was a formidable opponent, a youthful thirty-six, slim and strong, of average height and looks but possessing expressive golden eyes, a warm smile, and a ready laugh. His wit was quick but never unkind, the type it was impossible to find offensive. Bud found it no surprise to learn that the spritely Miss Moore was interested in Frederick Hunt, despite their age difference.

"Ay and she wouldn'a be human if she didna notice Hunt," Bud reflected, more than slightly jealous. Handsome enough, smart, hard-working and easy to talk to, Fred stood out among the coarse, poorly educated men who flocked to the area. Possessing a powerful energy and sharp intellect, Fred had risen to foreman of the New Lexington construction crew in only two years, and his ability to speak comfortably with people of all trades in the appropriate language for their class was a natural gift, indeed. Bud knew that now Fred was part owner of his own construction company, one with a solid reputation of quality work, impeccable ethics, and usually the lowest bid on every job. Like a chameleon, Fred Hunt adapted to his environment seemingly without effort.

It was clear Fred had a bright future ahead of him. Already twenty years in the construction field, Fred hired and supervised many men, some of them ten or more years his senior. That could have made him unpopular, but it didn't because he knew when to defer to the judgment of the men on his crew, when to give credit to a worker for an innovation.

Good with tools, better with people, Fred Hunt was already at the top of his field. The well-known San Toy-Rendville project was a feather in his cap; he got the job done, saved the company money and ingratiated himself with his superiors. Accepting an opportunity for more responsibility, Fred finessed a loan at the First National Bank to buy in as a partner, and was now one third of Cable, Rowen, and Hunt Enterprises. His bids were often the lowest because of his extensive knowledge of the type of building associated with mining boom towns: he had built eight of them already. Respected and trusted, Fred Hunt had everything going his way.

It looked as if the object of Bud's affection might also be going Fred's way, Bud sulked. "All that and he's a Christian, too," Bud recognized... "Kind of hard t' hate the bloke." Why Fred was unmarried puzzled Bud and others but no one asked. It would certainly make Bud's life easier if he had been.

One of the most eligible bachelors in the Nelsonville area, Fred enjoyed his popularity. Often, the Friday and Saturday night dances would find Fred in the company of one of the daughters of coal barons or physicians, or occasionally a comely red-haired teacher from Nelsonville. He escorted ladies to Stuart's Opera House; he attended balls at the Dew House. Fred was a competent dancer, strong and agile, and was also known to have musical ability, to play several stringed instruments and to sing with a strong and pleasant voice. No, it wasn't any wonder that Jane and other women found him captivating; Bud frowned when he heard of these additional attributes his would-be rival possessed.

A few threads of silver gracing his temples, the mature and solid Fred was interested in women, certainly, but he also had a good head on his shoulders. Bud recognized that Hunt knew he needed to keep his wits about him, to focus on his work at work and on play only at play. He worked hard. Rumor had it that he also played hard, but no reports of bad behavior ever centered around Fred. The rivalry was about to commence.

Single girls, marriageable ones, that is, were a precious commodity in an environment filled with, at a ratio of four men to every woman, randy men of all ages. A girl of only moderate beauty would find herself in no way lacking for male attention. A pretty, emerald-eyed charmer like sable-haired Jane Moore was the target of dozens of young men, miners, furnace workers and laborers alike, to say nothing of shopkeepers and professional men. She could literally have her pick...and she clearly picked Fred and made no bones about letting him know it. Bud thought Fred Hunt had to be blind, knew he wasn't, and puzzled about his rationale.

Slim, graceful, and moving with both energy and style, Jane—named by her literate and romantic mother for the heroine of Bronte's *Jane Eyre*—enjoyed the attention, of course, of the single men and the admiring looks she received as she shopped in Nelsonville or helped out in the store her father ran…but her heart fluttered only for the venerable Mr. Hunt.

Finding excuses to come into the store on the Saturdays Fred was there visiting with Peter and helping out with customers, Jane would become uncharacteristically tongue-tied and shy and unable to put even the simplest of sentences together, or the opposite, to exhibit nearly manic energy, jabbering and fluttering about, his aura was so befuddling to her senses. It was as if he had cast some sort of spell on her, bewitching her with his presence. Bud stood back and watched, waiting for his chance.

If Fred was aware of Jane—and Bud suspected he was—his sense of propriety kept him from approaching his old friend's daughter, and of course, their age difference concerned him, so Jane's efforts to catch his eye seemed to her to be fruitless.

* * *

"What is wrong with him?" Jane asked herself. "What is wrong with me? The other men don't act like I'm invisible…" and she would frown, sneak one more look at his strong back and tanned muscular arms, sigh dramatically and give up her pursuit—but only for the moment. Young, feisty Jane Moore was a determined young woman.

On a rainy evening in February of 1903, Jane had reached her frustration tolerance level and was ready to leave the store in a sulky mood when she, distracted by the allure of Fred Hunt, backed into Bud Neeley, lost her balance and nearly tumbled over a bench. Bud's protective instincts toward girls, learned at home with his two younger sisters, propelled him to grab Jane around the waist, hauling her unceremoniously back to her feet, preventing a fall—and for his efforts, to receive a huffy "Let me go!" and a very withering look from the lovely but disgruntled Miss Moore, who was mortified that the object of her affection just saw her in a less than graceful moment.

Speechless both because of the near accident and because of the rebuff of the delicious Jane Moore, Bud tipped his cap, backed up a step, and mumbled, "Sorry, miss."

Brushing herself off, she haughtily marched out of the store as both Bud and Fred followed her ravenously with their eyes. Each noticing the other's attention, Bud and Fred nodded to one another, exchanged awkward, embarrassed smiles, and went about their business, Fred to wiping off his counter and Bud to his exaggerated examination of boots.

Peter Moore had missed the scene which had just unfolded but he looked up in time to see his daughter, in one of her tempers, stomping out of the store. "That girl will do herself in one of these days, with that wild spirit of hers," he remarked to Fred, not noticing Fred's blush nor the intensity with which he had watched the dramatic departure of Jane.

"She's all right, Peter. Just…uh…got herself in a mite of a situation there…" stammered the somewhat uncharacteristically flustered Fred.

Bud discovered that he was still standing in the same spot, with a boot in his hand but staring out the door at empty space. Recovering his composure, he completed his selection of a pair of boots and carried them to the counter where Fred was standing. Taking stock of the young miner, Fred Hunt remembered him from church and also from earlier visits to Moore's General Store. Bud was one who always paid his bills within a reasonable time, so he offered, "So, Bud, would you like me to put those boots on your account for you? Those will last you a good long time, they're fine boots."

"No, I can pay for them today, I can. Had a good week…" and Bud placed three dollars on the counter. He found it hard to meet Fred's eyes…

"Lots of overtime this week? I heard the new workers were coming in from Buffalo next week. My crew is working overtime too, trying to get the last two cabins ready for them," Fred offered as he wrapped up the boots.

"You heard next week, it was? I heard they wer'na' due until April…we're to be pulling overtime for the rest of the month," and Bud furrowed his brow, hoping Fred Hunt's information was wrong, and the infuriating Miss Moore temporarily forgotten. Good overtime was quite a precious commodity.

"Well, maybe I heard wrong, but we're finishing up those cabins this week anyway, just in case. You have a good week now, and watch out for those falling girls," Fred replied with one of his characteristic slightly crooked but contagious smiles and a private wink.

Returning Fred's devilish smile and fighting off a blush which threatened to cover his handsome Irish face, Bud took his package, saying "I'll just do that. You have a good week too, Mr. Hunt, and I'll see you next Saturday."

Leaving the store, Bud was sorely distracted by the little incident with Jane and by her very intoxicating presence, and as a result, nearly ran smack dab into the captivating wench again, the young lady having stopped to gossip with her friends outside the store. Realizing that she had already seen him, even though he wished himself invisible, Bud braved her wrath by meeting her eyes and smiling boldly. "Uh…top o' th' mornin'…again, Miss Moore. This seems to be our day to collide with each other!"

Meeting his eyes but with a blistering look, Jane cocked her head his way, spitting out, "Yes, and you're certainly clumsy for a miner. I hope you are more careful with explosives than you are with your feet, or you aren't long for this world," and she turned haughtily away from him and back to her friends, who were gaping hungrily at the very handsome blue-eyed miner, wondering what was wrong with Jane not to see how incredibly attractive he was.

More than a bit perturbed now, Bud headed back to his wagon, but not without a glance over his shoulder at the headstrong but very intriguing Miss Moore. Thinking to himself, "Missy, I might just have to tame that wild temper of yours," Bud decided at that moment to make Jane Moore his own. Once Bud Neeley wrapped his Irish mind and will around a plan, no one could put it asunder: Jane Moore had best watch out!

Chapter 9 – The Plot Thickens

[Spring 1903]

"Why doesn't he see me? What do I have to do to let him see how much I love him?" she wailed. And Jane Eyre Moore slammed her hand against the railing in frustration, the pain of the new bruise adding to her unhappy tears.

"Drat, drat, DRAT that man!" she hissed under her breath to no one in particular as she gracelessly plopped down in the swing on the front porch of the house she shared with her mother and father. An only child, Jane was used to getting her own way. This dilemma, this man left her befuddled. She sobbed into her handkerchief for awhile, and then, out of energy, her sobs turned to spoiled sniffles, the kind which used to drive her father crazy when she was a child. But no one was here to comfort her or reason with her, so without an audience, the tears dried up, and a pout took their place.

She had just left Moore's General Store, the company store her dad Peter owned and ran for the mining company, and one more infuriating encounter with the man who tantalized her teenaged fantasy, haunted her dreams, the magical, mystical Frederick Hunt of the golden eyes. Although he was never rude to Jane, Fred made a point of being cool and casual with the adolescent daughter of his best friend, acting more like an uncle than a suitor, undoubtedly the only behavior he felt was appropriate, but this wisdom was lost on Jane today, in one of her snits.

"The devil with his appropriate behavior! I have to come up with a plan which will just knock some sense into him," Jane fumed. She had just about decided to come right out and tell him how she felt, tell him he was the only man for her, tell him to open his incredibly hypnotic eyes and see what was staring him in the face…then, once again, she had lost her nerve and become a fluttering wreck as soon as he came close to her, her heart racing, her hands clammy, her head swirling.

"He makes me…what? Crazy? Stupid? Senseless? Oh, I don't know…I can't think…oooohhhh…" Jane sulked, and went back to her plotting.

In spite of nearly twenty years age difference between them, Jane had made up her mind to have Fred Hunt, to win his heart and addle his mind until he just had to propose to her or face the wrath of her father. Unquestionably the most eligible bachelor in the county, Jane just assumed Fred Hunt was hers for the taking—didn't she always get what she wanted? But her plans, thus far, had brought her only embarrassment and more frustration. She babbled like an idiot, tripped over things and people ("And wouldn't you know, the one time he WAS looking at me, that idiot miner had to make me look stupid!" Jane fussed), and generally made a fool of herself in front of the man she so longed to impress.

"Soooo…what can I do to get his attention?" Jane thought to herself with a sigh. "Could I walk up and bump into him accidentally? Or how about this? What if I flirt with another man so that he can't help but see? And if he cares at all, that should make him realize he has to make a move…I'll bet that miner would play along…" A smile played with her pouting lips as the idea began to take shape.

* * *

The very desirable Frederick Hunt was indeed aware of Jane's feelings for him, more than aware of her "crush" as he saw it, too much so. She flitted around in his head more than he intended. In his dreams, too, much to his dismay, she teased him and beckoned to him then pushed him away, leaving him frustrated and angry. Perplexed by his own feelings, he hadn't allowed himself to consider them, both out of loyalty to Peter and because of her age.

"She's only seventeen, for God's sake! What am I thinking…" but he realized he wasn't thinking at all, pounding nails with a fury. He had left the store right after his unsettling experience, watching the woman he wanted be rescued by another man…and realizing how jealous it had made him. "Work…that's what I need…" Fred fretted, and he hurried to the building site.

Even though she made feeble excuses to come into the store when she knew he was there, even though she preened and primped in front of him, and even though she had boldly sidled up to him and looked into his eyes with the heat and intensity of another type of woman totally, Fred was determined to maintain his composure. He'd been spending more time in prayer than usual, asking for the strength to resist this temptation…but she even haunted his prayers.

"Little miss, you're not making it easy, coming in the store looking like dessert…" Fred grumbled as he nailed a ceiling beam in place with more force than necessary. Working outdoors was where Fred was most in control; this home, like all others that he built, was receiving the best that could be had, the Fred Hunt magic touch which had become a standard other construction companies could only strive for, rarely achieve. The strenuous physical activity helped to ward off those demons he was battling…not very successfully, though, and he felt out of control. Jane robbed him of that control. That made Fred Hunt furious.

In his natural element, the construction business, Fred was always captain of his own ship. But his concentration was poor today. When she nearly fell earlier, his heart had jumped into his throat and he was about to leap over the counter to rescue her, had that miner not done the job first.

"Thank goodness for you, Bud Neeley. I was about to make a really big mistake…" and Fred Hunt forced cat-like green eyes, silky black hair and the face of a very captivating elf back into the farthest reaches of his brain. That was becoming harder and harder. He found her appearing to him like an apparition when he was least prepared to deal with his wayward thoughts. Not used to being captivated by a woman, these "appearances" were driving him crazy.

Fred had been courting a widowed schoolteacher from Nelsonville, Esther Wood, for nearly a year now. He loved spending time with her. Pretty, funny, and intelligent, the high school rhetoric teacher Esther was the perfect companion. They often attended shows at Stuart's Opera House, or parties thrown by other business people in the Nelsonville area, and she sparkled, made him proud that she was on his arm…culture rubbed off on Fred and he quickly assimilated new experiences, adding them to his repertoire of conversation material.

Last weekend they had attended a political speech, by a Roosevelt politician hoping to capture a senate seat vacated by the sudden death of its previous occupant, and when Esther asked to shake hands with the politician, he discovered that he, a man who never cared for politicians, was being "courted" by this senate hopeful, and he attributed much of that interest to his charming lady friend.

Esther flattered Fred, made him feel powerful. The fact that Esther also occasionally allowed him to spend time sharing her bed was definitely a plus for the lusty Fred Hunt; he was always discreet and Esther knew that her reputation wouldn't be besmirched, so she enjoyed their rendezvous as much as he did.

Unlike some of the other available young ladies who would love to share Fred's bed, Fred was proud to take Esther to dances at the Dew House or concerts on the public square. She was a good dancer, well educated and interesting to talk with, and his friends all envied him his cultured, charming friend. Best of all, she was patient with Fred, tolerant of the occasional rants he went on when something seemed out of kilter. She let him rant until he had run out of words, then quietly sorted through his thoughts with him until both of them understood his position on the issue—he hadn't even known he had "issues" until he started seeing Esther.

She was a comfortable place for Fred to be...he felt safe with her; he respected her; he loved spending time with her—he wished he loved her. Unfortunately, that was the problem. His heart was not involved with Esther Wood, only his mind and his body.

Even his body had begun to betray him, as he noticed the effect that Jane Moore had on him, and he didn't like it. He opted to spend more time with Esther, but even that hadn't helped. Jane was in his blood and it infuriated him. Feeling that it was only a matter of time until he said or did something irretrievable, Fred found himself in a serious quandary. To speak to his friend Peter? To marry Esther? To give in to his increasing desire for the devilish Jane Moore? The first was terrifying. The second, unfair to Esther and himself. He liked Esther too much to marry her... The third seemed inevitable but his conscience would be forever sorely tortured...what to do?

* * *

As Bud rode slowly home to the bachelor miners' quarters just a few hundred yards from the entrance of Longstreth Mine #4, his mind focused on the captivating face and body of Jane Moore. The pony trotted homeward, a route so familiar to both pony and owner as to require little thought; accordingly, Bud allowed his fantasy free rein. And what a fantasy it was, enough to leave him breathless. "Whew! What a colleen that one is! She needs a tamin', that's for sure," thought the agitated young miner, recognizing to his surprise that her very unruly and disrespectful nature, instead of alienating him, charged his blood and fueled fires he had never felt before. His interest in her shocked him; she was not the type of girl his da would have called "marryin' material." But that was indeed what Bud intended for this fierce woman.

As the lengthening shadows signaled late afternoon, Bud discovered that he had totally misplaced the three-quarters of an hour which had passed since his second encounter with the young demon, his mind occupied, somewhat addled by mesmerizing green eyes, a face which flashed from rage to humor and back to rage in an eye-blink...and the powerful impact that brief physical contact with her had inflicted on his senses.

"It's time I found me a woman. Didna' me ma say that just before I left home? 'Course, I think she was meaning someone she knew, someone more like her…but hey, this'n's the only one I want." That realization came with sudden clarity, jolting Bud upright in the saddle.

"This woman" was clearly foreign territory for Bud Neeley; that may have been part of her attraction. Unaccustomed to women who speak their mind, to spitfires, Bud was a bit befuddled but a whole lot fascinated. His gentle mother, saddened by raising three small children alone, smiled rarely despite her new marriage, and always wore the countenance of martyred grace and humility. His sister Charlotte had an entertaining sense of humor but was always deferent to men, being raised as she was by her mother alone, with her brother and occasionally her grandfather Clancy the only males to interact with. Grandda Clancy's spirit had been broken by Aiden's death and by forty years in the coal mines; consequently, the time he could give his granddaughters was limited and usually took the form of a lecture on proper behavior for a woman…and Bud was just a brother, for heaven's sake. No, "family women" didn't count.

The man of the house from the age of eight, Bud knew how to work hard for a living, how to protect the women in his charge…but he had no one to teach him how to act with another type of woman, one who would spark his tinder, or even to explain the strange, new sensations he was feeling. What little he knew about women came from listening to other miners talk, and, making him blush, Bud was wise enough to know that much of what he was hearing was just boastful imaginings.

Somewhat stunned by the realization that he had found a woman he really wanted, Bud finished his ride home a sober man indeed. It was painfully obvious that Jane Moore had Fred Hunt in her sights, as it was that she considered him, Bud, a nuisance. "Well, I'll just have to find me a way to fix that, now, won't I?" Bud mused to Petunia, his pony. "But where to begin?" As Petunia offered no answer, Bud squared his mind around the dilemma and decided to pray on it and to think really hard, think what might bring the difficult Miss Moore around to a more charitable impression of Bud Neeley.

Chapter 10 – Love Hurts

[Spring to fall 1903]

"Uh-oh. This can't be good," he thought, as he nailed another roofing board into place. He pretended not to see Jane Moore's graceful buggy cresting the hill and heading toward the house he was working on. "That woman is asking for trouble…and she's liable to get it," Fred grumbled. She was in his thoughts too much as it was, in his fevered dreams, too.

Not since Sara Brown had a woman so totally captivated Fred Hunt, rendered him nearly helpless to resist her. And the fact that she continued to throw herself his way was making his determination to avoid a relationship with his best friend's daughter—very young daughter, at that—much more difficult. He had tried to ignore her, to no avail. He had asked for an answer in his prayers, but as yet, hadn't found one. She was bold, crass, irreverent…and totally irresistible, making him battle more than just his conscience.

When she came into the store last week, though, Fred suddenly recalled, she was different, strange somehow, and it puzzled him. She had always flirted with Fred before, made excuses to get close to him…drove him crazy, to be exact, with her obvious attraction to him. Last week, as she danced in the door, he had steeled himself to resist her onslaught, set his mind on inventory, using the inventory as an excuse to go to the store room when she came in. But then she was suddenly there, and just so casual, not making any effort to attract his attention, smiling once but moving on…leaving Fred baffled, and, although he hated to admit it, disappointed. In fact, she had gone over to that young miner, Bud Neeley, and apologized for being curt with him last month when he caught her, kept her from falling.

It was weird, now that he came to think about it…she moved in on Neeley the way she had always done to him, even laid her tiny hand on his arm and looked up at Neeley with those amazing eyes. "The poor fellow was tongue-tied," Fred recalled. "He stood there with his mouth open, trying to say something, and nothing would come out. The way she was smiling up at him…it was pretty damn clear that he wanted to devour her right there in the store."

Damn the woman, damn damn her, Fred thought—she has that effect on men, all men, evidently. "Hmmm… it really was weird, she didn't come over to me at all…I wonder why…" And he did wonder, suddenly, and had to admit that he had missed her flirtations, missed having her close, having to resist her, a thought that scared him down to his socks.

Stealing a glance over his shoulder as the object of his distress came closer, he caught his breath: the brilliant March sunlight was playing a trick with her raven hair, shimmering off her crown with the appearance of a halo…but this girl was no angel. Flirtatious, even downright shameless at times, she had spared no effort at placing him in situations which could result in physical contact. Bumping into him, brushing his arm, situations which turned his knees to jelly, weakened his resolve with a sultry gleam in her sensual green eyes. Then it seemed she just gave up…but now she's back. "What's going on in her pretty little head?" Fred wondered. "She is playing some sort of dangerous game…"

Even this far away from him, she worked a spell, destroyed his concentration, shook his faith, turned his thoughts to lust…and she was coming closer.

"Oh, damn!" He wasn't going to be able to pretend he didn't see her much longer. "The brazen thing is going to keep coming! What is wrong with that woman?" he wondered, not even noticing that his thoughts had changed her, over the course of the past several months, from "that girl" to "that woman."

"Twice her age, for God's sake…what is she thinking?…I could be her father…" but he shook that thought off quickly; his feelings for her were certainly not fatherly. As she reined in her horse just at the foot of the ladder which held Fred precariously near the top, he feigned surprise: "Oh, Miss Moore, hello. I didn't see you…"

Stepping solemnly, slowly, from the buggy, she looked so surprisingly sad, so unlike the Jane Moore he had come to know, that he could hardly breathe. Lifting her tear-filled eyes to his, she pleaded, "Fred, I need to talk with you. Please. This is important." And the three other men on the roof huffed, smirked at each other and at Fred's discomfort.

Shooting them a withering glare, he began to descend the ladder, praying for will power, praying that he could stand firm in his determination to keep her at arm's length. And he had to admit—both to God and to himself—that he didn't want to keep her at arm's length anymore. This was neither the time nor the place for this conversation, nonetheless, and he intended to tell her so…but she just stood beside the buggy silently, sadly and his heart melted at the pain in her face.

Sighing, Fred reached the ground and stepped hesitantly toward Jane Moore, no longer Jane the child. Clearly this was Jane the woman, and even worse, the woman he wanted, wanted to comfort, wanted to hold, wanted to take to his bed. His mind jolted as that last thought struck home: "...oh, God, please...my woman?" Leaving him stunned and motionless...

She reached out hesitantly to touch his arm, and he could swear that sparks flew, the intensity of her passion was so evident. "Not here, Jane. Not now. I can't do this here..." choked out the disoriented Fred, realizing that he had revealed much more than he intended.

Her cloudy face turned soft as she recognized the intensity in his voice, the bare emotion behind the words, recognized the acceptance in his resigned air. "Then where and when?" she whispered, her voice husky.

Trapped by his own weakness, he realized his guise of indifference was shattered, and he felt vulnerable—but strangely exhilarated. "Tonight. By the statue." And thus he stepped into the ring of fire which she had set ablaze.

* * *

It was warm for March, but Ohio was unpredictable that way. Knowing he may have set a ball rolling which could easily careen out of control, nevertheless, Fred, washed, shaved and dressed in a handsome flannel chamois-colored shirt which reflected the golden flecks in his caramel-colored eyes. His heart pounded as he walked the three blocks to the Civil War statue which sat at the edge of downtown, his stomach queasy at the moral battle which raged within him.

"What the hell am I doing? This is totally crazy!" he told himself, hesitating for a few seconds, tempted to turn around and go back to the hotel where he had a permanent room, knowing it would break her heart but perhaps for the best of reasons...yet it was as if he were being pulled by a magnetic field, and he strode on, powerless to stop.

"Those damned eyes of hers just look clear into the back of my soul. Why does she have so much power?" he raged silently. He had always been able to keep his emotions under control; women, he enjoyed, treated well, but kept them from knowing him, the true and unfettered him. But Jane Moore, she somehow stripped him of his defenses, left him out there in the open.

Fred Hunt was a good and moral man, raised to respect God's laws, one who believed in the Golden Rule, in the Ten Commandments, one who was fair in all his business dealings, and one who had, up until now, been, if not celibate, at least discriminating in his liaisons, wise with his heart...what was happening now was as foreign to him as the air flight from Kitty Hawk which was reported by the *Athens Messenger*, totally outside his comprehension.

Ridiculous, out of character…and downright stupid, he decided, was this meeting with young Jane Moore, yet his feet seemed to move on with a will of their own. By the time he reached the statue, he had managed to work himself into an angry state and was fully prepared to unleash his anger at her for causing him all this worry…and then he saw her, tiny and helpless looking, with a waif-like innocence about her and worship in her eyes, totally different from the woman he called "brazen" in his mind just that afternoon. Yet another facet of the gem called Jane… Befuddled again by the many personas of the lovely Jane, his anger dissipated and a resigned smile took its place.

Looking up to see him smiling affectionately at her, Jane's face lit up with love and trust, a look which finished melting his heart. He held out a hand to her which she took, pulling him down beside her on the bench. For several seconds, neither of them knew what to say, so intoxicated were they by each other's presence and so overcome with new feelings, that they just sat facing each other silently, each studying the other's face intently as time stood still.

Reacting then to a primal force, the couple drifted forward toward each other, seemingly without willing it, simultaneously falling into their first kiss, and by so doing, incinerated Fred's good intentions and sealed a covenant between them which had begun several months earlier.

Whatever he had planned to say was lost in the moment; whatever she had planned to say had become unnecessary, and they sat silently, hands clasped, eyes locked, hearts beating wildly, oblivious to others who passed by the bench, oblivious even to the passage of time. How long they sat there, neither of them could have told, but during the silence a bond was forged which they knew would take them down a path which would be memorable and totally new for each of them.

Later, walking hand in hand along the edge of Monday Creek, moonlight framing them in its silvery glow, Fred finally found his voice. "What is happening? How can this be? We really can't do this…"

"Shhhhh. We can. You know how you feel. I know how I feel. What else is there?"

And as he looked down into her eyes so full of love and worship, he almost believed she was right, that what they felt was all that mattered. Almost…

* * *

It was inevitable, Fred decided later, that they would become lovers, despite his honorable intentions. But inevitable or not, it was the most terrifying situation he had ever been in, being out of control, being so overcome by emotion and passion that nothing else seemed to have any significance, not his friendship with Peter, not their age difference, not even his religion...nothing.

As he walked with her into his room for the first time, it felt so right, nothing but right; the raging battle with his conscience receded into the haze of the passion he felt for her. The battles resumed every night, long after she had left for the evening...and battles they were, waking him at 3 a.m., torturing him with visions of burning in hell, of degrading Jane's purity, of giving in to his basest urges, and he would resolve again to end it...but he pushed those images aside immediately, the moment he met her eyes the next evening.

For the rest of that summer, Jane Moore and Fred Hunt explored each other, their bodies blending into the twilight romance of new love, hidden in Fred's room every evening, talking and laughing with an intimacy far more personal and overpowering, even, than their desire...and by fall, Fred had to admit that he was madly and hopelessly in love with this gamin of a girl, and he had absolutely no idea what to do about it.

There was no way Peter would allow him to marry Jane. He wasn't sure that was what he wanted, anyway, their philosophical differences were so great. It was almost as if he was being tested by God...whatever he held dear she felt was trivial; his religion she regarded as primitive and restrictive. He believed a wife would be, should be like Dorothy, home centered, wife and mother above all; Jane intended to go to college, to have a career. She believed women should vote, should hold political office, should work wherever they wanted, should be equal partners in all areas of life.

He greatly respected her ambition, yet he knew he would feel threatened by it and would ultimately stifle her, whether it was what he intended or not. In short, he recognized that they would eventually destroy each other.

On a more practical note, he also knew it was only a matter of months until he had to pick up and move again; the construction project was nearly finished, had, in fact, taken longer than he thought it would. (He even wondered whether it was his relationship with Jane which had made him unintentionally drag his feet on finishing the project...) No matter how hard he tried, he couldn't visualize Jane Moore, the spoiled daughter of a middle-class merchant family, used to having what she wanted when she wanted it, living the vagabond life of a contractor who followed the coal mines. And he knew, even as he lay in her arms drinking in the scent of her, that the end was coming for them and that it would be the hardest thing he ever had to do, that he had to break her heart…and his own.

He faced her silently in his bed, still drenched from their lovemaking, and traced the contours of her sleeping face with his fingertip…and an unexpected tear escaped from his eye. Afraid she would waken and notice, he sat up, grabbing his shirt and pants, dressing in the dark and sitting beside the bed in the only chair the room possessed, watching her sleep, feeling the enormity—and the agony—of his love for this tiny woman. His decision seemed preordained.

And so it was that Fred Hunt, man of integrity, man about whom no disparaging word had ever been said, packed his gear, instructed his crew to finish the current project under the supervision of his best foreman, and boarded a three o'clock train, stealing out of Nelsonville like a felon, leaving no forwarding address. And so it was that Jane Moore, arriving at his room for their evening rendezvous to find his room empty with no signs that he had even been there, found herself abandoned, devastated, totally alone, broken in heart and spirit. As she sat huddled on the floor of the hall outside his door, weeping miserably, she attempted unsuccessfully to deny what she knew, that Fred Hunt was gone from her life…and that she was two months gone with his child.

Chapter 11 – For Better or Worse

[Autumn 1903]

As Bud was coming off his shift at the mine, early autumn twilight had just begun to streak the brilliant sky. Trying futilely, out of habit, to wipe away the coal dust which had imbedded itself in the oil of his overalls, he looked up with a start to see a sleek black buggy, drawn by a dainty chestnut mare, turn into the grounds in front of the wheelhouse…and to recognize with astonishment the object of his affection, Jane Moore as the driver.

Making a frantic effort to clean his coal-streaked face before Jane could see him looking like an escaped convict or worse and adding more streaks for his effort, he was even more astounded when, after speaking briefly to the guard on duty who pointed Bud's way, she drove her buggy toward him. His two pals, laborers working for the same miner he did, hadn't noticed her yet, their interest on picking up their paychecks, but it was impossible for Bud to be in the same county as Jane Moore, let alone within fifty yards, and not be aware of her. His heart picked up its pace.

Hating for her to see him this dirty but knowing there was nothing he could do after ten hours in the bowels of the earth, his vision stayed riveted on her as she approached, baffled as he was as to why this shopkeeper's daughter, one who never knew hard labor or the effort it took just to survive, one who was never dirty and had every hair in place at all times, would be on the grounds of a coal mine, getting coal dust in her luxuriant hair and on her expensive frock…then his bafflement turned to amazement when she saw him and waved. Standing stock still as if he had suddenly grown roots, Bud looked furtively left and right over his shoulder to see if it could be someone else she was waving to, and recognizing incredulously that he was her designated objective, tentatively waved back.

Their last several encounters had been less than satisfying for Bud. He adored this girl, worshipped her, in fact, found her appearing more and more in his dreams, in spite of her moodiness and quick temper, but she always seemed to find him a nuisance…except that one time, six months ago, in Moore's General Store, where she seemed really to like him. He could still feel the way his heart had pounded and his throat constricted as she came up to him, peering up at him flirtatiously from beneath her black lashes, a capricious smile playing with her lips. But before he had time to get his hopes up that she really was interested in him, that interest had faded, so he decided with great dismay and disappointment that he must have misread her intentions.

When her visits to the store stopped suddenly, Bud had stopped going to Moore's as much as possible. Seeing her had been the high point of his week; deep within the mine, he often plotted and planned what he would say to her the next Saturday…and then always lost his nerve, settling for a quick exchange of inane pleasantries…then she stopped coming in. Bud thought he knew why…

So what in the world was she doing here? Everyone knew she and Fred Hunt were courting…well, not courting, exactly…but somehow intensely involved…everyone except her father, that is. Peter, Jane's dad, suffered from a malady that attacks many fathers, the inability to imagine his child—female child, especially—in a grown-up relationship. He remained willingly or unwillingly oblivious to what was obvious to the world around him, that his baby girl Jane and his best friend Fred were seriously smitten.

To Bud, she was cordial but distracted. They chatted, discussed weather, but nothing more. During the summer, her usual moody disposition seemed to change to one of perpetual sunshine; Bud was romantically naïve but not stupid and he attributed her moon-struck behavior to Fred, especially since her mood change coincided with a corresponding change in Fred, who also seemed to be walking around in a perpetual haze. Yes, he was jealous, but not angry; Fred was a worthy gentleman, mature, well-established and a far more educated and worldly man than he.

Not that Bud had totally given up…just that he had dropped back to reconsider his options, uncertain whether he could compete with Fred Hunt, or even whether it was worth his effort to try. Until she disappeared altogether…

But here she was. What could be the reason? The coal dust swirled around the buggy and Jane in devilish little eddies, but as she drew closer, Bud could see, with great concern, her look of apprehension, quite unlike the countenance she had worn since spring. Although he had never been in love before—that he knew of, anyway—Bud suspected that these feelings he always experienced when Jane was around were love. They were too intense and too unsettling to be any less. Seeing her now like this, disturbed in spite of the broad smile she seemed to have on as an adornment rather than as something that came from within, made his heart ache.

Jane reined in the chestnut directly in front of Bud, so there was no question now that he was her objective, but for what reason Bud couldn't imagine. Although he couldn't help but be suspicious, his feelings for her made it impossible to walk away or to feign indifference. Concern for her welfare overrode his cautiousness.

* * *

As Jane approached Bud, her stomach turned over in fear. Tension and wariness rippled in his face; Jane scrutinized the high, prominent cheekbones, masculine and handsome in spite of the grimy streaks, the thick dark eyelashes, almost but not quite girlish, which framed his amazingly intense deep-water blue eyes now looking at her with concern…and it made her heart ache, both with anguish at her immediate flash to another pair of intense, beautiful eyes, golden, not blue—and also with guilt at what she was about to do.

Steeling herself, she spoke to him softly. "Hi, Bud. Can we talk for a minute?" she asked, feigning cheerfulness.

"Of course, but not here, seein' as it's so dusty 'n' all…wouldn't want ye to get all dirty…" he answered with just a hint of brogue—which she suddenly found charming.

"That doesn't matter. Come with me and we can talk over at the mill. There's no one working there right now," and she patted the leather seat beside her.

Uncertain as to what to do, Bud looked down at his clothes, at the clean seat of her buggy, at Jane, then, gulping and absently brushing off his oilcloth overalls and shrugging his shoulders, climbed up the single step to the seat beside her. Relief washed over her momentarily. She signaled the chestnut to move forward and they completed the semi-circular drive that fronted the mine, pulling out onto the narrow but substantial gravel road, Bud silent beside her.

Bud was terrified, his mind busy with speculation while his body quivered at her nearness. This was the first time Bud had ridden in a buggy with a woman—any woman—and it was not at all the way he had pictured himself while experiencing his first ride. No, he saw himself shaven, spotlessly clean and driving his own elegant coach with a white steed worthy of fairy tales and a maiden gracefully garbed in satin and lace. Instead, he was the passenger, and a filthy passenger, at that, in a worn but still serviceable gentleman's buggy…trying desperately not to stare at the driver, his one and only passion.

As they rode silently toward the deserted mill, neither of them attempted small talk, Jane because of the weight of the task before her, Bud because he had no idea what to say. The silence was awkward, heavy, nearly palpable, but neither of them broke it.

As Jane turned the chestnut into the drive of the flour mill, the sun continued to set, bathing them in an eerie purple light. She reined the horse to a stop, pulled the hand brake, and turned slightly to face the now-terrified Bud. As if they had a mind of their own, twin tears began a path down her pale cheeks and Bud was so overcome with worry that, forgetting his griminess, he instinctively reached toward her to wipe away those tears, leaving coal streaks in their place. "Oh, I'm sorry…I've got ye dirty now…" the words escaping him in the intensity of the moment.

"It doesn't matter. Oh, Bud…I need your help…please…" And more tears erupted, breaking Bud's heart right on the spot. Whatever she would ask he would gladly deliver, cut off an arm? Walk barefoot over coals? Just not to see her cry…

He found his voice buried deep in his misery. "What do ye need? Please, Jane, don't cry…I'll help ye in any way I can…don't ye know that? Ye must know that I…" And he pulled her to him, coal grime, tear-soaked face forgotten, as she sobbed into his shoulder. "What is it, dear? What's troublin' ye so?"

For another minute or two she sobbed as he held her, rocking her like a baby and crooning, "There now, it'll be all right…there, there…" His love for her nearly burst his heart from his chest as she cried in his arms. Gradually the sobs began to subside, trembling taking their place. Basking in the feel of her, he wished that they might sit like that forever, his arms encircling the woman he loved, but finally she quieted and pulled back to look earnestly into his face, knowing the enormity of what she was about to ask him to do but sensing too that this was a man for whom no request was too large…and she began her halting, heart-breaking story.

* * *

Jane Moore became Mrs. Patrick Neeley two weeks later, in the tiny Catholic church at the outskirts of Buchtel. Her father walked her down the aisle, his jaw grimly set into a grimace which was supposed to resemble a smile, while her mother openly wept in the first pew. Only a dozen well-wishers attended; Jane found it agonizing to repeat her concocted story of love at first sight to explain the hasty marriage.

Bud invited two of his miner friends, who were seated, awkward in their Sunday suits, just behind his sister Charlotte, the only one of his family who had made the long train trip for his wedding. Although his mother trusted Bud's judgment in all things, her deep alarm over the sudden nuptials kept her home, not wanting her doubts to mar her only son's special day. Finding it difficult to hide her feelings, Elaine, Bud's mother, thought it best not to participate in something she suspected she might disapprove of. Knowing as she did the instinctive protector of women her son had become upon his father's death, Bud's mother had a nagging sense of foreboding. She had never heard mention of this woman Jane until the letter arrived announcing her son's plan to marry her the following week. And so, sending her love and best wishes in a letter with Charlotte, Elaine prayed for her son's happiness and for his future…and stayed home with her husband and Polly.

Charlotte, sitting there in the left front pew on Bud's wedding day, could see in her brother's face, as he waited at the altar and then followed his bride's progression toward him, a radiance that could only come from love…and she too said an extra prayer for her brother's happiness. Bud had always been the one to look out for the women in his life and Charlotte had no doubt he would be a fine husband to this woman he obviously worshipped.

But was this petite, solemn woman right for her generous, trusting brother? Would she, as she was promising now, love, honor, cherish, and obey him until death do them part? Where was the joy, the exuberant excitement brides were supposed to feel? Where was her smile, for heaven's sake? In her face, Charlotte saw affection, respect, and trust…but did she see love when Jane looked at her husband-to-be? The fact that Charlotte couldn't answer that disturbed her to her core.

As Jane and Bud exchanged vows, Charlotte looked back over the past week. Gracious enough when introduced to Charlotte, Jane seemed to have a mysterious sadness about her that seemed incongruous with the joy that being married should bring. Planning the ceremony, fitting her dress, the woman her brother was marrying was efficient and agreeable…but not giddy, not weak in the knees delirious the way Charlotte's best friend Gretchen had been when she married her true love the previous month.

"Going through the motions" was the phrase that occurred to Charlotte, not really feeling what she was saying. This fear struck Charlotte to her core, for Bud was her idol, her protector, her best friend. But Bud clearly chose Jane, clearly adored her and wanted to be married to her, and that fact had to be enough to focus on. Charlotte shook off the visions which disturbed her, put on a happy smile and watched as her brother married the woman he loved. One could only trust in the Lord and in Bud…and hope for the best.

"…I now pronounce that they be husband and wife. They whom God hath joined let no man put asunder…" And so it was to be. Jane Moore had become Jane Neeley and she and her beaming groom ran from the church to their waiting freshly washed and flower-bedecked buggy, a wedding gift from Peter, and from there to the life they had vowed to share with each other. The wedding was over; the marriage was just beginning. Two dozen guests waved as the couple rode off to begin their honeymoon in the tiny three-room married miner's quarters Bud had just rented. Peter Moore stood grimly watching. His wife couldn't bring herself to stand with the well-wishers…

Chapter 12 – Jane Moves On

[Summer 1907]

In June of 1907, as master miner Bud Neeley labored deep in the Buchtel shaft, his wife Jane labored as well, struggling to give birth to her third child in the back of a wagon which served as make-shift infirmary for the crew of Sunday Creek Mine #2. Supported by an efficient Negro mid-wife Cora Corbin who had delivered two babies already that day there in the shadow of the towering breaker, Jane, totally frightened and feeling helpless, labored on a hard cot which was dirty and disheveled. She would much have preferred to have her baby in the hospital in Nelsonville which had just opened, with clean doctors and white-clothed nurses to tend to her.

Between pains, she focused on her husband and their life he had created for her. Dear Bud, he did so much for her, tried to do everything in his capacity to make her happy and comfortable…but paying hospital expenses were totally beyond his capacity, and thus, she had never asked; thus, she lay here, amid filth, in total terror. But she was young and healthy, and after all, childbirth was a natural process, wasn't it? Wasn't it?

"Oh, please God, let it be over soon," she prayed silently and tearfully, until gripped by another pain, she lost control and wailed pitifully.

As her time drew closer, Jane grew even more afraid. Neither of the other two babies had been difficult births, but she could tell this baby didn't want to come into the world, a mother knows those things. Echoing her fears silently, Cora, the sweating midwife, tried not to let her worry show as she strained to turn the baby into a better position for delivery, the sweat dripping from her chin onto the rough blanket, but Jane recognized the look of grim determination on Cora's face. A competent midwife, she had, after all, delivered Jane's other two children…and never looked like this. Jane moaned as Cora forced the baby's head down from its rotated position, and she wept, both with fear and exhaustion.

The midwife had grown fond of this tiny, frail-looking woman and hated the fear she now saw. "Don't fret, dear," Cora encouraged her, "...old Cora'll get this young'un born, you jist hang on."

But Jane didn't hear her, lost in pain and terror; she lay sobbing and writhing...and, desperately missing her mother who had died of yellow fever the previous summer. Jane cried bitterly and felt totally alone.

* * *

Three hundred miles away, Jane's father Peter worried about his daughter, knowing her time was near and that he was helpless to ease her life in any way. Peter took his wife's death very hard, and without her quiet strength to come home to, dreading his empty house, in fact, he began to spend every night drinking in taverns in Buchtel and Nelsonville. He became a well-known bar patron, oblivious to the whispered gossip from those who had known him when it looked as if he had it all.

Peter Moore was well liked and respected, but no one would step up and intervene as Peter drowned his sorrows in a bottle. Now he rued the day that he had established himself as unreachable.

As his friends predicted, Peter's life had deteriorated as lives do when overtaken by alcohol, and he had finally sold his interests in the general store he ran for five years and moved on to open one for a new coal strike in Indiana, determined to pull himself back from the brink of Hell and into the responsible, respected businessman he had previously been. Hung over and shaky but determined to fix his life, Peter left Buchtel forever, telling Jane he would come for a visit as soon as the new store was established, knowing he wouldn't; things between Peter and Jane had been strained since her sudden marriage to Bud.

Peter Moore, intelligent and insightful, had begun to put together the sudden disappearance of his friend Fred and the unexplainable frantic behavior of his daughter—and didn't like what he had figured out. It was only a father's protective blinders which had prevented him from seeing the passion which careened back and forth between his daughter and his trusted friend Fred Hunt; obviously, that much-too-late awareness, after Fred's hasty departure, had prohibited Peter from being any help to his grieving daughter as he watched, hands tied and heart in a masher, while she struggled to survive her heartbreak.

Peter had watched helplessly as his daughter's usual fire died, as she ceased being his fighting tiger of a girl and faded, shade by shade, into a resigned, focused woman, sadder by eons, wise now beyond her years. Where was his little Jane, his baby?

Accordingly, Peter found it hard to be with Jane and her husband, couldn't look her in the eye or take pleasure in his first grandson, Ronnie. He took some satisfaction from the fact that Bud Neeley obviously loved his Jane without reserve and was a faithful, hard-working Christian husband…but he was a miner, a man who would live a brutal life, probably die young, who would never be able to provide for Jane in the way a gentleman could…and this sorely chafed against Peter, making it difficult to show his son-in-law the respect he undoubtedly deserved.

Jane offered nothing to make it easier for Peter. She had fallen, surprisingly easily, into the role of miner's wife, living simply, without luxuries, working hard in her tiny two-bedroom home without running water to make a life for herself, her handsome husband and rapidly growing family…and it tortured Peter beyond reason.

Bud had managed to move his family into a slightly larger cabin when the second child was born, but the miners' quarters were a far cry from what Jane had known as a child. Peter regretted sorely now his teasing, disparaging remarks when Jane as a teenager had talked of college and a career. If only that had been possible… If only he had seen sooner what was happening with Fred Hunt… Thus, a tortured father punished himself daily and nightly.

Without his wife to act as a buffer between him and his daughter, Peter believed that he was better off out of the picture altogether, leaving Jane to the unbelievably hard and dismal life she seemed to have chosen for herself. His wife had always been able to see what had escaped him; she knew, somehow, instinctively what to do for Jane…but even she had been speechless and grim when Jane had chosen to marry Bud Neeley.

* * *

As she labored in the wagon, Jane longed for her father's protective arms, missed him terribly, but her pride hadn't allowed her to plead with him to stay, to weep in his arms as she had as a child, to confess the truth about her marriage—and her oldest son, Ronald, the one with amazing golden-flecked brown eyes so unlike the green of his mother's or Bud's blue. Ronald was her heart's delight but looking into those eyes often stirred pain buried deep within her. Ronald and his younger brother Tom were waiting with Aunt Charlotte to see their new brother or sister…and Jane was alone, both physically and emotionally.

As another pain gripped her, she pushed with all her might, letting out a shriek which split the air around the mining camp, turning the heads of the men working on the surface in spite of the din of the machinery around them, causing them to blanch under the coal dust. Nearly in unison, they said a quick, silent prayer for the small woman struggling in the wagon. There was an air of tension in the camp anyway: two of the miners' wives had died in childbirth already this year, leaving their lonely and bewildered husbands to care for children; the men hadn't realized they could lose their wives. The miners whose wives were currently expecting were, consequently, choked with fear and uncertain of what lay ahead for them.

But as the mineworkers listened uneasily for another cry from Jane, they heard instead the tiny, warbling bleat of a newborn baby. Breathing sighs of relief and uttering prayers of gratitude, the workers resumed their duties wordlessly, exchanging tiny smiles which vanished just as quickly, hidden under masculine miner bravado.

Back in the wagon, Jane lay, sick and weak, cradling her tiny son in her trembling arms, tears of relief and love wetting his tiny face. Cora, relieved as well, wiped the sweat from her own brow and then from Jane's, patting her arm, crooning, "See, girlie? Di'n't I promise this chile'd be here soon? And ain't he a fighter for sech a little'un?" He was indeed, her third son: red-faced, lusty, bawling vigorously, enough to bring a hint of a smile to his mother's exhausted face.

Briefly examining her new son, counting fingers and toes, tracing his tiny face with her finger, Jane smiled wanly through her tears, then her head fell weakly back on the cot, her eyes closed as the need for sleep overwhelmed her. Cora continued, stroking her hair, "You sleep a bit, dear, then we'll give that tad a bit of a feed and help ye both on home."

All Jane wanted to do was sleep for a week—but she knew she had to regain her strength quickly, because she had to make her way back to the row house she shared with her husband and their two older children. The house, made of Nelsonville block like the others in the row, cold in the winter and too hot in the summer, had grown unbelievably crowded with the two boys; Jane had no idea how they were going to find even more space for this tiny life...and how she was going to find the reserve strength to care for them all.

To Jane's deep relief, Bud's sister Charlotte had come to help with the other children while Jane gave birth. Jane had grown to love Charlotte dearly. She wished Charlotte could stay forever, but she, too, had a husband who needed her back in Pennsylvania. Bud, a devoted husband and father who didn't care what was considered "men's work" and what wasn't, had planned to be there to help Jane through this birth, but an accident in the coal tipple two days earlier had injured two men from Bud's crew. Consequently, all the other men had to pick up the extra duties, extending their usual nine-hour working days to twelve and even fourteen hours. President Roosevelt had managed, in 1902, to get a bill passed which limited a miner's day to nine hours, but all mines worked longer when a crisis arose…and mines were fraught with crises.

Bud was a senior crew member though only twenty-three due to his eleven years working his way up from breaker boy to fully qualified miner. Therefore, he had no choice but to take one of the longest shifts. Jane understood, but felt frightened and resentful, nonetheless, to be alone to care for the older children and a brand-new baby; accordingly, Charlotte's presence had been a godsend. Charlotte always lent a quiet strength and stability to a household which was on occasion chaotic.

Jane trusted her sister-in-law and found her presence a soothing influence on the older children. Charlotte loved to read to them and to sing to them, all activities which Jane tended to neglect in her frustration of coping with her ever-growing family duties. As an only child, Jane Moore Neeley had been doted upon by both parents and, accordingly, learned very little about sharing and responsibility. Married at only eighteen, she had little preparation to manage a household, let alone become a mother a half a year later.

Life had been a crash course for pampered Jane Moore, one she had risen to embrace to the best of her abilities. Nevertheless, without her mother's love and her father's support, she often felt like an incompetent child playing at the role of married woman, mother of three.

Jane frequently wondered what would have happened to her if Bud had been less of a decent man, if he had loved her a little less; she knew the Lord had smiled down on her when He presented her with a loving, hard-working husband with the character of Bud Neeley. She thanked Him every night in prayer, prayer a comfort she had learned from her devout husband, Bud, one of his many gifts to her.

That she still longed for Fred Hunt, that she occasionally pretended that it was his arms around her at night, Jane hoped the Lord would forgive her for those transgressions. By day, she made it her primary responsibility to be a worthy wife and mother—Bud deserved no less. She had learned in the past four years to love the handsome Irishman she had married, to look forward to his coming home at night, to lying beside him in their bed. She had learned to do without many of the luxuries she had taken for granted as the only child of a middle-class family; Bud made her life as easy as he could, working more hours than he should, buying her a new dress or bonnet when she seemed sad, holding her close when she needed to be held, helping with the children…and knowing when not to ask questions when faraway looks crossed her face or an unexplained tear marred her beauty.

* * *

Word had already reached Bud in the #4 shaft that Jane had delivered and was alive. This crew had an unusually tight bond; many of them had worked together for years, coming over to Buchtel from San Toy or Rendville. Bud knew someone would get word to him, and he was right. Jerry Todd, just a year younger than Bud and a friend, based on mutual membership in St. Luke's parish, had braved receiving discipline for leaving his post as a laborer in a breast close to the opening of the shaft, but his friendship with Bud was more important, and he knew how worried Bud had been about his increasingly fragile wife. As Mike Corey, a laborer building a new pumphouse on the surface, carried the news to Jerry by previous agreement, Jerry had promptly scrambled down into the mine to re-assure his friend that he was a father yet again.

Many of the men in this camp worried for Bud and his pretty young wife. This was her third child in only a little over three years, and the miners all knew Bud was frightened for her. And she had no parents, no sisters to worry over her…

"Is she all right? Do y' know if she's all right?" Bud anxiously asked Jerry, who had delivered the message, risking the loss of his job to carry the information deep into the breast in which Bud worked with another miner butty and two laborers. The other three men stepped respectfully away, as, trembling visibly, Bud received the news he had been fretting about all day. Their ears strained, however, for good news; Bud was a very popular man in the mine, with a twinkling in his blue eyes and a good word, delivered often in an Irish lilt, for all his crew.

"Dunno, man. They jus' tol' me t' tell ya th' kid was born," and Jerry Todd shrugged his powerful shoulders, embarrassed by Bud's obvious display of emotion, and turned to return to the shaft, calling over his shoulder "Don't worry, man. She'll be okay…" hoping he was right; he knew Bud believed the sun rose only for his Jane.

"Wait!" Bud pleaded. "Can ye tell her…tell her I love her? Please? An' tell her I'll be home as soon as I can…please!" The desperation in the young man's voice touched the normally unemotional Jerry's heart and he turned back for a moment. It was no secret in the mine or in the church how crazy Bud Neeley was about his green-eyed spoiled wife. The fact that she now seemed so frail was alarming, not only to Bud but to his friends as well. Her health had deteriorated with the birth of her second child so soon after the first, and the sparkle which usually filled the room when Jane entered it had disappeared.

Although Jane and Bud rarely socialized, when they did, both of them found themselves at the center of conversation groups, as others just naturally gravitated toward the intelligent, cultured woman and her charming husband. But her vigor seemed to have faded recently. And now there was another child... Bud missed that snap of energy she always displayed; he often blamed himself for her loss of vitality.

The anguish in Bud's face melted Jerry's tough façade, and he responded, "If'n I can find someone to cover for me, I will. Never you fret, you hear?" With that, Jerry began to scramble along the track which would take him back to the surface.

Bud stopped to wipe the wetness from his face. He knew it wasn't manly to cry, but what was "manly" was of no concern to him; his fear for Jane was overwhelming and his relief that she had survived the third birth left him shaking and weak. He had promised God that, if He just let Jane live through this birth, he, Bud, would work even harder to live in His image.

Checking that no one was watching, embarrassed at his display of emotion—the others worked on without him, making a great show of not listening—Bud lowered his head, offered a prayer to the Virgin Mary to protect his family, crossed himself, wiped his face again, and fighting back nausea and dizziness, resumed his tedious and very dangerous task of packing explosives into the vein of coal, struggling to concentrate on the task at hand. Trembling hands and explosives were clearly not a good combination...but Bud carried on, nonetheless.

PART 3—SARAH

Chapter 13—Sarah Washington

[Summer 1907]

Sarah Washington smoothed the wrinkles out of her faded apron with her strong, calloused hands, looking at the sky hopefully. "Lordy, we need rain somethin' terrible," she said to herself, eyeing the somewhat promising clouds, dark at the bottom and heavy looking. "Mighty peculiar thing, weather," she thought, "half a year ago there was so much rain the poor little valley flooded real bad, and now, no rain for weeks…"

Casting a glance at the small cornfield she and her husband Jeremiah had planted behind their Nelsonville house, Sarah frowned with worry. The drought would make the kernels too small to be of dinner table quality. If the corn failed as a grocery item and had to be consigned to cattle feed, Sarah knew it would be nearly impossible to find the extra money they needed for school clothes and shoes for Marcia and Paul. That was unacceptable to Sarah.

Although living inside the city limits, Sarah felt at home only with some land to hoe, soil to sift through her long fingers. Farming came naturally to Sarah and Jeremiah, raised on adjoining farms in Marietta. But farmers had no control over the weather; the weather had been fickle for the past year. Farmers can till the soil, plant the seeds, weed and watch over the tiny plants…but only God could provide water. "Lord, would it be too much work t' spread that rain out a bit, 'stead of sendin' it all in one big bunch like y'did in April? But ours not t' reason why…" Sarah reflected, never one to question God's will.

One of only ten Negro families in Nelsonville, her children and the Corbins were the only ones in the First Street School. Being of color made them stand somewhat apart from the other children already without being made fun of for their worn garments; Sarah was determined the children would have decent clothing and shoes to wear.

Both children excelled in the classroom. Marcia, long and lanky with hair that never wanted to behave, was ten and in the fourth grade, reading at sixth grade level, well-liked by her teacher, accepted by her classmates…although she rarely went home with any of them, except for Cassie Jefferson and their neighbor, Katie Corbin.

Paul, already displaying his father's striking looks and affable personality, was eight, in second grade, with math his greatest strength. He didn't much care to read, unfortunately. Their teachers were good women, caring, fair. Sarah wanted more for her children than she had for herself. "Never satisfied, that's your problem..." she chastened herself. Somehow, though, Sarah knew there was more. She read voraciously; she knew there was more.

At tough times, Sarah would remind herself that her mother Hannah had considered herself fortunate just to escape the blacksnake whip, spending her childhood as a slave on the Hartney plantation in Roanoke, Virginia. Hannah hid the scars on her back...but the ones on her spirit had never faded. Hannah's parents and her husband Eli's parents had made their way to Ohio at the end of the Civil War to let their children grow up free and without the stigma of slavery...but the children of both families were still terrified of being captured and returned to the South as runaways; they heard chilling stories from Hannah and other former slaves, of whippings, rapes, lynchings and worse. Sarah and her sisters could barely imagine what the "and worse" consisted of...

Emancipation hadn't come comfortably to the plantation owners; many were bitter enough to use the guise of the Ku Klux Klan to punish former slaves for their "crime" of receiving their freedom. "Free" was just a word in many Southern states. The South had gone straight from slavery to segregation.

Sarah was born in Marietta, Ohio, just across the Ohio River from West Virginia, in country which had never known slavery, a free child of freed parents. Marietta had long been a "safe haven"—one of many stops on the Underground Railroad, a lifeline for endangered and indentured slaves.

Nevertheless, even though Sarah and her two sisters had grown up free, the stigma and shame of slavery—and the fear of renegade slave hunters who make a living rounding up any black person to deliver as a "runaway"—had caused the girls' parents to be wary of white people they did not know and to caution the children to be quiet, courteous, and respectful at all times, a demeanor common to freed blacks in states which, unlike Ohio, had been forced to abandon slavery against their will.

The posture of a "proper nigger" was ingrained from infancy as protection against punishment: head lowered, hands clasped behind the back, eyes to the ground, posture non-threatening, and language full of "Yessums" and "No sirs." Sarah hated it. The posture offended Sarah's high-spirited nature, and with her height and regal bearing, it was difficult to slump and look subservient, but she and her sisters had heard many tales of masked raiders coming in the night to round up any Negroes they could find and transport them back to the South to be sold at the now illegal but still existing slave auctions. Slump they did.

They had also heard that young black women were often used as mistresses or worse…so offended or not, Sarah followed the unwritten code of conduct and encouraged her younger sisters to do the same. It made her shudder to think of what her kin had suffered.

Little by little, however, Hannah and Eli had relaxed their vigilance; eastern Ohio had been good for them and most free Negroes found jobs in the mines, the lumber mills or the surrounding businesses, and were residing in decent housing, many of them helped by sympathetic white families. Sarah and Jeremiah had married when she was sixteen, he twenty, their parents friends from early childhood with much in common.

Sarah had also grown up as close friends with neighboring white children, Nell Rush and Louise Brackner, the daughters of the saloon keeper and the blacksmith of the southern part of Marietta. Sarah, bright and inquisitive, sobbed when Nell and Louise went off to school, leaving her unexplainably at home with her mother. Sarah begged to go to school too.

"Why, ma'am? Why can't I go to school too?" Although she begged, and couldn't be consoled, not even with Hannah's excellent oatmeal cookies, Hannah had no answer for Sarah, just a sad shake of the head and a strong hug to ease the pain. Hannah was well read and eagerly taught Sarah and Jessie to read and write; nevertheless, Sarah vowed that when she had children she would see that they got to go to school the same as the white children.

Sarah lived to learn, however. Learning was like air, like water, to Sarah, a necessity. Fortunately, Nell was a dramatic little thing, who loved to teach Sarah the lessons she had learned that day. Also fortunately, both girls were very quick to learn and it was to Nell's credit that she asked her father to buy some of the older books that the school had replaced so that she and Louise could hold school for Sarah and her sister Jessie, who was then six to Sarah's eight. Grateful to her friends, Sarah read every word of those tattered books, her fingers tracing each word lovingly, and then began them again, wrapping them in scraps of cloth left over from Hannah's sewing to protect their covers from any more devastation.

Like a person on a long fast, starved for more and more learning, it wasn't long before Sarah was an accomplished reader and even hungrier for more books, more knowledge. She read *Uncle Tom's Cabin*, and wept as she read; she read Soloman Northrup's true saga, *Twelve Years a Slave*, a horrifying story of kidnapping and torture, which served as partial inspiration to Harriet Beecher Stowe. She read of William and Ellen Craft who had walked a thousand miles to freedom, disguised as white peasants, and she made their struggles her own.

Reading was still the adult Sarah's passion. Her most recent heroine, now that she was a mother, was Mary McLeod Bethune who had, three years earlier, established a college for colored women in Florida. It was Sarah's fondest hope that Marcia could attend college, could have a life which wasn't limited by the color of her skin. Marcia was a quick student and had already expressed the desire to go to college. Her mother's heart broke at the thought that that dream might never come true.

Sarah loved the lyrical prose of Washington Irving and Benjamin Franklin as well, and although she had to struggle hard to understand their lofty language, forced herself through the Puritan documents in an effort to understand the minds of the early settlers of America. She found Cotton Mather frightening, but was, nevertheless, mesmerized by his hellfire and brimstone rantings. As a child, Sarah had lived many lives through the characters she admired, and suffered with the downtrodden of both colors.

* * *

But now, while Sarah's mind was back in Marietta, and her eyes were on the corn and the brown grass, she didn't hear her husband until he spoke, making her jump. "Sarey, girl, you look like you're a-wandering again. Where are ya?" Jeremiah placed his huge, muscular arm around her shoulders and kissed her cheek lightly.

"Oh, you go on, mister, my thoughts are my thoughts! You can't know everythin' now, can ya?" She gave him a playful punch to the ribs before she bent to pick up her laundry basket and, shaking off her reverie from a few moments earlier, moved toward the clothesline tied between the house and the oak tree. The tall, handsome Negro man watched her with translucent hazel eyes, his Sarah. With an affectionate smile on his rugged brown face, Jeremiah thought, "I got lucky with that woman, Lord I did."

The first time he noticed his beloved Sarah, she was all of ten years old, hanging up the family's wash behind their humble house in Marietta, her face serious yet calm, her lanky body strong and well formed, much like their daughter Marcia looked today. Sarah had worked quickly at her task, all the while keeping a watchful eye on the younger girls Jessie and Bettina; at that moment, Jeremiah knew by instinct that someday she would be his wife.

Jeremiah helped her father Eli tend the small collection of animals—five cows, a bull, a handful of goats and chickens—and the fields of corn and soy beans which bordered his family's property, helped for the past year, but somehow, he had never noticed the exceptional oldest daughter, her being just a child to his fourteen years, nearly a man. But this day had been different, as he saw her framed in the early morning sunlight, working diligently at her task. It wasn't her beauty which stopped him cold, more like her spirit flowing out around her, making him suddenly aware of a quiet power seeping into him from her.

And as he had determined at that moment, so it was to be, that Sarah Robinson had indeed become his wife six years later. He thought of her now, thirty years old, as beautiful and powerful as she was at ten, more so as life experiences gave her wisdom. Thinking of his wife always made him smile…her spirit still infused him with joy and vigor…and frequent desire, he had to admit. Her power still gave him strength; he would protect her and the children with his life, if need be.

* * *

As Sarah worked at her task, Marcia came running from the front door, calling "Mama, Paul isn't helping me with the veg'bles. Tell him to help me, Mama," bringing a tiny smile to Sarah's face, hidden, of course, from her stormy-faced 10-year-old daughter.

Jeremiah shared the smile, whispering, "I'll jist leave ya to deal with that young'un, missy!" and slipped away to his chores behind the house. Marcia kicked at the dirt sullenly, scowling at her 8-year-old brother as he swatted at her with a long twig.

"You go on, now, Paul Michael, leave your sister alone or she might just take care of ya good," Sarah cautioned her playful but frequently annoying son. "It's just as much your job as hers to snap them…those beans for supper…unless you'd like to skip a meal, of course…"

With a final swat, the youth and his sister stomped back into the house, as Sarah heard snatches of "…did not," "…did too" drifting back to her. Shaking her head in the eternal posture of the mother of two children close in age, Sarah went back to her laundry. She mused, "Those young'uns'll be the death of me…" but as usual, felt her heart swell with love and pride at her strong, handsome family, and with worry that when school started, Marcia and Paul would be singled out, not for their very good brains, but for their color and their worn clothing. That started her mind working again, thinking of ways to pick up an extra dollar or two…

She already took in laundry from two widowers who were raising children alone; what they paid her wasn't enough for the physical labor involved, but Sarah knew how hard life was for a man without a woman, especially one with children to raise, so she made do. Both gentlemen were courteous to her and appreciated the neatness of their children's school clothes, courtesy of the ironing Sarah did on her own time and for which she had never asked to be paid.

Could she take on more laundry? What other possibilities were there for a black woman? House maid, perhaps, but her own family's needs would make it really difficult to take on a position that demanding. She could cook well, and had considered asking at the Colonial Restaurant or the Dew House if they needed another cook…as yet, she hadn't been able to make herself take that big a step.

Jeremiah didn't want her to work more than she already did; she knew he felt that he was letting her down as a husband and provider if she had to take a job. While she didn't want his pride to suffer—he worked hard at the elementary schools while school was in session and farming their small patch of land in the summer—she hadn't told him how little money was left from his job, and since school would be starting in two weeks, she needed money now. Such a dilemma…

Chapter 14 – The Underground Railroad

The story of the black citizens in Nelsonville had begun many decades earlier, as men, women, even entire families, arrived in southeastern Ohio to escape the yoke of slavery.

Taking up as little space as possible, and working long hours in the mines, the iron furnaces or the fields, Nelsonville's first black residents had established a toehold for those who came after…courtesy of one amazingly courageous group of people, most of whose names are still obscure.

They were the brave, defiant abolitionists. They were black and they were white; some were even red, although few knew the key role the Seminoles and other Native Americans played. They lived in the North and they lived in the South, even the Deep South. They were Catholic, Quaker, Protestant, and Jew. They were wealthy and they were poor, professional and laborer, working as mine workers, preachers, teachers, laborers and homemakers. They were young and they were old and every age in between. Many of their identities will never be revealed, so well did they hide their efforts. They had nothing in common yet they had everything in common. The basic belief undergirding their common goal was later expressed eloquently in the words of Abraham Lincoln: "As I would not be a slave, so I would not be a master."

They were magnificent, the conductors, the station masters, the connections of the most mighty and most righteous yet the most unsung of all civil rights movements in the history of the United States of America. They took their inspiration from Sojourner Truth, from Harriet Tubman, from Susan B. Anthony, but also from Gus West, George DeBaptiste, John Curtis, Ellen Craft and the famous Quaker Levi Coffin—names known only by those affected by their bravery or located in dusty records in a safe house.

Many homes used as safe houses may never be discovered, as conductors destroyed evidence of their routes to avoid being found out and thereby lose their liberty or even their lives…many depots sprung up overnight and disappeared just as quickly.

One of the most inspiring stories of the Railroad, one of Sarah's favorites, involves George DeBaptiste who was, in approximately 1850, a well-to-do black businessman from Detroit who used his ships to transport runaway slaves to Canada, labeling his "cargo" as "black wool." Affiliated with the intriguing DeBaptiste saga is a courageous and intelligent runaway known only as "Jim" who escaped to Canada, stayed only a few months, returning to Kentucky to request reinstatement as a slave, a behavior unheard of in the South. Unbeknownst to the Kentucky owner was Jim's plot, his motive in this peculiar saga.

The story goes like this: In a heroic and clever effort to disarm the slave-owners, Jim relates to the surrounding plantation owners and all who will listen that Canada is an unfriendly place and that no one should consider going there. He claims that he made a terrible mistake by running away, and most especially, by running to Canada. His owners and other white plantation masters, lulled by his passionate discourse, use him as a model, having him talk with their slaves, thinking that they are thus safeguarding their "property" from the urge to escape and head north.

After a year of secret meetings with other local slaves to plan a daring coup, Jim then escapes again, taking with him this time not only his wife and children but also fourteen other slaves, again using DeBaptiste's willing assistance, leaving his owner totally dumbfounded! Jim's name grew to heroic proportions ever after.

Sarah's family most enjoyed the touching but amusing legend of Henry "Box" Brown who devised a way to cram his body into a cloth lined shipping carton only two feet square and have himself "mailed" to an abolitionist in Philadelphia. In spite of being in the box for several days and being tossed around the way cargo normally is, upon opening the box, the worried abolitionist was greeted with a simple "How do you do, gentlemen?" and Henry Brown slowly unfolded himself, a free man. What price freedom?

Whether blatantly defying convention and running slaves over borders in the bottom of wagons, digging "invisible" basements in the homes in free country, or simply raising money for the cause of freedom and humanity, the abolitionists and those directly involved with the Railroad risked their lives, their property, their families—but never their souls—on the correction of man's greatest inhumanity to man, slavery, human bondage.

From Florida to Ontario, they created secret rooms, tunnels, dry wells and cisterns, to aid in the cause. Ohio was one of the key states in the movement, situated as it is north of the Ohio River, but also because of the many canals and railroads, the flourishing commerce which carried coal, ore, lumber and other goods in all directions, including the favorite direction of escaping slaves, north, of course, to Michigan and then into Canada.

It is pretty well agreed upon that the name "Underground Railroad" came from some sort of word-of-mouth legend, but exactly what the legend was seems to be in dispute. One story says that an escaped slave named Tice Davis ran away from his owner in Kentucky and was followed by a posse to the Ohio River where he virtually evaporated from sight. The leader of the posse wondered if the slave had "gone off some underground railroad."

Or another version, close enough for all intents and purposes, follows the previous story line but attributes the name to the slave's owner, who is quoted as saying "I swear, that nigger got aboard a railroad that runs underground!"

Either version of the story expresses the frustration, not only of the owners, the posses, and the slave bounty hunters who were losing huge commissions, but also of the historians who have since immortalized the Underground Railroad. Facts are few and far between; data is as hard to find as are the hiding places of the many brave Negroes who risked terrible discomfort, exposure, disease, and even death to make the United States live up to its Constitution, establishing that "all men are created equal." Although there was no "railroad," the terminology is apt, and the "train" made hundreds of successful journeys.

Sarah took her children to one safe house in her hometown of Marietta and tried to instill in them the awe she felt for what had transpired fifty years earlier…but being children, Paul and Marcia found the hiding crevices of the strange old house creepy and asked to be taken outside.

Some of the tales of violence Sarah read would chill the blood. There is the story of a magnificent Negro named only "Joe" whose beauty, strength and obvious intelligence commanded prices in excess of $5000 on the auction block. Joe was bought by a plantation owner who chatted with Joe, treated him nearly as an equal during the journey to Joe's new home, then called him out early the next day to be whipped ceaselessly, until blood stained the grass beneath Joe's feet. When Joe begged to know what he had done to deserve to be flogged, his owner's response was, "Nothing, Joe, you're a good nigger. Part of owning a good nigger is showing him who's boss…"

A few months after this incident, Joe escaped through the Underground Railroad, leading a group of slaves to freedom, with the help of many stationmasters; the bounty on his head was so high that it was exceeded only by the bounty on the head of Harriet Tubman, leader of nineteen "passages" on the

Railroad. According to legend, Joe remained free. One can only hope legend is true.

Leader of the slave retrieval movement Harriet Tubman herself was injured seriously when just a child by a ruthless master who threw an anvil at her when she was too slow at her task, fracturing her skull, rendering her unconscious and leaving her dull-witted and subject to fits of sudden sleep for many years. As she grew up, however, her high intellect gradually came back, unbeknownst to her masters, and she used that intellect to benefit her people; her physical strength increased to the point where she could, if need be, and frequently did carry a full-grown man who had become too weary to run any farther as she led her people—Moses style—to freedom in New York or Pennsylvania, earning her the nickname "Moses of the People."

A relentlessly tough woman when crossed, historians report that she frequently brandished a pistol and offered only two options to weary slaves who pled for a rest: "Keep moving or I'll shoot you myself!" Harriet Tubman was Sarah's first hero and she acted out scenes with her sisters in which she brandished a "pistol" made of a tree branch!

Through her ordeals and her magnificent acts of bravery, Harriet Tubman never failed to be humble and to attribute her amazing deeds to the power of God, taking little credit for her bravery or her cunning. Tubman prayed constantly, whether in a trial or a safe moment, asking the Lord for strength, for guidance, for a miracle for her charges and never for herself for the scores of daring escapes she orchestrated. Serving later as a Union spy and an army nurse with an amazing cure rate using herbs and roots, Tubman rarely received any form of monetary remuneration, and was frequently reduced to near starvation; nonetheless, she thanked her Lord for giving her yet another day. She was Sarah's ultimate role model for the practice of her faith as well.

Both of Sarah Washington's parents had been born into slavery and had ingrained in her from infancy the injustices born by their parents and friends. Her nervous mother Hannah had never thrown off the onus of slavery, never allowed herself to smile or laugh without immediately looking over her shoulder to see who might be listening, who might report her as an unruly slave, one who needed to be watched. Old habits die hard.

Now living free and safe in Nelsonville, Sarah recognized that her life was truly blessed, living in a free society…yet she also knew that many of the "freedoms" which her white neighbors took for granted were as yet denied to her. She knew better than to attempt to have a soda at Greene's Confectionary; no sign told her "For Whites Only," as many other such signs proclaimed in

Nelsonville, Logan, and Lancaster. Nonetheless, Mr. Greene made it painfully clear that she was not welcome.

She knew which stores in Nelsonville would cheat her because of the color of her skin and which ones were color blind. Sarah couldn't afford to ride the train to Columbus, but she knew that if she could afford it, she would be given a seat of much less comfort than her fellow travelers who were white. Cora Corbin was asked to give her seat to a white man, much younger and stronger than she was after several hard days of delivering babies. Knowing it wasn't worth it to refuse, if she wanted to come home safe to her own family, the exhausted Cora had ridden the rest of the way to her stop north of Lancaster sitting on the floor by the door of the smoking car.

Sarah looked with pride at the oversized brick fireplace which now helped to heat her home in winter, but which had, sixty years earlier, been the hiding place for three or even four escaped slaves on their journey to freedom. Sarah's home was one of the several in Nelsonville which were known to have been safe houses, and that thought brought her much comfort.

At night, Sarah had conversations with the ghosts of those brave souls who had risked their own lives for people of color to have a chance at life. Those ghosts comforted Sarah and gave her inspiration, telling her to be patient, and good things would follow one day.

Patience came hard to Sarah, though. She could deal with the suspicious looks of some—fortunately, not all—of the white housewives when she entered the Markham's Dry Goods store, knowing that if she was respectful and subservient in manner, the other ladies would leave her alone. And Mary Rose Markham, petite as a kitten but with lively blue eyes of a color Sarah had never seen before, had always treated Sarah the way she treated all customers, with a reserved friendliness and conservative kindness.

Mr. Markham even called out to her when he saw her enter the front door, asking about her children, calling them by name: "Mrs. Washington! How nice to see you! Is Paul still playing baseball? That Marcia seems to win all the spelling bees, my brother Charley tells me!" His blue eyes—remarkably the same cornflower blue as his wife's—twinkled when he smiled and Sarah found him the most delightful of white men, in a town where white men were known to make crude comments to comely black women. Instead, he made her feel welcome.

Sarah knew where she could shop comfortably and where she had best avoid. As savvy to human nature as she was intelligent, Sarah did not borrow trouble…but the subservient, deferential demeanor she knew was expected of her still stuck in her craw. At times when she was met with a silent challenge from a white person, it took all Sarah's willpower to make her turn her eyes downward and take on the posture of a colored woman who "knew her place." Tall and attractive, it was difficult to become invisible, to appear as non-threatening as a house plant; Sarah liked to carry herself shoulders back, head high…but her better judgment usually told her to slump and shuffle along when in the visual field of hostile whites.

"How long? How much longer will it be 'fore these white folks learn th't th' war is over?" she often mused to herself. She loved Nelsonville, nevertheless, and had made a happy home for herself and her family; if the role she was cast in was uncomfortable, she had only to think of her mother's childhood, feel ashamed of herself for her displeasure, and behave as a "proper nigger" should so as not to attract undue attention to herself.

Chapter 15 – Sarah's Excursion

[Autumn 1907]

It was shopping day, one of Sarah's favorite days, especially when the shopping was at Markham's! She slipped out her front door just after 10 in the morning, after Paul and Marcia were in school and Jeremiah was working at First Street School, her dishes put away and dusting done. Clean was just short of a compulsion for Sarah; "neat as a pin," her mother Hannah would have called Sarah's house. The walk to Markham's took nearly a half hour, up and down Fort Street Hill, across the public square and finally right on Columbus Street. A long walk, and that left Sarah alone with her thoughts, the characters from her books conversing inside her busy mind.

In the tradition of the famous heroine Harriet Tubman who made nineteen trips from the South to Pennsylvania to help slaves find their freedom, Sarah accepted as her solemn duty being a champion of her people. She also recognized, however, that many of the white folks she encountered every day were as much champions of the oppressed as she herself was, and that white folks in general were not the enemy...if not provoked, most of the white citizens of the town she shared with them accepted her and smiled at her when they passed on the street. She always nodded courteously, but it had recently become Sarah's hobby to cautiously seek out the eyes of the white citizens of Nelsonville to see if she could read in them evidence of sympathy or antagonism.

She had mentally catalogued most of the people she did business with into "hostile," "friendly," "neutral" categories, based often upon nothing more than their body language. Frequently, she was right in her assessment of those she encountered. Nelsonville had long been a "free" community, but freedom was a relative thing, with the right to attend schools and own property, but not yet applied to voting, nor necessarily to living where one pleased. It certainly did not pertain to participating as an equal in government, in commerce, in recreation. Not uncommon to find signs in the windows of stores that stated that "Whites Only" need enter, Sarah knew that there were no laws which could legislate kindness or humanity. Some of the stores which bore no signs trumpeted the same message.

As she walked briskly down Columbus Street on the last leg of her voyage to Markham's Dry Goods, Sarah had to pass the sundry whose owner, Wilton Smith, she knew to be a member of the Klan, the most frightening and the most ruthless of clandestine racist brotherhoods. The Klan, as far as common thought was concerned, was dead…not so, Sarah knew.

She could feel Smith's hostility radiate outward as he looked up from his service counter to see her pass by; a narrowing of his cold, ice-gray eyes was the only outward sign of his hatred, one a disinterested observer might not notice, but Sarah knew well the stories of his midnight ventures with his "brothers" into the part of Nelsonville known to the racist sector as "Niggertown." Smith and his cronies went armed with bottles filled with kerosene and crude wicks fashioned of old cotton garments, these missiles carried in the saddle bags of the dark horses. Looking at him now, she could almost see the ghostly shadow of a white pointed hood hover above those hate-filled eyes. An involuntary shiver coursed through Sarah.

He ventured by night, of course, under the cover of darkness, darkness the friend of cowards, to throw his deadly gifts through the windows of unsuspecting black families, and accompanied by five or six others who shared his poisonous thinking, behaving as a group in ways which perhaps would be unacceptable to any of them as individuals. To Sarah, this was blatant cowardice, mob mentality, no better than the famous and frequent lynchings which had gone on—and still went on—south of the Ohio River.

As she passed his store, a jolt of defiance struck Sarah, and she straightened her back, pulling herself up to her full 5'10" height, lifted her chin, slowed her pace and turned her head ever so slightly to meet those deadly eyes for one second, two seconds, narrowing her own eyes to match his…and then to move on up the street. A tiny smile teased her lips; "Miz Tubman'd be proud of me this day, yessir she would," thought Sarah Washington as she reached the door of Markham's, quite pleased with herself.

Entering the cavernous store she loved so much, Sarah's nose was assaulted by the latest in lilac fragrance—always lilac—being offered by Mary Rose Markham. A touch sweet for Sarah's tastes, she admitted to herself that it was a pleasant girlish scent, very suitable for the diminutive Mrs. Markham with her robin's-egg-blue eyes and delicate features. A woman like Sarah was better suited to the vanilla which she occasionally dabbed between her breasts, a wholesome, earthy scent, much like the woman herself, who knew hard labor but still enjoyed the gentle touch of her man when the lights were out.

Looking toward the case of perfumes, powders, and polishes, Sarah pensively considered the type of life which lent itself to those luxuries…but only for a moment, then her practical self resurfaced. Catching the eye of the dashing Mr. Markham, Sarah offered a broad smile and a nod of the head.

"Why, there's Mrs. Washington come to see us! How are you this beautiful day? And how is Mr. Washington feeling these days? Over that cold yet?" sang out Billy Blake Markham, from his pet position, standing surveying his empire from the back of the long aisle, his left elbow resting, as always, on his right hand and a cigar between his fingers. Sarah appreciated the dry goods store owner more than he would ever realize; remembering their conversation two weeks ago when she had casually mentioned that Jeremiah was having trouble shaking a cold, Mr. Markham treated her like a person—not a colored person—and like a woman worthy of his time and interest, worthy of his respect. To his credit, Billy Blake Markham had always been color blind.

"Yes sir, Mr. M. and thank you for askin'," Sarah called.

A day trip to Markham's, even though the money didn't stretch very far, always left her feeling satisfied, and she knew a great deal of that satisfaction came from spending time in the warming aura of those twinkling blue eyes. Sarah liked Mrs. Markham very much, as well, but their relationship was more professional; Mary Rose was the brains, the bookkeeper, the quiet force which grounded the affable Mr. Markham and kept his generosity under control. But both of them treated Sarah with courtesy and personally helped her to find the fabric she needed, or the dress for Marcia, or perhaps an occasional new coat for herself with a lovely scarf or pair of gloves she was able to afford only rarely.

Sarah did love fine things. She often stood wistfully examining the display windows which Mrs. Markham had adorned with the latest in New York fashion, an activity not unnoticed by both Markhams.

Although rarely out from behind her desk and her bookkeeping duties, Mary Rose Markham was energetic and effervescent and loved to work with the customers, when time permitted, and with the merchandise; her handiwork often captured the eye of the shopper who thought she was finished buying for the day, bringing her back into the store for one more purchase.

When the Markhams saw Sarah later wearing a garment she had purchased from Markham's, usually on end-of-season sale, no matter how simple the dress may be, both remarked that Sarah's height and beauty made her a walking ad for

Markham's, slim and strong yet carrying herself with an unmistakably feminine grace and an elegance worthy of a Paris runway.

"Wouldn't she grace the cover of those new magazines, Billy? Do you think someday colored women can show how beautiful they are? It seems like a crazy world sometimes," Mary Rose had whispered to her husband as she admired Sarah's height and carriage one day exiting the store, wearing a silver linen skirt and pale pink blouse she had just purchased from the sale rack…the clothing had never looked better, both Mary Rose and Billy Blake agreed.

"She would that. Too bad…" Too bad, they agreed, that a woman of color couldn't be a model for magazine ads, for she would be magnificent: statuesque, elegant, with high prominent cheekbones and skin the color of lightened coffee. And when she held her head high and cocked her head just slightly as she did when listening intently, both husband and wife found her not only beautiful but magnetic.

Although gingham and cotton fabric was all she usually could afford, Sarah would have been positively regal, in silk and washed taffeta, with colored sashes of brocade and exquisite lace decorating the bodice, as was the fashion of the day. A pale rose evening garment matching that description was currently on display in the showcase window, graced by ivory silk stockings, and stunning jewelry of crystal and opal; Sarah gazed longingly at the dress on her entrance to the store this morning, as Billy Blake and Mary Rose Markham exchanged a sad, knowing smile…no, it would never be showcased on the magnificent Sarah Washington, not in this lifetime. Pity…

* * *

Today's visit to her favorite store was going to be a bit harder than usual for Sarah because of the way the drought had reduced her clothing budget. Sarah needed many items herself, but planned to go without so that Marcia could have two new dresses and, if possible, some new stockings to begin the school year. Even at ten, Marcia had become particular about how other children saw her, and was self-conscious about her height, destined as she was to be a half-head taller than the other children in her class…courtesy of her tall, stunning parents. Height, as an adult, was an attribute; at ten, it was a curse, making one stand out even more. As Sarah reached the middle of the store, the section where the children's garments were displayed on racks, she was startled to see Mr. Markham right beside her, only an inch or so taller than she.

"Look over here, Mrs. Washington," he whispered, "I put a few items under the counter which I thought you might be able to use for that pretty young daughter of yours. We were going to take them to the church for their bazaar, but I remembered your Marcia and thought they might just fit her. What do you think?" and he pulled out two white shirtwaist blouses, a brown kettle cloth skirt, six pairs of white cotton stockings, and a package of undergarments, last year's merchandise, but much more expensive than Sarah had ever been able to afford, lovely quality merchandise.

"Oh, but I couldn't..." she began.

"Shush, now, yes you can, you would be doing us a favor. That youngster of yours is in the same class as my youngest brother Charley and he tells me she might be the smartest person in their grade. Of course, he also tells me she's the sweetest girl...and he doesn't much like girls yet. We wouldn't want the smartest, sweetest person in the class to go wanting, now, would we?" And he winked. Sarah's heart skipped a beat.

"Mr. Markham, those are wonderful clothes but I don't have the money...the drought, you know..." Sarah shook her head, embarrassed, unable to continue.

"Did I mention money? No, I want you to take these off my hands. Take these for Marcia, then you can use your corn money for some pretty material for new curtains or maybe a blouse...for you, my dear."

Speechless, Sarah's eyes filled with tears; she barely resisted the urge to hug the man she now worshipped, who knew, somehow, just the right thing to do. "Is it all right with Miz. Markham? I wouldn't want you to get on her bad side..."

"It's more than all right. She picked out the sizes for you. Never you mind about my bride..." and he winked at her again as he bagged up the clothing. "Now, what else can we find for you?"

"Well, maybe just that dress over there on the sale rack, the yellow one. Marcia can use it for school before it gets too cold and for church...and do you have any new patterns, d' y' know?"

"That's my wife's department, but why don't you come look in the cabinet and see what you can find." And he placed her purchased dress with the bagged clothing on the wrapping counter as he made his way back to his spot, calling over his shoulder, "You tell Marcia to keep my brother in line, you hear?"

Nearly overcome with gratitude and embarrassment—her frugal nature overcoming her pride, fortunately, Sarah quickly selected a sensible dress pattern, and three yards of wine-colored gingham, which the hired girl Audrey cut for her, then made the short trip by Mrs. Markham's stool which allowed the tiny

Mary Rose to see over her tall, crescent-shaped oak desk where she labored over the store's books...and help her husband survey their domain.

As Mary Rose looked up and smiled, Sarah overcame a lump in her throat and forced out, "Hello, Miz. Markham. I want to thank you for the nice things you and Mr. Markham gave me. They're really goin' 'ta come in handy. The drought made it so hard, y' see, and you...well, you just can't know how much I appreciate..." and she ran out of words as tears filled her eyes again.

"Don't you think a thing about it, Mrs. Washington. Maybe you can help us out some day, what do you think?" and Mary Rose flashed her broad, dazzling smile at Sarah, who nodded, murmured "Anytime, ma'am, you just ask, anytime..."moving away to pay for her purchases, and walking quickly away before she embarrassed herself more by throwing her arms around these wonderful people.

"They're definitely the 'friendlies,' those two," Sarah murmured to herself as she cleared the door of Markham's, two bundles under her arms. "Why they want t' help me, I don't know...but for sure, I'll help them back one day...I will..." And she wiped a tear from her eye.

* * *

So preoccupied was Sarah with her thoughts that she didn't notice Wilton Smith and his hostile glare while she passed his window. She didn't see his lips curl in disgust, or hear his furious words, "Uppity nigger bitch, who does she think she is..." as a plan formulated itself in his fermented brain.

The bundles began to grow heavy as Sarah finished the nearly four-block walk to the end of the Public Square so she rested for just a minute on the wooden bench that had been placed in front of Stuart's Opera House. It was still in the 90s, only a few days before October began, and a typically humid Ohio Indian summer afternoon. Perspiration ran in rivulets down her back and beneath her long skirt as Sarah eyed the Square. She loved this block, especially the 15-foot fountain which made her feel cooler just by watching the water cascade from the three-tiered structure. The urge struck her, as it always did viewing the fountain, to kick off her boots, hike up her dress, and run through the cool water. Smiling at the image, she shook it off. "Not a good idea, t' get me arrested for bathin' in public..." Sarah thought with a chuckle. It was a cooling thought, nevertheless.

As she always did, Sarah admired the handsome marble monument, a tribute to fallen Civil War heroes who had given their lives for Sarah's freedom. On some of her shopping expeditions, Sarah crossed over to the monument and said a silent prayer of thanks for those fallen men who held as dear a place in her heart as the abolitionists did.

Taking her husband's handkerchief from her pocketbook, Sarah wiped the perspiration from her face. As she did so, her eyes strayed back the way she had come, and she noticed that a small group of white men were looking her way, standing in a tight circle in front of the Dew House less than a block away. As she was about to look away, she noticed that one of the men was Wilton Smith, and that he looked practically demonic as he gestured her way and spoke under his breath through his scraggly black beard to the other men.

"That man's the Devil himself…" she thought to herself as her stomach lurched and a shiver ran up her spine in spite of the heat. Sarah picked up her bundles and began her hurried journey up Fort Street hill, wanting right then to be anywhere except where that evil Mr. Smith was, especially with his cronies, who tended to take their cues from Smith. "Like one o' those rotten apples, that'n…" she muttered to herself.

She had made it past the Fort Street Cemetery where Daniel Nelson, the founder of Nelsonville, and most of his family reposed looking out over their realm, and was cresting the hill heading home to Beatrice Street when something came flying past her head, startling her, making her drop her packages. Angrily, Sarah turned to see what had nearly hit her and whipped her head back to see who had thrown it, but the broken bottle which lay at her feet gave no indication of the direction from which it had come and no one was in sight. She hoped that the missile was tossed by a careless mischievous kid who was skipping school.

Sarah continued up the steep hill toward her house, feeling perturbed that her wonderful afternoon had taken a nasty turn. As she stepped onto her front porch, she released a huge sigh, both from the fatigue of retreating rapidly uphill in the 90 degree heat, and from relief that whatever threat she had imagined seemed not to have materialized. Her adventure had taken most of the day; it was time to get back to her housework before Jeremiah and the children came home.

Entering her house, Sarah released the breath that she didn't realize she had been holding, and leaning back against the door, she attempted to throw off the sense of foreboding which had plagued her since she saw Smith and his cohorts with their heads together. The house was nearly as hot as the outdoors; in spite of the open windows, no air was moving. Sarah moved sluggishly through the central hallway to the kitchen on the back of the house, dropping her packages on the cobbler's bench, and reached to open the back door in hopes of capturing a renegade breeze.

Stepping onto the back stoop, she picked up a large crockery bowl and filled it with water from the pump in back of the house, then carried the bowl into the kitchen, setting it in the window, the only window which seemed to have a slight movement of air. "There, now, blow over the water, will ya?"

Shaking her head at herself, knowing the temperature wouldn't drop one degree, but the bowl of water making her think it was cooler, Sarah sank into the straight chair at the end of the table, picked up an envelope lying on the table to use as a fan, and closed her eyes for a moment. The heat, the hurried journey uphill to home, and the pent-up stress combined to make her weak and in seconds she was dozing in the chair.

* * *

Slam! "Ma! Where are ya?" *Slam! Crash!* And Sarah startled awake to the sound of her rangy son Paul banging in the front door.

Shaking off the fog, Sarah called, "In here, son, in the kitchen…what're you yellin' for?"

"Sorry, Ma, I din't know where ya were…" and her handsome dust-covered eight-year-old threw his gangly arms around her neck. Hugging him close, Sarah had forgotten her edginess earlier as she drank in the boy-smell of her youngest.

"Where's your sister?" Sarah queried. "Weren't ya together? Where's Marcia? What time is it?"

"Dunno. She wuz behin' me, but Katie hollered at her an' she run off," Paul muttered in the unmistakable manner of an eight-year-old, part sulk and part distracted.

A strange feeling of unease rose again in Sarah's throat, and gently pushing her son off his hanging place around her neck, she rushed to the front door, pushing it open so rapidly it banged against the wall, calling, "Marcia! Marcia, girl, where are ya? Answer me, ya hear?"

Paul had followed her to the porch and he now sidled up against her, asking, "Wha'z wrong, Ma?"

"Nothin', son, I just want to know where your sister is…" and turned her worried face back to the street which she had rushed up an hour earlier. The tension eased from her face as she saw her long-legged daughter and her friend, the roly-poly Katie, running up the hill as fast as they could, looking afraid that they were going to get a bawling out. Marcia's legs took her up the hill at nearly double the pace that Katie could maintain, bringing a chuckle to Sarah's relieved mind.

"It's okay, Marcia, wait for Katie!" and reaching for Paul, she sank into the ancient rocking chair on the porch to wait for the out-of-breath travelers.

As Marcia and her friend clumped onto the porch, Sarah reached her other arm out for her daughter, pulling her into her lap where Paul was already ensconced and then stretching her hand out to Katie, she said, "Okay, young'un's, I was bein' silly. I just got scared when I couldn't see you, and your brother lost ya, too. Anyways, what've you been up to today? Katie, your ma was home, wasn't she?"

"Yes, ma'am. We wuz just playin' house with my dolls 'n' havin' a tea party, then Paul said that wuz girl stuff 'n' took off 'n' then we heard ya hollerin' 'n' then we hurried..." And Katie ran out of breath and plopped down on the porch.

"Well, now, how would you young'uns like some fresh lemonade? I can make some in just a minute, if you stay here on the porch for me. What do you say?" To enthusiastic replies of "Yum!" and "Lemonade! Yummy" Sarah re-entered her home, silently admonishing herself for her foolishness. "Bein' a mother's not easy...things scare you..." She took out a small block of ice from the icebox and began to chip it into her mother's pitcher.

As she worked on the ice, her mind was flooded with memories of watching her mother Hannah performing the same activity and talking to Sarah and her sisters about her life back on the plantation in Virginia. The cook had occasionally snuck out a pitcher of lemonade to the slaves after the evening meal had been cleared away. Hannah had talked on and on of how cold and sweet that treat was and how much she wished she could have it any time she wanted.

Sarah always wanted to know more but her instincts told her not to ask. Sarah knew that her mother had many hurtful memories of her first fourteen years, years spent as a slave. That memory of the lemonade was one of the only good things she seemed to remember. As ice filled the pitcher, Sarah reminisced about the dark look her mother had gotten on her face when she talked about her childhood, a haunted look which frightened Sarah, and she wondered again how one human being could believe it was right to own another human being.

Frederick Douglass had written, in 1881, "Someone has well said, we may easily forgive those who injure us, but it is hard to forgive those whom we injure. The greatest injury this side of death, which one human being can inflict on another, is to enslave him, to blot out his personality, degrade his manhood, and sink him to the condition of a beast of burden." Douglass was eloquent and Sarah had memorized these lines. She thought of them again as she labored over her menial task, and thanked the Lord that her miseries were minimal, compared to those of her grandparents.

Shaking off her reverie, Sarah began to cut and squeeze lemons over the ice in the pitcher, and again her mind wandered to earlier summers and earlier times, times when she longed to do the things white children did, go wherever she wanted, especially school. These longings had never been satisfied, even though, thanks to her childhood friends, Sarah's education had taken place in the kitchen of her home rather than in a classroom.

She loved to read and her favorite book was *Harriet: Moses of Her People* about the amazing Harriet Tubman, not only a conductor on the Underground Railroad but also a spy for the Union Army during the Civil War, and Sarah's idol. Sarah loved *Uncle Tom's Cabin* and other reports of the struggles of her people. She had recently read W. E. B. DuBois, a new voice of colored people, but she felt uncomfortable with his anger. A shocking thought popped into her head: "I wonder if I could write a book…a book for colored people t' take hope…t' put hate aside…" and a seed of inspiration was planted. The lemonade was taking shape… and so was a plan.

Chapter 16 – Racial Unrest

[Summer 1908]

In the summer of 1908, the temperatures were sweltering and so was racial tension. In states north of the Mason-Dixon Line, towns and cities which had been in full or at least partial support of abolition found themselves unprepared to deal with equality. Black men owned businesses; Negroes prospered alongside whites…occasionally even more than whites. Hundreds of black families had immigrated to the North around the same time that thousands of immigrants from Europe made their way to the Pennsylvania-Ohio-Indiana-Illinois farming and mining regions, finding jobs and beginning new lives. New jobs couldn't keep up with the influx of new workers. And a seed of discontent began to sprout and take root.

In Springfield, Illinois, a series of events snowballed into a cataclysmic crisis, which had a ripple effect all over the North.

On Independence Day, a black man of a criminal nature broke into the home of a prominent white citizen, threatened to rape his daughter, and although chased from the house, when caught by the homeowner, the perpetrator brandished a knife, slitting the throat of his victim. This was a grisly crime, even for a city the size of Springfield; the victim was able to identify his assailant—a well-known Negro criminal—before succumbing to his wounds. During tense times between blacks and whites, this crime proved to be the spark to ignite a powder keg. Unfortunately, the perpetrator was a black man who was accused of attempting to rape a young white girl, the worst crime imaginable in the post-Civil War era, or, for that matter, in any era.

The suspect was arrested; he, the surly black man named Jim, languished in jail for a few days awaiting trial, but the story was reported and sensationalized by the local newspaper. As those things frequently happen, the story was picked up by several newspapers in surrounding states, the *Athens Messenger* and the *Nelsonville Tribune* included. The Wilton Smiths of the world like nothing better than to see their biases justified; nevertheless, the poisoned fruit might have withered on the vine had not another Springfield event occurred.

Three days after the attempted rape and murder, the wife of a prominent Springfield businessman reported hysterically that she had been "raped and brutalized" by a black laborer from her husband's company who supposedly had "dragged her from her bed and outraged her." That man, too, was arrested, and although protesting his innocence most vehemently, was thrown into the same jail, which already held the other black "rapist."

As the report of yet a second atrocity traveled by the grapevine, the telegraph and the newspaper syndicate, a rumble of fury began to circulate in the white community of Springfield and in the white communities of towns and cities far away from Springfield. Predictions that the "niggers" would get off if taken to trial fueled the flames. A lynch mob assembled and grew to nearly a hundred armed vigilantes. Anger already simmering over the job situation sought a scapegoat. Temperatures soared into the nineties, taking with them the tempers of the crowd. A frightened white Good Samaritan warned the sheriff that the mob was on its way and he quickly put the two suspects, with guards, on a private wagon to be taken by train to be jailed in a nearby town to protect them from mob "justice."

When the lynch mob arrived at the jail to find their prey escaped from the lair, their fury exploded. The hapless wagon driver who assisted the sheriff to get the fugitives out of town was shot and killed, then, tasting blood, the rabid hunting pack moved toward the black business district, burning and vandalizing every store in its path. Many black families awakened to find their stores in flames and their homes and lives in jeopardy; many fled on foot, on horseback, by wagon…any conveyance possible to prevent loss of life as well as business, the majority of whom never returned to Springfield.

Still not satisfied, as mobs operating on blood lust are not easily sated, the predators moved on to the home of a well-liked and respected elderly black businessman in his eighties who had had the audacity to marry a white woman…over forty years earlier. The couple had lived in relative peace, raising their children, until his wife had passed away a few years back. When confronted by a murderous mob, the elderly widower defended his home, shooting two vigilantes in the process but was stopped with a bullet, bringing the death toll to four.

As the pack of angry men ran out of things to burn, many members of the Negro community—those who hadn't fled for their lives to another state—began to form a protective group, which helped somewhat to quell the violence, as did the quickly assembled local militia. It wasn't, however, until the Illinois National Guard arrived that the riot was ended, with the final tragic count resting at seven dead, five whites caught in the fire of their own compatriots, and two blacks.

Both black and white communities were outraged, each blaming the other for the atrocious behavior of their race, but the final irony was yet to be revealed. Horrified by what had ensued since her rape accusation, the white businessman's wife broke down and admitted that she had lied, that she had reported a rape when none occurred—to cover up an affair she was having with an associate of her husband's. This was a shocking and confusing turn of events, reported everywhere throughout both the North and the South.

* * *

In southeastern Ohio, black and white citizens had co-existed for a century, if not comfortably, at least at a guarded truce, tense, somewhat twitchy at times but with few incidents of the magnitude of what had taken place in Springfield. Many black families had come to Nelsonville with the expansion of the five major coal companies, which had mines and offices in the county, and to work with the parallel businesses, the iron furnaces, the brick factories, and the canals and railroads. Life was comfortable for many black workers, barely poverty level for others.

Sarah and Jeremiah Washington were among the lucky ones, while not at all wealthy, able to count on the next meal, shoes for their children's feet, and a safe and dry roof over their heads. Well liked and respected as the custodian for two elementary schools, Jeremiah also earned extra money doing odd jobs for several elderly people, both black and white, and during the summer, did farm work, both on his own small patch and for neighbors.

The whites with whom he had contact described him as intelligent, hard-working and respectful, all qualities which made him an acceptable associate, and they figured, if he was good enough to work around their children, then he must be trustworthy. He was trusted; only behind his back did his employers add the suffix, "...for a colored man." After the Springfield race riots, Jeremiah found only a little added tension from the families for whom he worked during the summer while school was out; in general, it was business as usual.

Sarah too had made a comfortable place for herself in Nelsonville, not only through her extensive involvement in the schools where Marcia and Paul attended, but also as someone who was frequently seen shopping (she did love to shop, especially at Markham's) and at political speeches or public gatherings on the Public Square.

The library staff knew her by name, set new books aside for her. She was a voracious reader, often finishing books within a few days; she read Frederick Douglass, Booker T. Washington, W.E.B. DuBois, as soon as new treatises became available. She also read classics by such authors as Charlotte Bronte, Nathanial Hawthorne, Charles Dickens…she pored over the words, expanding her vocabulary, expanding her comprehension of the human experience.

Ever since her unexpected inspiration the previous fall, Sarah had thought often about the plight of her race and of her place in the overall picture. The events of the past Independence Day had given her further cause to pursue her belief, her desire to write a book which would tell of the struggles of her race, that and her frequent brushes with the most hateful of men, Wilton Smith. Sarah followed the newspapers faithfully. When they couldn't afford to buy one, Jeremiah often brought a newspaper home from the school where he worked. The race riots of July 4, in Springfield, Illinois, had been frightening reminders that the peaceful relations between black and white were tenuous, at best.

By sheer determination, she had improved her speech, both her diction and her vocabulary, to sound more like mainstream white rather than small-town black. She read out loud when no one was home, listening to herself, criticizing herself when she dropped the ending of a word, pronouncing that word over and over until she was satisfied. Little by little, Sarah Washington was beginning to sound more like the literate, educated people whose books she inhaled, memorized, took to heart…in short, like the person she wished to be.

Sarah had tried to write the book she believed was in her soul, but found it frustrating to search and search for the words to say just what she wanted to say. So she would read a chapter by Douglass, then try to write a chapter which sounded just like Douglass…and wound up discarding it as a cheap imitation. Often she had decided to give up the quest…but when the frustration of the moment passed, she would find her way back to her desk, her pencil and tablet. A page at a time, she was beginning to accumulate some thoughts on paper which just might, someday, be that tinder to spark her book.

In the meantime, no one—not even Jeremiah—knew what Sarah was planning. She continued to be active with schools, to spend her evenings helping Paul and Marcia with homework, occasionally correcting their grammar and diction as well as her own. Both children received straight A's in school; both had caused no problems which would single them out in any negative way, and Sarah was indecently proud, of her children, of her hard-working husband…and of herself, learning to thrive in a town with buried racial tension without succumbing to the spirit-breaking racism.

Sarah Washington was friendly, appearing to be sufficiently reserved, and respectful; just what the white families considered "her place." If she occasionally held her head too high or failed to drop her eyes when in the company of whites, most but those with deepest racial prejudice considered her subservient enough to be acceptable. Her presence at political gatherings hadn't yet sounded an alarm; Sarah was wise enough to keep to herself her conviction that all women, white and black, should be able to vote and participate in local government. These thoughts she shared rarely, even with Jeremiah. Instinctively, Sarah recognized that her life's work would be directed toward the strengthening of her race and her gender—how she would do this work was as yet secret…even to Sarah.

* * *

As the news of the events of Independence Day and the days following reached Nelsonville, it was filtered through whatever the prejudice was of the reader; peace-loving folks of both colors offered prayer for lives lost and for those who were trying to reconstruct their lives, and talked of their hopes that this one ugly incident would be the end of it.

Angry men, some of whom had recently lost jobs to blacks, had an altogether different take on the situation. Burl Rogers and India Kensington, foremen of Longstreth Mine, one in Buchtel and one in Nelsonville, had, in early June of that year, taken a trip with several wagons to Alabama, a rich source of willing labor, bringing back more disenfranchised black sharecroppers who believed that "North" was the symbol of success.

The effort to recruit young and strong black men to work in their mines when the mine workers' union had struck, supplying the mine with willing scab laborers, had unwittingly thrown kerosene on fires of hostility which had to this point been smoldering. Both men awoke in the wee hours of July 8 to find their barns and sheds ablaze, the flames accelerated by gallons of kerosene, and were barely able to escape with their families and their lives before the flames reached their homes. Newly promoted to chief of police, Gene Linbach was a recognized racist whose hatred of blacks had propelled him upward in the police department. Responding to the fire, Linbach let Rogers and Kensington know that they should consider themselves fortunate. No charges were filed.

Clyde Corbin, Cora's husband and a close friend of Jeremiah and Sarah's, had the previous summer opened a blacksmith shop at the south end of Nelsonville. News of the burning of Rogers' and Kensington's places traveled fast. Being awakened by fire whistles coming from the south and fearing the worst, Clyde and Jeremiah rushed to the shop in time to stop a small group of masked riders from destroying the shop, extinguishing the small fire set by an ineffective bottle bomb before it could take hold of the wood-frame structure, but the nearest neighbor, an elderly black barber's establishment, was already in ashes.

Clyde sprinted two blocks to his father's home, followed by Jeremiah and two other men who had joined the rescue team, woke the elder Mr. Corbin and took up positions on his front porch, all of them armed with a makeshift weapon, a hoe, an axe, a board…and one very old muzzle-loading rifle which probably would have done more damage to its shooter than its intended victim. There they waited until dawn; the vigilantes, like vampires and other bloodsuckers, seemed to have run out of steam with the morning light.

By the light of day, Nelsonville's black community took stock of its damage and counted itself lucky that no one had been injured. Sarah Washington and Cora Corbin checked on their friends and neighbors, finding all homes and families safe. The carnage seemed to be limited to the business ventures of industrious blacks. Sarah pondered the message that was leaving: "You can live here. You can raise your families here, but you won't prosper…not in our town." Tears of fury coursed down her face as she helped sift through the rubble of the barber shop.

Two businesses were completely destroyed, two others damaged, but except for black painted letters saying, "niggers get out" and similar expletives, that was the extent of it. Springfield had not been reprised.

The community's emotional damage had been much greater, however; stressed and saddened parents had to find words to explain the unexplainable to children that morning, why the color of their skin had made them victims of hatred. Law officials worked all day and into the night taking damage reports. Several skirmishes broke out between men who were previously on good terms; ugly names were exchanged and threats made, ending friendships and planting seeds of mistrust.

Human nature has an amazing way of healing itself, though. In the aftermath of the July disturbance, an unsettled peace returned to Nelsonville. In the tradition of pioneers of the earlier century, many neighbors converged on the scene of the burned-out stores, offering their services to rebuild. Burl Rogers' property had taken the worst hit, but friends rallied to his side, making plans for the rebuilding.

Kensington and his family made the painful decision to leave Nelsonville for good and return to Akron.

Clyde Corbin was brought to tears more than once at the offers of assistance, which came from white folks as well as black, and he accepted whatever was offered. His damage was minimal, so the work was finished in no time and Clyde's benefactors moved with him to see what, if anything, could be done about the barbershop. Its gray-haired and stooped owner had escaped slavery as a boy and made a life as a freeman in Ohio. Now he was devastated, weeping; he had hopes of passing the business, the American dream, to his two sons and retiring soon—now there was nothing to pass on. The crew had other ideas, however, and by the time the elderly owner arrived back at his charred business after checking on his ailing wife, much of the burned timber was removed, the two ancient but still usable barber chairs cleaned up and declared sound. The red and white pole, the symbol of his trade and those who practiced it, was replaced…standing by itself on a makeshift platform, but standing proud, nonetheless.

"My, oh my, don't trag'dies bring out the best in folk?" declared the snowy-haired barber, shaking hands with everyone who had rallied to the scene. As he shuffled through the remains of his shop, he found several scissors and razors undamaged, a mirror which had fallen but remained unbroken, and with a chuckle, he stropped the razor on his overall leg, and held it up to glint in the sun, declaring, "Shave, anyone? Let dem cowards come back by disaway agin' n' we'll show 'em what fer!"

As the weary but motivated workers laughed, the tension eased, and from the rubble Jeremiah's baritone voice broke into. "We shall overcome…we shall overcome…we shall overcome one day…" and one by one the rest joined in. Black men, white men and children picked up their pace, determined to restore the barbershop to its previous condition. Song after song, load by load, the rubble was loaded into the back of Tim Dooley's milk wagon to be taken away to the dump, as the choruses continued long into the night. The wagon returned with lumber and in the ashes of the wreckage a phoenix arose, built of courage and determination.

As the day ended, the barber was back under a sturdy roof, proud and defiant, weeping again, but this time with gratitude. Many white citizens of Nelsonville had a crash course in Negro spirituals that day, and by nightfall, were singing along with vigor.

As Jeremiah stopped to wipe his face, he looked at what lay before him, a unified crew of workers singing and laboring, and tears began again, as he raised his eyes to Heaven, saying, "Thank ye, Lord, fer the spirit y' put into these hands and them others. We be doin' yer work this day fer sure…"

That night, after her exhausted husband had fallen into his bed, Sarah Washington sat at her desk, lighted only by a candle, and laboriously recorded the events of the last twenty-four hours in her journal…

PART 4—A CAUSE FOR THREE

Chapter 17 – Jane Meets Mary Rose

[May 1909]

Jane wondered why she was so out of breath, but after looking around, she realized that with unseasonable early May temperatures in the high 80s and humidity even higher, everyone else she passed on the street looked as if they felt the same way, like wilted lettuce. She hadn't been on this street before, although she had been to the Opera House for a suffrage meeting. Pausing to breathe, and glancing around, she was captivated by the squared-off false fronts all the buildings on Columbus Street possessed; just like the one on her father's store in Buchtel, but his store was frame…these buildings were brick! Two of them had what looked like little turrets, better suited to the castles in her favorite illustrated book of the medieval King Arthur than a busy modern metropolis like Nelsonville.

Just ahead, Jane noticed the full glass windows with the Roman letter M painted in gold, and thought to herself, "That must be it. Markham's. Yes, there it is…" as she, relieved to be leaving the heat, approached the entryway to the store she had been hearing about from her friends at the sewing circle. Many of the miners' wives came into Nelsonville to shop whenever work in the mines allowed extra money. They told Jane that the Markhams were generous with credit, allowing them, when necessary, to pay just a dime a week if money was tight.

Her gratitude for the shade of Markham's entryway faded, though, as a wave of humiliation nearly stopped her in her tracks. Jane was still the proud person she had been at seventeen, despite the twists her life had taken. But she had to keep walking: money was tight right now; the mine was exploring a new breast of coal and work in the older breast had all but stopped for the time being. Jane had three children to feed.

Jane was proud of her needlework, but had never considered selling any of it, thinking of it as her handiwork. But her family needed the extra money to tide them over…and Carrie Loggins had mentioned selling some crochet work last month. "Never hurt to ask, I guess…" Jane considered.

Entering through the beveled glass of the right hand door, Jane felt dwarfed by the cavernous entryway, ceilings 14 feet high and painted black, framing the sparkling interior of Markham's Dry Goods. Doing a quick mental comparison with her dad's general store—mostly unfinished wood floors, shelves and counters, utilitarian storage—she decided that she liked what she saw, gleaming wood floors, polished glass counters and strong iron racks as far back as the eye could see, displaying blouses, dresses, children's clothing, and farther back, myriad shades of fabric and household linens.

Jane had always enjoyed the unique smells of stores; her dad's store, though, tended to smell more like pipe tobacco and snuff, not to mention coal oil and sweat, but that was logical—it catered to miners. Here, more feminine scents teased her nose, powder, cleaning solutions, even cologne. Yes, the ambience was altogether different here, as might be expected.

Squinting to peer into the rear reaches of the store, where her friend had told her she could find Mrs. Markham, Jane spotted her there, nearly swallowed by the tall, half-circle of a desk which she perched behind on a tall stool. Carrie had told Jane that Mrs. Markham was a pretty little thing and very sweet. Jane wasn't exactly intimidated by the fact that she was about to approach the business owner…to ask for money. No, not intimidated, perhaps, but a whole lot embarrassed…

As she lingered halfway back the right aisle, Jane's eyes were drawn to an open archway which seemed to connect Markham's with a totally different store. Through the arch she could see displays of shoes and boots. "What a surprise! You wouldn't even know that other section was there, looking from the outside…how strange," Jane mused, peeking through the arch to discover what looked like an entire second store, attached only by the archway. "I wonder why it's arranged like this…" she wondered.

What Jane couldn't know was that Edward Markham's brother Clarence ran the shoe store. Since a family feud over something silly that no one remembered, a year earlier, he had distanced himself from the rest of the Markhams and now ran his store as in independent entity, going so far as to change the name from "Markham's Shoes" to "C.M. Shoes." Only the one arch remained, perhaps representing a subconscious hope of being a bridge…but so far, it hadn't served that function. It was only a matter of innate trust and deeply buried family love which had kept that one small link intact…but even it, that five-foot opening, was partitioned off and locked when the stores closed for the evening.

Shrugging off her curiosity, Jane moved on toward Mary Rose's desk. As she approached the desk, she noticed a dainty, cozy recessed area just past Mrs. Markham's desk, which featured tiny display racks of thread and colorful yarn, another of needles of all sizes and shapes, two rocking chairs with a small table between, littered with needlework magazines and catalogs. "Hmm. This store is full of surprises..." Jane thought, as she stepped toward the opening.

Giving in to her curiosity to see what was featured there, Jane passed the desk and stepped into the needlework alcove, her eyes scanning the shelves, finding them replete with knitting needles, squares of assorted fabric...and there, on the right, a floor-to-ceiling shelf displaying finished needle crafts of all sizes and varieties: knit booties and scarves, crocheted doilies and tablecloths, embroidered napkins and pillowcases...but, to Jane's delight, no tatting!

As she moved closer to examine the quality of the finished items for sale, her heart soared to see the amazing prices Mrs. Markham had placed on these beautifully crafted items! "Yes, this just might work out..." Jane murmured, a smile dimpling the corner of her mouth.

Just at that moment, Mary Rose Markham looked up from her ledger and noticed the dark-haired young woman who seemed to be lost in her needlework section, with a bemused smile. Catching her eye, Mary Rose called warmly, "Oh, hello! Do you like to sew? Some of those items are here on consignment...would you like to see them?"

Jane met the gaze of store owner, smiled broadly, and replied, "As a matter of fact, I do like to sew, and I was hoping to talk with you about that very subject! Consignment, you say? How does that work?" As Jane took the three short steps to Mary Rose's desk, at the same moment, Mary Rose hopped down from her tall stool. Startled, the two women stood eye to eye, exactly the same height, not a common occurrence for either woman, both of whom were used to looking up at everyone; emerald-green eyes peered into sapphire blue.

Both seemed slightly amused by their mirror imagery; at any rate, the atmosphere was suddenly friendly and charged with positive energy, as Mary Rose said, "How do you do. I'm Mary Rose Markham. Do I know you?"

"No, ma'am, but my friend Carrie Loggins shops here occasionally and she recommended that I look for you. My name's Jane. Jane Neeley. Pleased to meet you," and held out her hand, a gesture unusual for a woman, but well-received by Mary Rose Markham. The latter liked forthright people, especially women and, most especially, women as small as she, who could so easily be eclipsed by larger people were it not for the dynamism each woman exhibited.

Grasping that outstretched hand, and noticing that it was strong and work scarred, yet well groomed and neatly manicured, Mary Rose replied, "Jane, I'm very happy to meet you too. Tell me about your needlework. Why don't we sit over in the needlework center while we visit?" Leading the way to the first of the rocking chairs, Mary Rose gestured to Jane to sit, which she did, sinking into a chair which fit her perfectly, her tiny toes actually reaching the floor…highly surprising for Jane!

For some reason, her embarrassment faded in the glow of Mary Rose's smile. "Mrs. Markham, I've never sold any of my work before. As a matter of fact, I never even thought about it. I love my work, but I just do it for myself, you know, to make the table prettier or sometimes to send to my husband's sister for a gift. But Carrie…well, she overheard me mentioning that…" She paused, sighing, then continued, "…that money was a bit tight, you know, and she suggested I talk with you…"

As Mary Rose listened intently, her face clouded momentarily when Jane dropped her eyes while discussing money. She sensed that this conversation was difficult for the proud, articulate young woman. She felt Jane's embarrassment and tried to will her to be at ease. There was a strange sort of telepathic communication passing between them; Mary Rose knew instinctively this was a woman who would be her friend.

Jane continued, "…so, if I showed you a few pieces I brought with me, do you think you could…take a look at them?" And her voice trailed off as she looked into those amazing blue eyes which were intensely seeking her own, radiating a warmth and concern which Jane felt more than saw, sensed more than heard.

Responding to Mary Rose's enthusiastic nod, Jane passed three handkerchiefs she had carefully edged with lace to Mary Rose, who took them gently and held them close to her face, examining the intricate stitches as if they were the most precious of treasures. Jane waited silently as Mary Rose fingered the exquisite lace which bordered the handkerchiefs, hoping she wouldn't find the work too clumsy. She needn't have worried.

"Jane, these are just beautiful. My mother used to tat, but my fingers don't seem to want to catch on. I try but…well, I'll stick to knitting. Yes, please do bring more pieces in. Do you have any more? Your work is delicate yet it looks so strong. That is amazing! I am certain that we can sell them for you here. How much do you think you would like to have for these handkerchiefs?"

Wide-eyed, Jane stammered, "I…I…have no idea, Mrs. Markham. What do you think they are worth?"

"Let's put fifty cents on each of them. When they sell, I keep only 10 percent and the rest is yours. Is that satisfactory?"

Jane's mouth fell open. "Fifty cents? You really think someone would pay that much? Yes, ma'am, that is more than satisfactory! I can bring more tomorrow...if that is okay..." Her voice trailed off, a bit embarrassed at her enthusiasm, but Mary Rose seemed as excited as she was, so Jane's embarrassment evaporated in the comfortable atmosphere.

"Well, that's settled then. Bring whatever you have and we'll see what it does! So, now, Jane, why don't you stay and visit a while? We've been really slow today...the heat, I think...and we can pour some lemonade and get acquainted. I would love to get to know you. I have so few friends close to my age. Come, I have a small icebox in the back and we can have a cool drink...and just talk. Oh, maybe I can show you my husband's book corner. Would you like that?"

"Yes, ma'am, I'd love some lemonade and I love to read, anything, just anything. The store carries books? How wonderful!"

Frowning, Mary Rose said, "And, Jane, one thing..."

"Yes, ma'am?"

"Call me Mary Rose, please. 'Ma'am' makes me think of my mother-in-law! She's a love, of course, but I am definitely not a 'ma'am'! Not for a few more years, anyway," and she chuckled, leading the way to the book nook, Billy Blake's project.

Blushing and following her, with a chuckle of her own, Jane replied, "Yes, ma'am...I mean, Mary Rose. I understand. Oh! What amazing books! Oh... I love this section..." Jane fingered the spines of several classics, to Mary Rose's silent approval. "So can I help with the lemonade? This is such a fabulous store. My dad ran a store in Buchtel..."

"Oh, really? What kind..." And the conversation never lagged for a second for the next hour. Billy Blake came back from his appointment, measuring the windows of his friend the postmaster's new apartment above the post office, coming in the front door wiping the sweat from his forehead, to hear the most delightful of sounds, the musical laughter of his Mary Rose and the equally captivating laughter of her petite companion.

Amused, he cocked his head and approached the book corner unnoticed, watching for a moment the delightful animation of this gamin of a woman who had so captured the attention of his wife, her black hair swinging free, his wife's blond tresses immaculately in place, dark contrasting with light in these two lively diminutive women. Knowing by instinct that Mary Rose's judgment was sound, he "harrumphed" a time or two, to be noticed and introduced to his wife's new friend.

"Oh, Billy! You startled me! Billy Blake Markham, please meet my friend Jane Neeley. Jane, this is my husband." Jane rose from her chair, holding her hand out to the surprised Billy Blake, who wasn't quite sure what to do with it…so he shook it earnestly, saying, "What a pleasure to meet you, Mrs. Neeley. Are you new in town?"

"No, but this is the first time I have come into your wonderful store. Your wife has been so gracious…oh, my, I didn't realize how much time had passed. I've kept her from her work long enough! I must get on home and let the two of you get back to work," as she visually scanned the store, noticing that it was still empty.

Amused, Billy caught the significance of her glance, and, looking around as well, adopting a mock serious expression, he announced jokingly, "Oh, by all means, Mrs. Neeley, we must get back to all our very hard work…"

Laughing aloud, Jane decided that this fun-loving man was indeed worthy of her new friend, Mary Rose Markham, and she followed his lead: "Oh, yes, and over here. How do you do, Mr. Smith? And Mrs. Snedley, how are you?" Jane nodded to invisible customers as Billy Blake and Mary Rose shook their heads and snickered.

"Well, it's usually busy this time of day…but perhaps everyone stayed away in your honor, Mrs. Neeley, so that you could have my wife all to yourself." Billy Blake's blue eyes twinkled as he peered down…way down to her five-foot height. "At any rate, I am delighted to know you and I hope you will stop in often." Billy headed to the back room to write down his window measurements before they exited his brain.

"What a nice man!" Jane observed to her new companion, watching his back as he retreated. "And again, thank you, Mary Rose, both for the lemonade and for allowing me to show my work here. I'm very proud that you like it. But I must go…oh, my, yes! My husband will wonder where I am…I left him with all three boys!" She offered her hand yet another time to her new friend, who took it confidently this time.

"Three boys! I can only imagine how frantic he must be!" Mary Rose chuckled, "I am so blessed to have found an amazing woman to help me with my youngsters, not that Billy couldn't handle them if he had to…but it is a blessing to have a third person the children trust and relate to. The children hardly miss me with Sarah there. So, Jane, I'll look forward to seeing you tomorrow. Maybe we can chat some more then, too. I would like to hear all about those boys. I have three children myself…so until tomorrow …"

"Goodbye, Mary Rose. I'll look forward to chatting more." Jane stood up, collecting her bag and moving toward the entrance, glancing around. "The store is so lovely. You must be very proud."

"Yes, thank you, we are." Escorting her friend to the front door, and watching her as she moved on down the street, Mary Rose smiled to herself, admiring the tiny, trim woman who was destined to play a significant role in her life to come.

* * *

As Jane Neeley made her way back to her buggy tied to a post near the opera house, she felt gratified, glad that she had made the decision to swallow her pride and ask for help. After five years of marriage to her handsome, hard-working miner and the birth of three children, it was hard to even remember the days when she was carefree, never worried about money…the days when she lived with her caring parents—who, she now recognized, spoiled her to distraction—in a home with luxuries, when food mysteriously appeared on the table through no effort on her part, when worn-out clothing were simply discarded and immediately replaced with new.

Jane suddenly felt disloyal, and ashamed of herself. Bud did everything he could for his family, and with no complaint; Jane fought the moods which plagued her, moods which she knew would wound Bud. As she stretched her food budget to the breaking point, as she darned and mended damaged clothing and socks, as she looked about their humble house…it was difficult always to be cheerful, to be supportive, not to complain. Yet she struggled to hide her occasional despair, hide the moments when she wished life were different, when she longed for an uninterrupted nap, a new dress, a ride in an elegant carriage with soft leather seats.

Even worse, she dreaded the days when she looked into her husband's loving blue eyes and the farthest reaches of her mind tormented her with a flash of honey-flecked eyes, aglow with love and passion. She forced those images away, but on occasion they snuck up on her, causing her to gasp with a real, physical pain. Bud didn't seem to notice when his wife's focus blurred; she hoped that was the case. Her husband was so good, so kind to her, so generous with his love and his time…he deserved better than intermittent loyalty.

Today was a good day. She had made a new friend, set a plan in motion to add to the family budget…and enjoyed being out of the house by herself, away from the boys. "Enough lollygagging, Mrs. Neeley. You have a family at home…" Jane muttered. Yes, it was time to go home. Bud would be at his wit's end caring for three boys under four, but he would fight hard to keep her from knowing his day had been difficult. Feeling a bit guilty for enjoying herself so much, she flipped the reins, increasing the pace of her old but strong dapple-grey, Lucky.

Her dad had told her once, when she was a child, that dapple-greys were lucky, so when Bud had brought home this gentle twelve-year-old retired carriage horse, Jane had loved him immediately and had named him Lucky. He was faithful, intelligent, never had to be whipped, followed the gentlest of commands and even tolerated the boys when Bud put them on Lucky's back for a walk around the yard they shared with the homes of six other miners' families. Lucky trotted on easily, south along the canal then east toward their home in Buchtel.

* * *

The store was still quiet when Billy Blake finished cutting the window blinds. Only two customers had been in since noon, a strange occurrence. But the quiet was nice at times. Both Markhams enjoyed solitude, were never uncomfortable when conversation lagged. As he carried his merchandise to the outgoing table, he glanced forward to where his wife pored over the books, calling to her, "Well, how do we look for the month, dear? Do you think we can afford the automobile?"

She looked up with a tolerant twinkle in her eyes, responding, "Oh, we might just be able to do that, if you really think it's a wise investment," knowing, of course, that Billy had his heart set on Henry Ford's new Model T. Ever since Edward and Elizabeth had bought the Buick, the little boy in her husband had longed to play with a machine of his own.

No one in Nelsonville yet owned a Ford automobile; there were several Oldsmobile trucks in service, as well as one other Buick, but a truck was a big, lumbering dinosaur of a ride. Billy wanted the airy, open lines of the Model-T, wanted to be the first to own one. Mary Rose wanted what he wanted…just because he was her Billy, so she had pinched pennies, both at home and at the store, being frugal by nature anyway.

The Nelsonville store was running smoothly; the Athens shoe store had always been self-supporting as was the Caldwell General Store. The newest Markham store, the Lancaster leather outlet, had started to pay for itself within the first three months, and was now set to be expanded into a full-scale department store…but the profit from the current store was easily covering the expansion. With her machinations, she had managed to set aside the $900, more than they needed for the automobile, and it took her only a year. She pretended to work some more figures on her paper, looking studious but noticing from the corner of her eye that Billy had stopped, an expectant, childlike hopefulness on his face.

"Well, what do you know? I think we can do it, Billy. What do you say when we go to Athens on Saturday to meet the contractor for the Lancaster remodeling job, we just stop at the new Ford place as well, if Sarah can stay longer with the children…and if we like what we see, we can put in our order?" Mary Rose was tickled to see her calm husband bubbling like a little child, like their effervescent Frankie! He was practically jumping up and down!

"Really? Do you think…really? It would be so nice to have the automobile before we open the Columbus store, and then if Dad needed me to go up some time when he wasn't going, I could…and oh, of course, I could take the children for their doctors' appointments in Athens without bothering Dad…really? We have the money?" He shouldn't have been surprised; his wife was a genius with money; not that he was any slouch, but she was just brilliant. Bending over her desk, he puckered his lips for a kiss, one which she met quickly with her own affectionate pucker.

"Yes, let's do it! I think it would be fun to be able to go that fast! You know, Billy, I read in the *Tribune* that the Model T can go over 20 miles an hour! Can you imagine? What fun it would be to feel the wind in my hair, no hat, no braids, just the wind!"

That image gave his heart a jolt: Wind in her face. Yes, he remembered well. Wind in her face was one of Mary Rose's earliest thrills, when she rode Sylvia, when her dad took her on river boats, she always threw back her head and loosened her hair so that the wind could whip through it unencumbered. She had looked like that, windswept and breathtaking, the first time Billy Blake had seen her and had fallen in love with her instantly, on the spot. A smile continued to tug at his lips as he remembered her that way.

Now, today, at their place of business, she was well-groomed, immaculate, every bit the professional woman who was beginning to take her place in the formerly all-male world of business…but beneath that suave exterior beat the heart of a pirate! She still radiated the same energy and excitement, in spite of having just had a baby in April, one month after moving into their new house, their dream house.

Hiring Sarah Washington as nanny had been inspired. It not only allowed Mary Rose to work with him in the stores, but also, took some of the stress out of her daily routine. Sarah was a wonderful woman, the right choice.

Admiring his wife who was now smiling at him teasingly, Billy Blake could barely contain the avalanche of love—and desire, if the truth were known—which surfaced at that moment, but resisting the urge to scoop her up in his arms, he planted another kiss, this one on the top of her head, whispering, "Thank you for being my wife, my partner, my best friend, to say nothing of the mother of my children…and most of all, the hardest job, for loving me."

His tenderness filled Mary Rose with joy, filled her eyes with tears. She answered softly, "You are very welcome, my lord and master," meeting his eyes, so filled with love. At that very moment, however, the front door opened and the third and fourth customer of the day entered, very nearly catching the Markhams in a moment a bit too intimate for public! Pulling away, Billy Blake winked at his wife, and called out in his usual manner, forever the charismatic shopkeeper, "Why, hello, Mrs. Gaylord, Mrs. French! How nice to see you! How can I help you?" and he moved away from Mary Rose's desk, as she too waved at the customers…but not before returning his wink.

Chapter 18 – Building for the Future

[May 1909]

On the following Saturday morning in May of 1909, Sarah and Marcia Washington banged in the kitchen door of the Markhams' Fort Street home, carrying a bag of fresh peaches and a rhubarb pie, two of the very few fruits which Billy Blake Markham hadn't managed to cultivate on his triangle-shaped half-acre property…at least, not yet. Give him time, Sarah knew, and he would…he could grow anything, bigger and better than anyone else in Nelsonville, another of Billy Blake's amazing talents. "Kids, stores, and vegetables…he can grow 'em all…" she thought often about her favorite white man.

At that moment, Sarah and her daughter were greeted by the boisterous Frankie, followed by Betsy, hard on his heels. Frankie leaped into Sarah's arms, squealing, "Save me, Auntie Sarah! A monster is chasing me! Help!" Although he nearly knocked her over, Frankie nevertheless always made Sarah laugh. She was so fond of his changeable personality, one minute a little grown up man taking care of the family, then the irrepressible all-boy creature which had just leaped into her arms a moment later! She spun him in a circle.

Betsy had wriggled up to Marcia and wrapped her chubby arms around the girl, giggling and babbling, "Me up, me up! Catch Fankie!" Even the pre-teen was tickled by this onslaught of the Markham brood, and she did what Betsy asked, lifting the toddler and spinning her around as well, to the youngster's delight.

Mary Rose Markham was coming down the steps from the bathroom and turning into the dining room, just in time to see her children flying in circles, and she laughed at the half-delighted, half-frightened expressions on their faces. "Gracious! What is happening? Is there a giant wind in here, maybe a tornado?"

"Yah! A tomato!" Frankie squealed.

The children were returned to the floor, stumbling a bit, dizzy from the spin, but belly-laughing, nevertheless. Betsy's bottom, well-padded by diapers, plopped on the kitchen floor, as her mother reached her to pick her up for a good-bye kiss while Frankie wrapped his arms around her waist. "You monkeys be good for Auntie Sarah and Marcia, now, do you hear? Papa and I just might have a surprise for two good little children." The young charges bounced in place. "Sarah, Will just ate and he is dozing in his crib, but I don't think he will be down for long, especially not if these two monkeys have anything to say about it," knuckling her older children's curly heads affectionately.

"No problem, Miz Markham. We can handle ten like these, right, girl?" Marcia nodded but didn't look quite as confident as her mother. "Marcia, take Frank and Betsy to the table 'n' show 'em the fresh peaches we brought…" Marcia did as she was told, and in a matter of seconds, peach juice was dripping from two chins.

"Okay, Sarah, we will be meeting with the contractor who is doing some remodeling on the Lancaster store and that will take…oh, two hours or so? Then I promised Mr. Markham that we would stop at the Ford dealership and take a look at that new Model T he has been drooling over for six months now…so it will probably be late afternoon before we get back. I hope that isn't a problem…?" One eyebrow raised, Mary Rose peered at Sarah, questioning.

"No, our menfolk left us anyhow—fishing—so we got the whole day. Take all th' time ye need…an automobile? Wouldn't that be something!"

"Yes, it would indeed. Ever since Mr. Markham, Senior, got the Buick, my husband has been wanting one…and, since Edward is a bit under the weather, we are driving the Buick today, so we can compare the two cars. Mr. Markham thinks the Ford is 'more fun'…we shall see! If, of course, it doesn't get us killed!"

"Oh, no, ma'am…wouldn't want that! You see he's careful, now, you promise…"

"He will be, Sarah. He will. Don't you worry. Just keep my brood happy until we get back. Bye now…" and she grabbed her sun bonnet hanging by the door, frowning at it. "I really hate to wear bonnets, Sarah. I'm not sure I'm supposed to be a grown up yet…I just love wind. But, it's a business meeting…and, I guess I can't show up with my hair looking like a haystack, so…bonnet, do your job." She fastened the strings just in time to hear the rumble of an automobile as it pulled into the lane which led past Billy Blake's pride and joy, the grove of walnut and hickory trees, to the rear of the house. Waving to her peach-covered children and Marcia, Mary Rose left by the back porch door, and climbed in beside Billy Blake, handsome in a Brooks Brothers suit and sitting tall and proud at the wheel of a 1904 Buick, an elegant vignette indeed.

* * *

Fred Hunt strode into the storefront quarters of his branch office in Athens at nine a.m., carrying a blueprint rolled up under his arm and a satchel filled with building code books and legal forms. The company's clerk/stenographer Molly Cavanaugh looked up from her desk, startled to see one of her bosses frowning and preoccupied. Surprised to see the illusive Mr. Hunt, she spoke to him, interrupting his reverie, "Why, hello, Mr. Hunt! I wasn't expecting to see you today! Do you have a meeting?"

He looked at her quizzically, retorting, "Uh, Molly, don't I still work here?" Then he felt bad to see the hurt look his flippant comment caused. "It's okay, Molly, I know I'm not here a lot. Yes, I do have a meeting, with the Markhams, as a matter of fact, at 9:30. Until then, I will be working on their designs in my office. When they arrive, will you show them into the conference room, then come get me, please?"

"Sure thing, Mr. Hunt. It's good to see you. Do you need anything else before your appointment?" Molly began to rise, eager to please the very attractive junior partner.

"No thanks. And Molly? You do a good job. Even though I don't see you often, Bill Cable keeps me posted...and, secret? He thinks you can walk on water!"

Blushing prettily, Molly protested, "Oh, no, Mr. Hunt, but that's very kind of you...I do my best." Settling back into her chair, she self-consciously brushed a stray hair back from her brow, embarrassed by his praise, but basking in it, nonetheless.

"I know you do. And your best is pretty darned good. I'll visit with you later, okay? And Molly, could you put on a pot of coffee for me, please?"

"Of course. Right away...and I'll bring you a fresh cup as soon as it brews."

"That will be wonderful. Perhaps the Markhams might want some, too, so make a big pot, okay?" Striding through the leather chair-lined front entry hall, Fred Hunt left the young woman wistfully admiring the view of his retreating form, and enjoying a wishful moment...but she knew better. This was her place of work. This is not a place to be capricious...so, shaking her head to clear the haze, she left her task of typing invoices on the massive new Royal typewriter to enter the small anteroom and cross to the coal stove with a burner which permitted a coffeepot.

Bill Cable, the senior partner of Cable, Rowen and Hunt, was in his office with the senior director of engineering for Athens County; seeing his partner pass by, he called out, "Fred, hello! Did you need to talk with Ron about the Markham project?"

"Hi, Bill. No, not this time. This one is in Fairfield County. Maybe next time. Hi, Ron. How's the building business in Athens?"

"Great! Hey, Fred, I heard lots of really nice comments about that office complex you did across the river, the Baldwin project? The owners love it and so do the tenants," the engineer called.

"That's nice to hear. Hopefully, there will be more like that one. I'll keep you informed. Bill, when the Markhams get here, you might want to sit in. They have some pretty creative…and, I might add, ambitious…ideas."

"If we finish up in time, will do, Fred, but don't wait for me. This is your 'baby'…"

Moving on down the hall, Fred stepped into his crowded masculine but comfortable office. Settling comfortably into a patched leather desk chair he had carried with him, sort of as a good luck charm, since his San Toy project days, Fred smoothed the blueprint out in front of him, anchoring it with a paper weight so it wouldn't roll back up. Perusing the front elevation, he frowned while considering the architectural variations he would have to create if an existing building, a warehouse on Cherry Street in Lancaster, was to be transformed into the light and open concept he and Edward Markham had visualized during their preliminary meeting. As he studied, his excitement grew. His architect seemed to have captured the concept well…but the Markhams had yet to make the final decision.

This would be the first time Fred actually had drawings to show the Markhams. Edward and Billy Blake, according to their first meeting last month, had initially hoped the existing structure which they had bought from Riley Napson the previous year would allow for the expansion they had visualized, but after operating out of that location through three seasons, both men recognized that the leather goods location had nowhere to expand. If Markham's, Lancaster, was to be a department store…it needed room.

Also, the exterior of the current structure had no appeal; Billy called its style "Nouveau Ugly," bringing a smile and a nod of agreement from Fred, who had stopped by the Lancaster location to see what, if anything, could be done. So, when the Markhams went searching for a builder, Fred was ready with a head full of ideas, immediately impressing both Markhams. Of course, they checked his references, which were impeccable, the icing on the cake.

Fred Hunt had just finished a waterfront project in Athens, an ambitious project, and father and son had taken an excursion to look it over. Impressive was their conclusion, innovative yet practical, just the type of look they wanted for Markham's. Thus, they hired Cable, Rowen, and Hunt, specifying a preference for Fred. It seemed the Markhams had gone shopping for a builder just as the builder had gone shopping for a project…and the match worked well. Personalities meshed, minds locked, and a partnership blossomed.

As Fred peered through his reading glasses at the building face, he hoped he had interpreted the concept Edward had described and presented it clearly…he usually did, but this gigantic department store building was a far cry from the saloons, the boarding houses and general stores he had been building for the coal companies. The Athens project had been a good foot in the door, but this one, if done right, could be the beginning of a much more exciting and, not a minor point, more lucrative series of projects.

The Markhams were up and coming, there was no doubt about that, and the son, Billy Blake, seemed to have the same business sense and ambition that Edward had. Yes, this one was important, he nodded to himself, as he flipped to the interior floor plan. "Ummm…yes, good. Umm hmm…yep…" Fred mumbled as he scanned the plans.

Barely fifteen minutes later, Molly tapped on the door; as he looked up, he saw a steaming mug in her hand and waved her in, returning to the perusal of his blueprints. She waited patiently for his attention, after placing the hot coffee on the side table. Molly Cavanaugh was used to the concentration which Fred Hunt employed when involved in a project. Noticing that she was still standing in front of him, Fred queried, "Was there something else, Molly?"

"Yes, sir, I was wondering if you had seen last night's newspaper…the article about the university wanting to build some three-story dormitories for students?"

His attention captured fully now, Fred replied, "No, I didn't get in from Chillicothe until midnight. What did it say? Something we should take a look at?"

"Well, I thought so. I brought the paper in with me…here." She handed the *Messenger* to her boss.

"Hmm, as usual, you have done your job and then some. Thanks, Molly, I will read this just as soon as the Markhams and I have finished up. They should be here any minute, so…Molly? Thanks. You are one in a million." And he winked, sending her heart lurching.

"You're welcome, Mr. Hunt. I hope it pays off…for the company, of course…" Retreating, Molly Cavanaugh paused briefly, her hand over her racing heart…and moved back toward her desk, just as the front door opened and the junior Markhams stepped in.

"Good morning, Mrs. Markham, Mr. Markham. Mr. Hunt is ready to see you. Won't you step this way? Would either of you care for some fresh coffee?"

Mary Rose smiled appreciatively and replied, "Thank you very much. That sounds wonderful. Billy?" Her husband nodded his head enthusiastically, gracing Molly Cavanaugh with a dazzling Billy Blake Markham smile.

"Right this way. Mr. Hunt thought you would be more comfortable in the conference room…more room to spread out. Here. Make yourselves comfortable and I will be right back with coffee…oh, and with Mr. Hunt, of course." Smiling, she stepped across the hall and again tapped on the door of Fred's office. "The Markhams are here, Mr. Hunt…Mrs. Markham and Mr. Markham junior."

Somewhat surprised but never shocked that the lovely Mary Rose Markham was attending while Edward Markham was not, Fred smoothed back his hair, still chestnut brown with a distinguishing shading of gray at the temples, picked up the blueprint he had been studying, stopped to nod at Bill Cable, gesturing toward the conference room, and followed Molly across the hall. "Billy Blake, always a pleasure, and Mrs. Markham, what a nice surprise!"

"Mary Rose, please, Mr. Hunt," and she held her hand out to him.

"Okay, then, make it Fred," and he grasped her outstretched hand firmly.

Billy Blake Markham had risen to his feet and held out his hand as well. "Good morning, Fred. This is going to be an exciting project, I believe. My wife has an excellent head for business and also for design. Thank you for allowing us this time in your very busy schedule. How is the Chillicothe project going?"

"Ahead of schedule, I'm happy to say!" Let's have a seat and take a look at these elevations; I think my designer and I captured your vision, but only you can tell me that…Is your father joining us?"

Mary Rose replied for her husband, "Mr. Markham Senior is a bit under the weather, so my husband suggested it might be acceptable if I sat in on the meeting. I hope you don't mind…"

"Mind? Certainly not! I understand you participate in the daily operation of the Nelsonville store, isn't that right?"

"Yes, I do. I must admit that I really love being involved in the stores."

"You are more than welcome to join us at any time," Fred said, flashing his charismatic smile at her.

Fred and Billy Blake took seats beside one another on the long side of the conference table; Fred unrolled the blueprints while Billy Blake eagerly leaned forward to see. Rising and coming around behind her husband, Mary Rose Markham peered at the drawings, her excitement rendering her even more vibrant than usual, Fred noticed. The gentleman in him felt slightly awkward that she was standing while he was seated, but she was clearly engrossed in the designs, so he began his detailed explanation while both Markhams listened attentively.

* * *

Two hours and two pots of coffee later, Billy Blake and Mary Rose shook hands with Fred Hunt and Bill Cable, who had joined them mid-meeting, and left the offices with visions of a magnificent, modern department store dancing in their heads. The Frank Lloyd Wright innovations had stood the construction industry on its ear five years earlier. Somehow, Fred's architect had been able to create just the slightest hint of the Prairie look, with a gently sloping roof over the portico and semicircular windows gracing the main entrance, but keeping in mind the winter snowfall issue, leaving a steeper pitch on the main roof. Still, it would be a modern-looking building, stylish yet practical…innovative, indeed, for Lancaster, Ohio.

Both Markhams found Fred Hunt to be not only an astute designer but also a personable and captivating man, one who seemed to be as infected by excitement as they were. "…and oh, Billy, the way he extended the entryway to include a covered portico! What a terrific idea! Never would have thought of that…" Mary Rose bubbled.

"I know, it's wonderful! More like a theater entryway…people will feel so pampered, like they are entering an opera house…I love it! He's good, don't you think?"

"Good?? He's fabulous! I hope we can keep him around…he works all over the state and in Pennsylvania and Indiana, I think he said…you know, we may just have to keep him busy enough to stick around!"

"Yes, he did say he would like to put down some roots soon," Billy pointed out. "Maybe we can provide him some motivation to put roots down where we can pluck the fruits from a very nearby tree!"

"Silly! But I know what you mean…wow! What a design he created! I'm glad the crew can start on it this week…you know, we might be able to get the new Lancaster store open by the end of summer! That's wonderful, Billy. You chose a really good man to do a really good project. I'm so proud of you."

"Dad found Fred, Mary. But I agree, this could be the man to work with for a long time to come. Now…let's go look at a car, what do you say? Or would you like to have some lunch at the Oak Street Café, first? We haven't done that for awhile and we are celebrating, after all."

"Oh, let's do that! Sarah said she was in no hurry…Jeremiah and Paul went fishing, and you know how they are when they get to the river with a bucket of worms and a couple poles. Sarah may not see them for awhile. Let's have a nice lunch and then…let's go buy a car!"

"Buy a car? Not just look at a car? Why, Mary Rose Markham, I do believe you are trying to turn my head!"

"If it isn't turned by now, there's no hope for you, my dear. We deserve a car! I can hear it now: The handsome and very elegant, sophisticated…and of course…successful Markhams now arriving in their sparkling new Model-T Ford…attention, everyone!" She kissed his cheek as he helped her into the passenger seat of the Buick, barely able to contain her excitement.

Chapter 19 – Sultry Summer

[August 1909]

"Hush, now, don't you cry, wee one, Auntie Sarah's gotcha," the hot, weary Negro woman crooned as she rocked on the Markhams' front porch in the wonderful wooden swing Edward Markham had brought it over from the house Billy Blake and Mary Rose had moved into while waiting for this house to be finished. It now hung proudly on the back porch which spanned the entire rear of the Fort Street home. From the swing, one could see the garden and fish pond Mr. Markham had put in, and admire the massive apple tree which shaded the north end of the house. Large and comfortable, this house had every amenity imaginable, running water, a roomy bathroom with claw-footed tub, even electricity. Sarah loved the house almost as much as Mrs. Markham did! The porch was covered and picked up an eastern breeze, aided by her rocking.

Although it was approaching evening, it was still warm and the late summer mosquitoes sought purchase on the tender young skin of the baby William; Sarah swatted at them, but they were fierce and persistent...typical late August menaces. Will squirmed and wailed, daring his nanny to quiet him, angry at the heat and the mosquitoes.

"Now, look here, youngster, all that screamin'—screaming—isn't gonna make it cooler...hush, now..." and the pace of her rocking picked up. "You just want your mama, don't you, little one? You aren't gonna be satisfied with me, no matter what, are you?" Sarah laid her head back on the cushion, her hand, conditioned by practice with her own two children, falling into the unconscious maternal instinct of patting, much like the rocking mothers do without thought years after their last child has left the fold.

She patted the back of the unhappy young man, who continued to whimper and squirm, but his fussing seemed not quite as intense as before. As his cries faded into mild, going-to-sleep murmurs, Sarah found herself beginning to drift off as well, the first welcome breeze of evening finding her there in the shade of the apple tree and one massive maple.

But her respite wasn't to last long…it rarely did. Frankie, a serious four-year-old looking intense, came to the screen door, peering out into the shadows, calling, "Auntie Sarah? Where are you?"

She replied softly, "Shh, now, Frank, I just got your little brother to sleep. Where's Betsy? Why don't both of you sit at the table in th' playroom an' have yourselves a tea party?"

"Naa, that's a sissy thing. I don't like tea parties," the usually good-natured Frankie answered, his voice more of a whine than usual. "I want dinner, Auntie Sarah."

Sarah sighed and, shifting the now-sleeping baby to one arm, she rose with effort, reluctantly giving up her comfortable spot in the swing. "Al' right, son, Sarah's coming. Help a bit with Betsy, will you? Soon's I put Will in his cradle, we'll fix some supper. Maybe we'll surprise your mama an' fix some for her and your papa too, what d' you say?"

"Oh, that's a good thing, Auntie Sarah; let's cook for Mama and Papa! What can we cook?" and he screwed up his face, thinking. She knew Frank's good nature would prevail; he was the one of the Markham brood who never caused a problem for her. Mature for his four years, Frank often took charge of his younger sister, who was cranky with anyone but him. Sarah loved him dearly.

Mary Rose had often marveled to Sarah at the special way Frankie had with Betsy's stormy personality, calming her, teaching her patiently to share, to be more patient. "It's as if he is the parent, Sarah, and I am just a bystander," Mary Rose puzzled. But both his mother and Sarah were often grateful for the solid, tolerant way Frank displayed his maturity. His whines were few and far between; when Sarah heard them, she wanted to accommodate his needs as quickly as possible, so dinner was a must…and now.

Noticing that the parlor clock read nearly 6 o'clock, and wondering where the last hour had gone, Sarah remarked, "My goodness, Frank, no wonder you're hungry! Come help me clean some vegetables," and chuckled as he darted ahead of her into the kitchen, rattling around in the lower cabinet to find a stock pot and a scrub brush, thinking "Lordy, that boy loves to help."

As Sarah laid the sleeping Will in his cradle, curly-haired Betsy looked up from her tea party and flashed one of her too-rare ear-to-ear smiles—Mary Rose's smile—at Sarah, "Lookie, An'ie Sarah! I gots cookie!" holding up a piece of old hard bread she must have gotten from the trash.

Stifling a gasp, Sarah reached for the "cookie" before it could go into Betsy's mouth, remarking quickly, "Uh, little miss, let's remember not t' spoil dinner. Come help Sarah, now." The two-year-old's face clouded for a minute, but the prospect of banging on the cooking pots—"helping"—drew her to her feet and, toddling ahead of Sarah, she joined her brother who was now searching in the pantry for carrots and any other vegetable treasures he could find in there.

It was the second night of the Lancaster Markham's Department Store grand opening, and Mary Rose had warned Sarah that they could be late. It was exciting to Sarah to see her missus light up like the new electric streetlamps brightening their Fort Street neighborhood when she talked about the stores; Sarah wished she had the courage to ask if she could help open the stores. She knew she could be real help, because she was strong and smart…but she feared the time wasn't right yet for colored women to work alongside their white sisters. "Only as a nanny…or a maid t'day…but some day, it'll be different. I wish 'someday' would hurry, though," Sarah mused as she searched in the icebox for the chickens she had cleaned and cut up earlier that day to fry for dinner. "Like Miss Ida Wells promised, some day…"

The chicken found its way into the iron skillet without the help of Sarah's mind; her hands could carry on without any real thought, and her thoughts were twenty-five miles up the Pike, with her Mrs. and Mr. Markham, smiling and shaking hands with new customers, cutting beautiful material for dresses for those pretty white ladies, wrapping up curtains and towels in brown paper…what a wonderful place to be! "I could do it, I know I could…I wonder if I should just ask…what would it hurt?" Not noticing the stock pot concert going on behind her, Sarah's thoughts raced up and down clean, polished wooden floors, nodding and chatting with fine ladies, to the cash register…"It must be even bigger than th' one in th' Nelsonville store…imagine that!"

Sarah loved the Nelsonville Markham's Dry Goods Store, and spent as much time in it as she could justify. She loved the way the store smelled, like dusting powder, cleaning wax, new linen…and the impression that one could go back, back forever as one looked down the long, straight side aisles to the very back, where Billy Blake Markham often stood, smiling and surveying his kingdom.

Sarah always loved to watch the sales girls Audrey or Lillian ring up her purchases on that giant register. Tall as the coal furnaces her husband Jeremiah kept stoked at the elementary schools and nearly as heavy, it had fascinating drawers and buttons, all trimmed in gold on the dark walnut wood, with all sorts of mysterious symbols on them. Sarah found it absolutely hypnotizing and sometimes she stood frozen, watching the clerks push buttons so that little bells would ring and drawers would pop open like magic. She would so much like to be the one to push those buttons and make magic happen…

Lost in her fantasy now, Sarah saw herself dressed in a smart grey suit with a gored skirt and shiny black buttons, greeting the stylish ladies of Lancaster as they came from the portico into the new store, peering into their faces as they told her what they would like to see…leading them to the right department, chatting, smiling… Mrs. Markham had taken her along one Sunday afternoon when she and her friend Jane Neeley traveled to Lancaster to check on the installation of the electric lights and, coincidentally, Sarah had stopped by to drop off some shirts she had taken home to iron for Mr. Markham.

Riding in the car was a thrill, but seeing the new store was like a dream come true for Sarah. As her employer and Mrs. Neeley had bustled around the store, checking this and that and chattering, she had stood wistfully in the center of the showroom, gazing about as if she were in a fairy tale! The store was like nothing she could have imagined, like something out of a magazine! Even though it was closed and quiet, she had no trouble visualizing it filled with eager patrons, fingering the wares. Visualizing herself standing proud next to her employer, Billy Blake Markham…her eyes closed as a mystic smile softened her face.

A sigh escaped her lips as she returned to the here and now. It was a wonderful dream…

But for now, she knew caring for the Markhams' three children and helping with the housework was good. It pleased Sarah to help these two beautiful golden people, and she was so grateful that Mrs. Markham felt Sarah could be trusted with her precious children. Those children were the center of Mr. and Mrs. Markham's world.

It was an amazing coincidence that the Markhams had decided to look for a nanny just as Sarah had begun to think of going to work. She was sure God had a hand in it, as He did in all things! When Sarah had stopped into Markham's last spring, looking for school clothing for Marcia to finish out the school year, Mary Rose and her husband had exchanged an inquisitive look and then a small, satisfied nod. The look was not noticed by Sarah at first, but when she paused, looking longingly at a rose-colored silk blouse in her size, then shook her head sadly, denying herself the pleasure of finery so that her children could have what they needed, she saw Mr. Markham nod at his wife, walk toward Sarah, take her arm and whisper, "Mrs. Washington, my wife and I have something we would like to talk to you about, if you have time."

Mr. Markham was her favorite white man in the world! If he wanted her time, it was his. And so it came about that Sarah Washington became the nanny and housekeeper for the junior Markhams. For five months now, she had been caring for Frankie, Betsy, and the baby William Blake Jr.—Will—and learning just what exceptional people her employers were, even more than she had thought previously. They had so much on their minds with this newly renovated store and another one—way up in Columbus—being stocked to open in two months, yet they always remembered to bring her a little gift along with the ones they brought Frankie and Betsy, when they had to be away for longer than normal days.

Sarah had quickly learned what made that marriage so solid: mutual respect and consideration, mixed with lots of laughter and boundless energy. Both Mr. and Mrs. Markham were smart and clever, but they never forgot that people come first, things come second. They loved their stores...both of them sparkled when they talked about the openings...but they always opened their arms and their hearts to their children, their parents, their friends...and to Sarah.

Yesterday, when Mary Rose came in, way past the time she had expected, she had given Sarah a gold bracelet! "Oh, Mrs. Markham, I can't...you don't need..." she had protested.

"Sarah, you work so hard and are so kind to the children, so Mr. Markham and I want you to have something you don't need, for once. Take it and enjoy it. It would please us."

So she took it, a little worried that Jeremiah would think she was displeased, that she thought he couldn't do enough for her...but to her surprise, Jeremiah put the bracelet on her arm, kissed her hand, and smiled lovingly, silently, proudly. That was her man, her wonderful man, knowing just the way to put her in a comfortable place.

A louder than normal crash startled Sarah out of her reverie, and she turned just in time to see Betsy pounding on the pot...with one of Mary Rose's silver candlesticks, the ones she had gotten as a wedding present from her mother and dad! "Oh, no, little miss, no, you don't! Your mama will skin both of us if you dent that candlestick!" and she rescued the treasure, replacing it in Betsy's chubby fist with a wooden spoon. "There you go, girl...bang away!"

She noticed Frankie was still patiently scraping carrots and potatoes, bringing Sarah to her senses; she poured water into a large pot...not the one Betsy was enjoying...and held it out to Frankie to put his vegetables in. "Good work, Frank. Those'll be good with th' chicken. Let's us boil 'em now, okay?" and he gratefully gave up his task, returning to the other kitchen chair and a wooden puzzle his uncle Stewart had made for him. "Such a good child," she thought to herself.

Twenty minutes later, the chicken was beginning to smell delicious, so Sarah covered it and moved the skillet to the back of the stove where the meat could simmer while she finished the meal. "Betsy, let's you and me put th' plates on th' table, an' Frankie? Can you get those tomatoes off the porch?" The meal was coming together, only a half-hour later than planned, and the kitchen was no more of a disaster than it had to be…so, feeling a little guilty that her mind had wandered so, Sarah sat with Betsy in her lap, playing patty-cake with her and Frankie while the chicken and vegetables simmered.

"You two are the best little people…next to my Paul and Marcia, of course," and she nuzzled Betsy's neck while Frank scrambled away from that "kissy stuff"; he was doubly relieved when dinner was ready to be eaten. The kitchen then erupted into a sensory delight, as Sarah and her two older charges served, sliced, chewed, and chattered, warm and comfortable.

* * *

Nearly ten p.m. found Sarah, the little ones peacefully asleep for the night, in her favorite place inside the junior Markham's home, in a rose-colored damask wing-back chair, one of a matched pair beside the fireplace in the massive sitting room, shaded floor lamps pleasantly bathing the room in warm light. She was totally enthralled in the biography she was reading of her newest heroine, Ida B. Wells, one of Sarah's role models in her crusade for fairness, both to Negroes and to women in general.

Born in 1862, Sarah read, of slave parents as she was, the heroic Ida Wells had taken over the rearing of her six younger siblings when Yellow Fever had claimed both of their parents. Lying about her age and determined to keep the family together, she had obtained a teaching job at the age of sixteen, and managed to conceal the fact that she was raising a family and holding down a full-time job when she should have been just a school girl herself. Sarah was currently reading about the incident which had inspired Ida to be a writer: while riding on a train on her way back to her teaching job, she was asked to vacate her seat to a white passenger. Refusing, she was forcibly removed by three white men, conductors and passengers, to the smoking car. She had paid for a seat in first class, and was now reduced to riding in the smoking car; furious, she got off the train at the next stop and found other transportation. Not stopping there, this brave young woman had sued the railroad—and won a settlement!

What a brave and foolish thing to do, Sarah mused. Ever since she had begun to read about brave Negro women who fought for a better life—Sojourner Truth, Harriet Tubman in addition to Ida Wells—and white women like Susan B. Anthony, Lucy Wells, and Elizabeth Cady Stanton who also picked up the cause, Sarah had become determined to find a way to make a difference as well, a difference not only for Negro women but for all women. But how? she wondered.

The kernel of a book she wanted to write was rattling around in Sarah's head as she read further into the biography, a book about slavery, about emancipation—about what freedom really meant. This idea had been teasing at her mind for several years now, and she had been writing little snatches of stories, ideas as they came to her. Sitting there in the pleasant quiet, Sarah had just about made up her mind to pick up pencil and tablet to tell the story of a slave's daughter who became a famous writer…as soon as she got home. The thought had her mind and heart racing…

"One day, Miz Wells, one day I'll do my part, I promise…" she muttered, just as the distinctive rumble of Billy Blake and Mary Rose's shiny Model-T Ford entered the lane to the right of where she now sat, relaxed but full of plans, weary from a hard day's work, but excited about tomorrow. Rising to meet them at the side door, Sarah pulled herself up to her full height, flashed her captivating, white-toothed smile, and held the door for Mary Rose as she struggled in with two large bundles, her husband just behind her with yet another even larger bundle.

"Whew! What a day! Oh, Sarah, it was wonderful! The people came all day, they walked all over, poked in every corner and shelf…I could barely scurry around fast enough to answer their questions! And Mr. Markham shook more hands than President Roosevelt! Whew! My feet hurt…oohhh, what do I smell? Oh, Sarah, is that fried chicken? Oh, bless you, bless you. I am so hungry, I could eat a chicken, feathers and all…" and heading toward the kitchen, dropping her bundles on the bench beside the door, the tiny dynamo of a woman barely stopped for a breath.

"Were the children any trouble? I don't hear crying. How's Will taking his bottle? Did Betsy break anything?" and she bubbled on as she sat at the table, unbuttoning her shoes, removing them and wiggling her toes dramatically.

Chuckling at her mistress' ramblings and her stockinged feet, Sarah followed on her heels, lifting the lid on the vegetables and beginning to dish out chicken, smiling over her shoulder at Billy Blake Markham who was still struggling to lock the door, shaking his head with amusement at his wife's monologue. "You sit, Miz Markham, Mr. Markham. Frankie and I made you some dinner…that boy wouldn't be satisfied 'til I promised I would feed you th' minute you came home…an' told you he fixed the vegetables. Mr. Will had a fussy spell—the heat 'n' all—but he settled down good; Miss Betsy…well, she was Miss Betsy…but we all had a good day."

Billy Blake had finally made his way to the kitchen and was collapsing into his chair opposite Mary Rose, just as Sarah placed a plate of steaming, delicious-smelling chicken and vegetables in front of him. Inhaling deeply, he exclaimed, "I don't know how you manage, Sarah, to juggle those three scamps, cook food fit for a king…and queen" with a wink at his wife, "…and still keep the house looking like no one under four lives here…but you are one of a kind. Thank you for this, this dinner. Mrs. Markham and I were prepared to eat a cold tomato sandwich and fall into bed!"

Sarah smiled at her adored Mr. Markham and his exhausted but still energetic wife who was gobbling her chicken leg in a very unladylike way, much to her husband's amusement. "It was no trouble, Mr. M. No harder t' cook two chickens than one…and remember, Frankie did the vegetables!"

"Oh, yes, wouldn't want to forget that, would we? Mrs. Markham's right, Sarah, the opening was fabulous! You should have seen the crowd! People came from as far away as Cleveland to check out the new store. I wasn't sure, you know, when Dad chose to expand in Lancaster…but when is he ever wrong about things like that?" He began to devour his chicken, and for a moment, the room was silent, with only the sound of cutlery on stoneware to disturb the silence. In the hunger-induced silence, Sarah's thoughts raced…

Absent-mindedly, Sarah cut another fresh tomato and a green pepper and placed them on a plate in the center of the table, poured both of the diners iced tea with lemon, then took her surprise, a fresh peach pie, out of the pie safe, as Mary Rose's eyes got huge. "Oh, Sarah, when did you have time to do that? Is that peach? Oh, I wouldn't have believed I could eat another bite…but bring that over here!" Despite her amusement at and affection for her mistress, Sarah's face clouded momentarily as she weighed her words…

"Uh, Mr. Markham, Miz Markham…d'you think maybe someday I could help you out in the store…the Nelsonville one…or another?" Averting her eyes, she worried that she might have created a problem and wished she had kept quiet. The silence was leaden.

Mary Rose looked at her, stunned, then at her husband, one eyebrow raised. Billy Blake spoke first, "Why, Sarah, I had no idea you wanted to do something like that! Well, let's see…Lord knows there are days when Audrey or Lillian can't be there…well, what were you thinking?"

Gratefully, Sarah answered, "The ladies…I like the ladies…well, d'ya think I could wait on the ladies? Would they be…well, y'know…upset 'cause I'm…y'know…" and her voice trailed off, her eyes downcast.

Mary Rose and Billy Blake looked at each other, then at her, then began, almost at the same time:

"Well, if they would…that's on them…" said Billy.

"Too bad…that's what I say…" said Mary Rose.

Billy continued, "Let us think about this for a few days, until we get recovered from the opening, okay, Sarah? I promise we will talk about it again." And he stood up to his full six-foot height, looking directly into Sarah's eyes. "We'll talk, don't you worry. And thanks so much for trusting us, for letting us know how you feel. We had no idea…"

Mary Rose agreed, "None at all. It's something to think about, isn't it?" and she too rose and headed out of the kitchen, calling over her shoulder, "The dinner was wonderful, Sarah. Thank you. Especially the pie…what a treat!"

Sarah mumbled, "Thank you. I wouldn't want t' cause you any trouble…" And she took the plates to the sink, noticing that she was perspiring very heavily, in spite of the wonderful breeze which now entered the window above the sink. "You two go on, now, up t'bed. I'll just clean up a bit and head on home. You've had a long day…" Embarrassed at the earlier conversation, Sarah bustled and made lots of dish noise.

"Good night, Sarah. And, oh, there's a little package for you on the desk for being so good to the children, and to us, of course," and Mary Rose, weariness showing in the slump of her shoulders, started up the stairway in her stocking feet, carrying her tiny shoes.

"Good night, Sarah. I loved the chicken. Say hello to Mister Washington, okay? Will we see you Saturday?" Billy Blake called from the hall.

"Yessir. Eight sharp. Thank you for the…present…" Finishing the dishes in a suddenly empty and quiet kitchen, Sarah noticed her own fatigue for the first time, but she left the kitchen neat as her proverbial pin, crossed to the desk, and opening the package, she gasped as she saw that rose silk blouse she had denied herself three weeks earlier. "Oh, Mr. Markham…" Sarah murmured, with tears in her eyes; lifting the soft fabric to her face, smoothing the blouse with her calloused hands, then tucking it neatly back in its wrapper and picking up her worn carpetbag, she turned out the lights and exited from the same door her employers, her thoughtful, wonderful employers, had entered a half-hour earlier. "Could it be…?" She wondered at her future.

Chapter 20 – Women's Suffrage

[September 1909]

Bosom friends Jane Neeley and Mary Rose Markham walked briskly across the Public Square on their way to the Opera House, giggling like school girls when an updraft threw their skirts into the air, exposing two pairs of pantaloons and very shapely legs. Fighting their skirts back into place, they looked both ways before stepping into the street to approach the Opera House. They were wise to look where they stepped: carriages and automobiles were lined up all the way from Columbus Street two and three deep and even around the corner onto Washington Street as their patrons disembarked to rush into the already packed theater. "Oh, dear, I hope we can still get seats!" Mary Rose exclaimed, viewing the crush inside the lobby.

"Oh, we will. We'll just look helpless and some men will get up," teased Jane. This was the second of a new series of women's suffrage meetings; there would be few men there, Jane knew. A dozen or so had attended the first one, but half of them had left before the meeting was over. Jane and Mary Rose had been seated near the back for the first meeting and were amazed at the level of excitement they had felt, even back that far. The audience had been electrified.

"I wish Sarah could join us," mused Mary Rose, as they followed the throng up the narrow stairs to the seating. "She really has a lot of good ideas of ways women could get the vote. Really, it's just silly that we don't..."

"I know. The times are changing. It won't be long before the world realizes colored people should vote, too. Did you know, Mary Rose, that colored men could vote right after the War and then some idiot took the vote away from them? That's so crazy. President Roosevelt thinks so too..."

Jane pushed into a crowded row with two vacant seats right in the middle. "Excuse me...oh, sorry, sorry...'scuse us" as she made her way to the seats.

The two diminutive women had been fast friends since their first meeting in Markham's that spring. Jane had missed the company of cultured women since her hasty marriage had put an end to her childhood and the environment in which she had been raised. Although she never got to go to college as she had planned, Jane kept her mind active and growing, reading every chance she had. Now, with Mary Rose as an ally, she had relaxed back into her earlier role of middle-class woman. At home, Jane was wife and mama, and she played that role well, too, to Bud and her three handsome and rambunctious sons; having an outlet in the form of her new friend took away some of that ache Jane had been suppressing for five years.

Conversely, Jane had gotten Mary Rose involved in women's issues, suffrage an issue for which the intelligent and outgoing Mrs. Markham was a natural, but had been previously uninformed. So it was a symbiotic relationship. Even had it not been, the two women had grown so fond of one another that if more than a few days went by without seeing each other, they grew moody and sullen. Both husbands encouraged the friendship; it seemed to be both stress-relieving and intellectually stimulating for the women. Billy Blake Markham and Bud Neeley, however, although they liked one another, found they had very little in common, so it was never a foursome.

To Bud's credit, Jane knew that he welcomed the sparkle his wife had re-acquired since her friendship to Mary Rose Markham had blossomed, so he did his best to make it possible for the friends to have at least one evening a week to visit, socialize, attend their meetings. Bud had fallen in love with a spirited woman whose spirit had been dampened by marriage, three children and a hard life as a miner's wife; his Jane was back and he rejoiced seeing her smile again. The fact that he felt a bit like an outsider didn't alter his determination to let Jane have the kinds of experiences she needed to keep her contented. He struggled to make it possible for her to pursue her interests.

Settling into the seats, the two women looked around them, as over two hundred women and a handful of uncomfortable-looking men began to settle down, waiting eagerly for the much-respected panel of speakers who had made Nelsonville a stop on their rally trail. The noise level was deafening, as the members of the audience chatted with their neighbors, speculating on what they were about to hear, on what they heard two weeks earlier, and as they caught up on gossip.

The friends accepted a program which was passed along the aisle, perusing it for the names of the speakers. "No one I've ever heard of…I wonder who this is," mused Jane, pointing to one of the names which captured her interest.

"I haven't heard of her either, but then, I just started following this movement when you told me about it," answered Mary Rose. "I was hoping that Mary Church Terrell would come to one of these. She started an organization for colored women, I read in one of the articles Sarah showed me, and a school, a college. In Florida, I think…Sarah would like for Marcia to be able to go to Mrs. Terrell's college. She would be a really interesting speaker. I'm not sure how Nelsonville would handle a colored suffragette…what do you think? Are we open-minded enough, do you think? Sarah doesn't think so…"

"You really like her, don't you, Sarah, that is?"

"She's wonderful, smart, funny, well-read…you should see her when she comes into the store to try on dresses. Did I tell you she asked us last month if there was some way she could work with us in the stores? I just didn't know what to say…we're still trying to figure something out. Billy and I both think she would make a perfect model, but I think she would rather be president or something…" Mary Rose finished, with a laugh. "Not that she wouldn't be good at that, too…"

"Why don't you invite her to join us for…something? I'd like to get to know her too. She was so quiet that day we went to Lancaster, but I'm sure she was uncomfortable. And you're right, she really is beautiful. Let's do something together…I don't have any colored friends. Oh, that sounded awful. I don't just want to know her because she's colored…you know…"

"I know what you meant. Very well, when I get home tonight, I'll ask her if she would like to…what? Where could we all go together? I never thought about…well, can colored women go places white women can? I don't know…" Mary Rose looked stunned. She thought of herself as a modern woman, and an enlightened one, but the fact that she had never realized how limited life was for colored women deeply troubled her. Her face clouded, thinking of Sarah and others like her, shut out of ordinary life, of activities she took for granted.

"Shhh. The program is starting…" Jane whispered, and Mary Rose's attention returned to the speakers.

* * *

Fred drove his new Oldsmobile into Nelsonville, grumbling to himself at the traffic, which had stopped him on the road next to the canal. "What is going on? Where are all these people going? Darn, I'm going to be late…where are these people going??" Fred's habit of talking to himself worked well to vent his frustration. The carriage and automobile traffic was worse than he had ever seen in Nelsonville, especially at night, worse, in fact, than he had ever seen it anywhere. Maneuvering around a long row of stopped buggies which blocked the intersection of Fayette and Madison Streets, Fred peered over his shoulder to see if there had been an accident or something. Seeing nothing but more vehicles, some moving but many just stopped, he shook his head in puzzlement, deciding to find a detour rather than fight his way through to get to the offices of Clavenger and Scott, the attorneys who handled the Markham-Hunt collaborations.

Turning sharply to get back out onto the main road, Fred noticed the traffic was lighter. "Good decision, Hunt, good decision…" he mumbled to himself, pulling into a lane which paralleled the large Markham's Dry Goods, working his way back through to the Public Square from the north.

Sighing with relief, Fred parked his automobile beside the First National Bank, grabbed his satchel and blueprints, and stepped out, entering the side door which lead to the roomy, elegant offices of Clavenger and Scott, on the second floor, above the bank. As he entered the door, the town hall clock struck eight. "Phew. Made it. On time, too…" Fred breathed. He didn't like to keep people waiting.

Noticing that Edward and Billy Blake Markham had already arrived, Fred smiled broadly and held out his hand, calling out, "Billy Blake, Mr. Markham, nice to see you! What in the world is going on out there?" gesturing over his shoulder to the Square.

"Oh, that's a women's suffrage meeting, Fred. Mary is there, with a friend of hers. It looks like most of the women in Nelsonville—and the whole county, for that matter—are there. Did you have trouble getting in?" Billy Blake queried.

"Boy, I surely did! I've never seen so many automobiles and carriages in one place before! I thought maybe there was an accident, or maybe Caruso was singing on the Square! Women's suffrage, huh? Interesting," he replied, shaking his head in surprise. "Well, are we all ready? It looks like we're all here!"

James Clavenger caught Edward's eye at that moment, indicating that they were ready inside the boardroom. The senior Markham said, "It looks like they're ready for us. Are you set, Fred? You brought the plans, I see."

Nodding in the affirmative, Fred followed the two Markhams. The three men strode single file into the boardroom, taking seats around a King Edward II oval table, a magnificent…and very heavy…piece of furniture. Admiring the gleaming wood, as a builder would notice, Fred hated to put his papers down, hated even to finger-print it, but noticing that Clavenger didn't seem to share his compunctions, and after all, it was his table, he shrugged and opened the floor plans for the Columbus store renovation, spreading out his cost sheet beside Clavenger's building code book.

The Markhams were ready for yet another expansion! Fred Hunt was proud and excited to be a part of this vision, this father and son team who seemed to have the Midas touch. The meeting tonight was to finalize the plans for the fantastic project, Edward Markham's biggest dream, the New York-style department store he had been visualizing since his first store in Caldwell. For this one, he was in a big, big hurry. Edward wanted the store to open before Christmas…a really rushed remodel! Fred knew it was possible, but he would have to pull all his men off other projects for two months. It was worth it. The Markhams were men on a mission! That the expansion had also been good for his reputation was a plus, but Fred Hunt believed he would have enjoyed watching this explosion, even if he hadn't made a dime! The excitement was certainly contagious.

Clavenger perused the papers very carefully, the lease on the building in Columbus, the building permit, Fred's drawings; the room was silent, as it always was when Clavenger was thinking. Pregnant moment…then the attorney's warm smile spread underneath his handlebar mustache…and Fred's heart slowed back to a normal rhythm: he knew they were home free!

* * *

"Now that was inspiring, don't you think?" Jane asked her companion. "When Mrs. Rhodes read that article from *Life Magazine*, I thought I would be sick! 'The standard of qualification for voting is already so low that no influx of women voters could lower it!' Really! How insulting! Oh, and that line about there being nothing the 'average American woman wants that the average American man will not give her if he can get it!' It makes us look helpless, like wilting plants, or house pets!"

"Really. It makes me wonder, though, whether men are going to take it well when women get the vote. I'm really lucky…Billy Blake knows I have a brain, has always treated me as his equal, but some women aren't that blessed," Mary Rose replied, as the women crossed the Square to the Colonial Coffee Shop where Billy Blake was meeting them for coffee before taking Jane home.

"What scared me the most, though," Jane continued, "was the letters from women who were so against having the vote. I don't understand that thinking. When women are fighting against other women, it makes the struggle so much more futile. That was discouraging, don't you think?"

"Yes, but that last speaker, Mrs. Woodson, made a really good point when she said that not all slaves were in favor of emancipation, because they had been sheltered from what life could have been for them and denied education and so on. I think that may be the case with some of these women, too, they're afraid of the responsibility. I can understand that, I guess. What was that woman's name Sarah told me about? Oh… Lucretia Mott fought for equal rights back in the 1860s, both for women and for Negroes, but when she succeeded getting the equal voting rights on the ballot, it was defeated. I wonder if women would have voted for their own rights if they could have," Mary Rose pondered, thinking about a conversation she had had with Sarah earlier in the week. Sarah had educated her quite a bit on the dual causes of Negro suffrage and women's suffrage; she found herself frequently thinking about points Sarah had made.

"Lucretia Mott? I've heard that name…oh, she worked with Miss Stanton, didn't she? I wish we could get someone like Mrs. Mott to come here!" Jane exclaimed.

"Yes, wouldn't that be something? The last speaker, Catherine Woodson?" Jane mused. "She seemed to be worried about whether men will make it their responsibility to 'teach us' how to vote and 'tell us' who to vote for, like we are feather-headed. Do you think it will be hard to convince men we have the capability of making our own choices? I don't worry about Bud or Billy Blake, of course, but the others? So many men think women are…just stupid or helpless without them," she continued, shaking her head, "or maybe they just want us to be that way…"

"Probably. But we'll convince them, one at a time. Well, I look forward to a fresh cup of coffee. I just might have some pie, too," Mary Rose offered, as they reached the Colonial and entered, noticing that the Markham men hadn't arrived. "Let's sit in that booth in the back so we can talk about the meeting and watch for Billy. Is that okay with you?"

"Perfect!" Jane gestured to the waiter that they would be taking the back booth, to which he grunted his approval with a scowl. "Friendly type, isn't he?" Jane muttered as the women settled into the booth, leaning against the wall comfortably, and chatting about the speakers they had heard.

The Markham children were safe with Sarah. Bud and his sister Charlotte were watching the Neeley brood tonight, so Jane was in no hurry, enjoying her evening with her friend. Charlotte visited often; she loved her nephews and her only brother, and it was no hardship for her to spend an evening in the company of her four favorite men. It helped Jane, these excursions, Charlotte knew, and Jane was grateful for her sister-in-law's generosity. When her mind was active, her mood lightened considerably.

* * *

At that moment, the meeting in Clavenger's office had just ended and the three partner- friends were coming down a dangerously narrow and dark stair, talking rapidly and excitedly about the grand opening of the store in Columbus next month. Fred had his head turned toward Billy Blake Markham, listening to his excited chatter about the grand opening; suddenly, Billy noticed the clock on the Town Hall and his eyes widened.

"Oh, gracious! I just have time to get to the restaurant and meet up with my wife and her friend. Say, Fred, why don't you come with me and join us for coffee? I'm sure the girls will have a lot to talk about, and we do too, don't we? You know Mary Rose will want to hear the details."

Pulling a gold pocket watch from his vest, Fred Hunt puckered his brow, pondering. "Well, I do have an early meeting, but…it's only a little after nine. Sure, why not? I have time for some coffee, and it is always pleasant to hear your wife's innovations. It's a good thing she doesn't want to be a builder…I would have serious competition," Fred declared with a laugh.

"Yes, you are so right. It's a good thing she's on our side!" chuckled the proud husband. "Dad? Would you like to join us?" Billy Blake inquired.

"No, son, thanks, but I think I'll head on home. Your mother had a headache and I promised her I wouldn't be late. Fred, it's been a pleasure, as always. You do great work. Son, give your bride a kiss for me…I'll see you tomorrow." Edward headed around the corner to his Buick which was parked behind the Dry Goods store, waving goodbye to his son and his builder.

"What do you think of the archway effect we planned for the main foyer, Fred? I saw a picture of Macy's and it seemed so…elegant, I guess," Billy Blake queried as they strolled the half block to the Colonial.

Delighted by the excitement in his client's voice, Fred responded, "You know I like it! It's easy to build, supports weight really well, and yet gives the illusion of open space. Much better than square openings…we learned that in the Lancaster store, didn't we?" Fred replied, entering the restaurant behind Billy Blake.

"You're so agreeable! I like working with you, to say nothing of the fact that you're a genius with a building! Oh, there they are, in the back…" and Billy walked toward the rear of the narrow restaurant, waving to the women and not noticing that his companion had stopped dead in his tracks, his mouth open, his face frozen.

As Mary Rose waved back, she didn't notice that Jane's face drained of all color. Jane's head swam as her eyes locked on his too-familiar golden eyes and time stood still. They stared, still twenty feet apart, their two companions not noticing the silence or the atmosphere, much like the aftereffects of an electrical storm. Billy continued moving toward his wife and Jane.

"Hi, my lord and master! We just got here. Oh, good, Fred's here too. Jane, I…Jane?" Mary Rose noticed, with alarm, her friend's pasty skin tones and her gaping mouth. Alarmed, she touched her arm across the table. "Jane? Are you all right?" Looking up at Billy, panic in her eyes, she noticed Fred's frozen expression, just as Billy, peering at one face then the other, caught on to the strange sequence of events.

Fred gulped, took a few more steps behind Billy Blake, and then stopped again, unable to go on…or to speak; although he tried, he moved his mouth, but nothing came out. His mind raced: she looked no different, maybe more beautiful if that was possible, even though she was as pale as a ghost. Finding his voice at last, Fred croaked, "Mrs. Markham, and…your friend and I have met, I believe," one eyebrow raised, his head cocked toward Jane.

"Oh? You've met Jane Neeley?" Mary Rose exclaimed, amazed and puzzled.

"Neeley? Jane…Neeley…yes, a long time ago…Neeley?" stammered the usually eloquent Fred, as names and faces slammed around in his mind.

Finally overcoming her paralysis, Jane spoke: "Yes, Mr. Hunt and I knew each other before I was married. Hello…Fred." Her voice wavered, her shoulders quivered, ever so slightly but she found a tiny tight smile which made its way to her lips, still numb and cold with shock.

Mary Rose and her husband exchanged puzzled, slightly alarmed glances and a shrug, then, to disarm the awkwardness, Mary Rose said, "Here, join us. We haven't ordered our coffee yet. Fred? Billy, what would you like?" she queried, frantically motioning behind Billy's back for the waiter, as the men sat, Billy Blake beside his wife and Fred awkwardly at the end of the table, as far from Jane as possible without being too obvious.

Fred Hunt seemed to be having trouble breathing. The room was suddenly stifling. He fumbled with his satchel, loosened his shirt buttons…thinking, "Those eyes…" His mind struggled for a toehold.

The two hadn't taken their eyes off each other, had barely blinked. Only vaguely aware of their surroundings, both looked as if they could take flight any moment. Rarely at a loss for words, Mary Rose Markham was anxiously searching her mind for topics of conversation. She desperately attempted, "What a coincidence, you two knowing each other…"

Sensing that wasn't a safe topic, she tried again: "Uh, we went to an interesting meeting tonight…" Then, noticing her words were falling into empty space, just gave up and, with a sigh, let the silence resound in the room, deafening them all, while Billy Blake gulped and looked totally confused and embarrassed.

The waiter arrived, breaking the tension slightly, as they all ordered coffee and pie, Mary Rose taking as much time as she possibly could with her selection, then chattering shrilly to her husband about the meeting, the weather, the car…just anything to keep the awful intensity under control. But Fred and Jane seemed oblivious to her efforts, seemed to see only each other. A light suddenly went on in Mary Rose's brain: this is no casual acquaintance. She narrowed her eyes and scanned first one face then the other, then back, and with that uncanny way two close friends have of reading each other, especially two women, puzzle pieces slipped silently into place. She nodded imperceptibly, sighed, and relaxed, putting her arm through Billy's. He was still stunned and totally baffled, but, feeling her hand on his wrist, he glanced her way, seeing her nod slightly again. Not sure what that meant, nonetheless, he relaxed a bit as well, and began telling her about the meeting, hoping that Fred would join in, giving him ample opportunity…but it was a monologue, nothing more.

Chapter 21 – A Daring Proposition

(October 1909)

Jane and Mary Rose spoke often of Sarah and other women like her, women with so much to offer the world. It became evident to both of them that there was no true equality in America. Slaves were no longer owned by white landholders; now they were enslaved by their color. Women had walked beside the wagons in pioneer days, built cabins, chopped wood, tended herds, protected their families. They had earned their place as students in colleges…but that was just about as far as their rights went. Women had no vote. None held political office. If they owned property, it was because they had inherited it from a father or a husband. None were police or fire officials. None headed coal mines, railroad companies, or industrial complexes. Only a brave few were doctors or lawyers or college professors. None owned major companies or served on the executive boards of banks or corporations.

There was no lower form of human life, as Mary Rose and Jane now perceived it, than a woman of color. Their meetings had become more than an avocation; they had become a crusade, for all women, but most expressly for women of color. This was a dangerous crusade, they were to learn.

As Jane regained her equilibrium temporarily lost by the re-entry of Fred Hunt into her life, she found that she was not only surviving, but was a much stronger person. No longer searching for Fred in Bud's eyes, Jane felt free from her past for the first time. Now she was able to see Fred Hunt when he happened to be working with the Markhams, smile and speak to him cordially…and walk on. Although a piece of her heart would always belong to her first love, that piece was now safely locked away deep within; her marriage was sound and her respect for Bud Neeley grew every day. She was a woman at last, no longer a frightened, spoiled little girl who expected to get whatever she wanted just because she wanted it. She had earned her adulthood, and it felt good.

This newfound strength allowed her to plow into her crusade for equal rights. She and Mary Rose had learned some unpleasant truths about Nelsonville and

Athens County. While the town and county were progressive and successful—models, in fact, of modern twentieth century commerce—they were secretly hotbeds of prejudice and racial injustice. Worst of all, no one with any power or authority wanted to acknowledge that fatal flaw.

Unlike the seething resentment evident all over the South, in southeastern Ohio the prejudice was veiled, denied. The statements which Jane and Mary Rose learned to hate the most were ones like "I have nothing against colored people…as long as they know their place." Where was "their place"? queried the two crusaders often. No one had an answer for that. Then, there was the insidious "Why, some of my best friends are colored people!" Yet lawn parties were lily white, ladies' auxiliary groups had no dark faces, and bridge and mah-jongg clubs were limited to white women.

It was beginning to be common knowledge that Police Chief Gene Linbach was very vicious to black men who had the misfortune of being on the wrong side of the law…or perhaps, just the wrong side of Gene Linbach. Mary Rose and Jane had compared the sentences of black men with those of white men convicted of the same crimes in the city of Nelsonville. Conversely, Terry Prentice was a good, honest man who had risen in the police force to the position of captain, but his efforts to neutralize his superior officer's malice were frequently futile.

When Gene Linbach was the main testifying witness for the prosecution, the black men served nearly two days for every one a white man served. Thankfully, there had been no public lynchings in over a decade, but when black children had the misfortune of disappearing, the police department, headed by Linbach, seemed to be apathetic in the search, unlike the frenetic energy put into the retrieval of white children. Worst of all, black on white crime seemed to solicit the maximum penalty allowed by law. Obviously, Linbach wasn't the only man in law enforcement who opted to "enforce" more vigorously if the perpetrator was a man of color.

Women seemed to have "their place," as well, and that place stuck in the craw of the suffragettes, both nationwide and local, Jane and Mary Rose among them. Mary Rose recognized the fact that her "place" beside her husband and father-in-law at all official Markham's business functions set her somewhat apart from other women of the town. The family attorney, their bankers, Fred and his partners all accepted her as an equal partner…but some of the wives, she knew, whispered behind their white gloves.

"Women are sometimes their own worst enemies, Jane," Mary Rose remarked one afternoon as they crossed the Square to share lunch at the Colonial.

Two matrons, peers of Elizabeth's, had just come from the People's Bank, and, although nodding and waving courteously to Jane and Mary Rose, hadn't hidden their mistrust—or even contempt—behind those artificial smiles. "What it is that bothers them, I have no idea, but I don't think they will be on our side if we try to get women's voting rights on the ballot this year," Mary Rose commiserated.

"Probably not. Have you thought about talking with them frankly? They seem to be intelligent enough to understand," Jane wondered.

"No. Maybe I should…it's just that look they get in their eyes, especially when they see me coming out of the lawyer's office with Billy and Edward…it's evident they think I am out of place…and for that matter, out of my mind." But it was clear: no one would put Mary Rose Markham…or any of her friends, for that matter, in "her place."

The friends had these discussions often. They read *Women's Advocate* faithfully; they perused local newspapers for ideas for discussion groups. Their Wednesday afternoon teas had become liberation meetings. They had taken old copies of *The Liberator* out of the library and examined it for ideas they could utilize. All of these had provided valuable insight, but both of them came to recognize that the most valuable asset to their cause could be Sarah Washington.

* * *

Sarah had been writing at her desk for nearly two hours, oblivious to the time. She was excited because an article she was working on was beginning to take shape. Her skill with words had surprised her; her habit of reading everything she could get a hold of had provided her with a vocabulary far superior to those of her peers. Nevertheless, Sarah continued to harbor fears that her writing would set her apart…uncomfortably so, not just from her black friends but even from her family. Yet the urge to write was too great to deny. It had become as essential as breathing. She would attempt to stay away from her tablet…but it would draw her back. The more she wrote, the stronger her grasp of prose became and the more she wanted—no, needed—to write.

Jeremiah still didn't know she was writing seriously; it wasn't that she was hiding it from him…not exactly. He was an understanding man. But was he capable of understanding this? Capable of understanding that she might bring trouble down on the family if she made her views public knowledge? Those questions worried her, made her hesitant to share with her husband the intensity of her feelings and her need to put them on paper.

The article she was writing told a badly needed truth about an assault and rape which had occurred—and been rapidly covered up—near Haydenville last week. The victim had been a pretty teenaged daughter of one of Jeremiah's co-workers, an honest hard-working black widower who served as janitor for the elementary schools of Nelsonville. The aggressor, a brick-mason—white—from Haydenville had grabbed the girl Cassandra as she fished in the creek behind her home, struck her repeatedly when she screamed, tied her shirt around her mouth to keep her quiet and then raped her less than fifty yards from her own home.

The child had survived the attack, managed to stagger home, hysterical and traumatized. When her father arrived home and heard the story, he had channeled his fury, hitched up his wagon, and ridden to the police station, his daughter quaking beside him, to report the atrocity. The insolent desk sergeant had made him repeat the story three times, each time badgering him for additional details, meanwhile looking Cassandra up and down, insinuating that the child had seduced the man, gotten frightened and created this tale. Although a report was taken, paperwork was filled out, and promises made, nothing was done, although Cassandra had been able to describe her attacker clearly, knew his name, even.

A night cleaning woman, hiding in a coat closet, had overheard the horrifying story, witnessed the cavalier manner of the sergeant, and taken the story public, telling every black man or woman who would listen. She had, of course, since been fired.

Cora Corbin was one who listened; she brought the story to Sarah, knowing that Sarah could—and would—write about it. Now, a week later, nothing had been in the paper, no posters were out offering rewards…in short, the incident never happened. But it did, Sarah declared, and she would see to it that the entire town…if necessary, the entire state knew about the mishandling of the incident. A child was brutally raped, her youth and innocence stolen and her life changed forever…and no one cared.

The truth would be told, she vowed. This was her quest, as she sat laboring at her desk. She knew her words would be unwelcome in many quarters, would force blinders off those who believed Nelsonville had no race problem, would make trouble for the police department…especially for blatant racist Gene Linbach. "That 'un needs to have trouble," Sarah grumbled.

She wasn't oblivious to the danger she was creating for herself, her family, her friends, her race…while she didn't seek out danger, she had vowed not to shy from it. This article would be sent to the *Nelsonville Tribune*, the *Athens Messenger*, the *Columbus Citizen* and to any paper that would accept it. Tonight was the night, Sarah recognized reluctantly, that Jeremiah and the children had to be told of her work so that they could be prepared for whatever might follow.

Just as she began revising her prose, she was startled by a brisk knock on her door. Checking the clock, she realized it was too early for Paul and Marcia…and they wouldn't knock anyway. Rising, smoothing her hair with one hand and her skirt with the other, she peered through the small glass window in the door. Surprised, she saw her employer Mrs. Markham and her friend Mrs. Neeley standing on her porch. Opening the door, she became alarmed that something had happened to one of the children. "What's wrong, Miz Markham? Is it Frankie? Miss Betsy?"

"No, no, Sarah, everyone's fine. Can we come in and talk to you for a few minutes?" Mary Rose inquired. "I hope we're not interrupting anything…" This was highly unusual, white women calling on a black woman…and it worried Sarah slightly, more for them than for herself.

Nevertheless, holding the door wide, Sarah replied, "Of course you can…I was…writing something. Come in, please."

"Writing? Another article? Can you talk about it?" Mary Rose asked excitedly as she swept by Sarah. "This is sort of what we want to talk about," she exclaimed, exchanging a look with Jane. Sarah had told her employer when she began to write, a year ago; Mary Rose had been both enthralled and surprised by the announcement. Since then, Sarah had confided in her about many of the pieces she had attempted to write, accepting her encouragement gratefully.

"Well, ma'am, it's about that girl I told you about…out in Haydenville?" Sarah trusted Mary Rose completely, and both had cried when relating the tale Cora had shared with her. "The police…well, they didn't do anything. So…someone has to…" Sarah commented, setting her jaw in firm defiance.

"Yes, you are right, someone does. That someone is you, I can see that. Sarah, Jane and I have been talking for a long time about something very much like that. That's why we're here." She paused briefly, weighing her words. "You have so much information and such wise ideas about Negro rights and women's rights, and we want you to work with us. Together, we can get more done, we think. And by the way…just because you work for me sometimes…doesn't mean we aren't friends. Friends don't call their friends 'ma'am' okay?" Mary Rose smiled and took Sarah's hand, pulling her down on the sofa beside her.

Finding it eerily prophetic that she had been planning her own secret attack on the white establishment just as these two strong, courageous women were planning one, Sarah found herself searching for words. "Work…how? You mean at th' meetings? I couldn't…they wouldn't let me…"

Mary Rose interrupted: "They would and they will because you will be with me, with us. We need you, Sarah, to tell some of the things you know. To share some of the amazing ideas you have shared with me. Trust me, Sarah. I can protect you."

"I do trust you. It's not that…it's…the children…my husband…I don't know if I can…" Sarah admitted. "He doesn't even know what I'm writing…I don't know what he'll say…or think…" Her face clouded with pain as she went on, "…an' it's not your job to protect me…I should be protecting you."

"First of all, the people of Nelsonville need to see the three of us standing together, as friends, as equals, fighting for the same cause. You are a writer. Neither of us can do that." As Sarah protested that she wasn't, Mary Rose continued, "Yes, you are. That last article you wrote about the children of slaves was wonderful. It needs to be published. You have so much to say. I want you to help us and we want to help you, don't we, Jane?"

Nodding vigorously, Jane agreed, "Really, Sarah, you are so good with words. And nobody but us has heard those words…so it's time for you to speak to the world. We're trying, but we have agreed on this: we need you to be the brave strong voice you are." Jane's earnest tone was reflected in her honest, intense green eyes, now locked on Sarah's face.

Looking from face to face, Sarah fretted, pondering how to respond. She respected these two women as much as anyone she had ever met…but what were they asking? Did they even KNOW what they were asking? With a deep sigh, she replied, "I don't know what I can do, but if you think I can help and you want me, I'd be proud to stand beside the two of you."

Thinking "Lordy, what have I done?" Sarah clasped the two hands which were reaching out to her.

"You won't be sorry," Jane promised. "The next meeting is next Tuesday night. Come with us. Just come, this time. Let people see you there, with us. Then we'll figure out the next step when we get to it. Can you do that?"

"Tuesday. Um…if you can find somewhere for the children…I hate to leave you with no one to watch the little ones…"

"We've already worked that out! So Tuesday night, 6:30, come on down to my house," Mary Rose said, "and we will take the car down to the Opera House."

"Yes'm…Yes, Mary Rose…" Feeling awkward with the first name, Sarah shook her head slightly, but seeing her smile, smiled back. "Yes, that'll be fine…I'll be there Monday mornin' for the children…you're still going to Columbus, aren't you?"

"Yes, and there's something about Columbus I want to talk to you about, too. We'll do that Tuesday night. Thank you, Sarah. I feel really good about this. I think the three of us can make a difference! We'll let you get back to your writing. Bye. Give 'em 'what for' in that article!" She stood and moved toward the door, Jane following.

"Yes…uh, g'bye." As the women left, Sarah stood very still, her head leaning against the door jamb, thinking. Wondering… Worrying…

* * *

Tuesday dawned bright with sparkling blue skies and puffy white clouds, but as the day went on, the clouds turned dark, the atmosphere taking on an ominous feel of a winter storm brewing. Throughout the day, the temperature plummeted and the wind picked up, until at 6 p.m., as Sarah stepped off her front porch, leaves and debris were hurled skyward, sending dust into her eyes and a chill through her body. Returning to the house to grab a shawl, Sarah had to make a second effort to force herself to walk down the steps, fighting both the gusts and her misgivings about her promise to attend the suffrage meeting

Sarah had long been an advocate of women's rights and a student of human nature, but stepping out in public with two white women? Was this a way to make a statement…or to call undue attention to herself? Or even worse, to put her two white friends in jeopardy? "If the people see me there and get angry…it could make trouble for the Neeleys and the Markhams. Oh, lordy, what am I doin'?"

Tempted to turn back, Sarah's sense of integrity forced her to walk on: she had given her word. It was only a five-minute walk to the Markhams' house; Sarah wished it was longer, giving her more time to think. Arriving on the back porch just as Jane and Mary Rose were coming out, Sarah adopted an attitude of cheerfulness which certainly didn't reflect her real feelings. "Good evenin', ladies. My, there's a nip in th' air. You two bring your coats…wouldn't want you to get a chill, now…" Her calm words belied her pounding heart.

"Oh, hi, Sarah. You are so right! Where did all that nice autumn sunshine go? Brrrrr! Just a minute, I'll grab my wrap," Mary Rose replied, slipping back inside to grab her black cape. Jane already wore a warm knit shawl which Sarah imagined she had made herself; her knitting was more than a hobby, it helped to provide warm garments for her and her sons.

Sarah also knew that Mary Rose had often attempted to give Jane clothing for herself and her family, things which were badly needed and she couldn't afford on her husband's pay, but that Jane was determined not to take what she saw as unfair advantage of her friendship with the merchant. Mary Rose prevailed only rarely. Jane was a proud woman, and one who was conscious of her husband's feelings, not wanting him to feel she was dissatisfied with what he could provide. Sarah understood that sentiment well...she also worried about Jeremiah when her employer lavished gifts upon her. But the giving of gifts made Mary Rose happy. Jane hadn't learned that yet, Sarah realized. Mary Rose Markham was the most giving person Sarah had ever known.

Suitably garbed now, Mary Rose climbed behind the wheel of the Ford, putting a pillow behind her back so she could reach the pedals. Sarah stifled a laugh. Jane climbed in next to Mary Rose, leaving more room for Sarah's long legs. It was another awkward moment for Sarah, riding in the car as an equal. Fear gripped at her stomach as they backed out of the drive and turned the auto toward the south. "What if people see..." went through her mind, immediately followed by, "well, of course they'll see...we're goin' downtown..." and she admonished herself for being silly.

It was still a thrill, though, to ride in an automobile. Mary Rose had learned to drive it almost as soon as Billy Blake had and had offered to teach Sarah to drive. That plan still offered promise. So tonight she wrestled her fears down and just enjoyed the sensation of rapid movement. They arrived all too soon at the Opera House; the downtown streets were now slightly more accommodating to automobiles as places to park them were being created. Not enough yet, but it was progress. Mary Rose found a place just around the corner on Washington. The women climbed down and fought the gale force winds which threatened to rip their cloaks from their backs, rushing to make it around the corner to be sheltered from the wind by the sturdy red brick of the Opera House.

Huddled with others waiting for the double doors to open, Sarah found herself more at ease than she had expected as, scanning the crowd, she saw a handful of brown faces mingling comfortably with the white. Releasing a pent-up breath, she accepted a program from an official-looking woman who was circulating through the waiting crowd.

Although she was a full head taller than her companions which made conversing difficult, especially with the pending storm, she found that they were including her in their conversation, pointing at a familiar name in the program, speculating about the masculine name scheduled to give a talk, chatting about other speakers they had heard. Sarah had attended one informal open meeting held on the square, and had also listened to President Roosevelt when he campaigned from the balcony of the Dew Hotel, but she had never been inside the famous Stuart's Opera House. She was beginning to get excited at the prospects the evening held. Much to her surprise, however, she found that she was as well informed about women's issues as were her companions, even better than some; her reading had certainly paid off.

The front doors opened just as a wave of sheet lightning electrified the sky, followed by a startling CRACK of thunder. The coincidence of events acted almost like a cattle prod, stampeding the crowd through the doors. Fortunately, the lobby was large enough to allow the charging crowd to fan out as it entered or people might have been trampled!

Once all were inside, nervous laughter revealed embarrassment at being startled into bolting through the doors, tension was relieved and calm restored. Jane led the trio up the stairs and into the theater, its elegance leaving Sarah speechless. The room felt to her almost sanctified, cathedral like, with its vaulted ceiling, rich ruby draperies and seating which faced, pew like, toward a central focal point. Her church was very humble, but she had seen drawings of magnificent churches in Washington, D.C., and London, among others, and this vast showplace had the same grandeur and the same ambience.

Very unlike a church, however, was the noise level. The space positively crackled with voices, contagious excitement. She felt the tempo of her heartbeat increase slightly as a well-dressed middle-aged woman stepped to the podium on the deep stage and began signaling for quiet.

* * *

An hour later, Jane, Mary Rose and Sarah were relieved that the storm hadn't further developed as they scurried back to the auto, chattering with excitement. Exiting the Opera House, they noted that, although the air was much colder than the morning had been, the winds had died down enough to allow them to walk to the automobile without being assaulted by the leaves and street trash which had flurried around them earlier. Once inside the vehicle, Sarah spoke first: "I want t' thank you both for inviting me. It was…inspiring t' hear the plans for getting th' vote. But those women who were goin' t' Washington t' talk with th' President…my! How brave!"

"He's pretty easy to talk to, they say. He respects women and has a reputation of being an eager listener. But, unfortunately, he won't be President much longer. Who knows what Taft will be like?" Jane replied.

"Good question. Former President McKinley was working on a bill to give women the vote when he died…I think I read that somewhere…" Mary Rose added.

"Well, Roosevelt's had lots of years to do what's right. But, to be fair, he has done a lot of 'right' things, like making all those parks national landmarks. And one man can't do it all…" Jane said, as the wind buffeted the Ford, making it hard to turn.

"Whoa, Nelly!" cried Mary Rose, as she fought the wind. "I didn't know wind could do that…say, maybe we should put up a sail!"

To a chorus of laughter, Sarah added, "We'd get home sooner that way…if that's th' way the wind blew us! Or maybe we'd end up in the canal! Wouldn't that be somethin'?"

All laughed again, but Mary Rose had to struggle enough to sober her momentarily. As the gusts subsided, she said, "Sarah, Jane and I have been talking about an idea that Billy had. Would you be able to go up to Columbus with us when the new store opens? I know you want to work with us and we want you to…but Billy and I had a special idea that you might like…"

"Columbus? My stars! I'd love t' go to Columbus…to work in the store, you say? How…it's so far up there…how…?" Sarah stammered in surprise.

"It depends on you and whether you can work something out with Jeremiah and the children…we know you haven't shared everything you've been writing with him, and it's none of our business, but…well, if you don't think he approves of the way you are telling the truth…he may not like our idea," Mary Rose suggested.

Her stomach feeling queasy, Sarah admitted, "I don't know. He's never said no t' anything I wanted t' do…but…I just don't know… What would I be doing?"

"Let's take one thing at a time. Can you talk with him, see how he feels? He was fine with you coming tonight?" Mary Rose asked.

"Uh, yes…he understands. When those men burnt Clyde's store, he was really surprised somethin' like that could happen here…and he was glad when I started talking about working for Negro equality. He would probably be fine with my articles…honestly, I just haven't had the nerve t' set him down and talk. But I will…tonight."

"That's good. After you see what he says about helping in Columbus, we can take it from there. Okay? We've got a month or so to win him over, if we need to. I think you will like what we have planned…but I don't want to tell you the whole story yet, I hope you understand…" Mary Rose said, as she pulled the

Ford into the lane beside her home, then, changing her mind, backed out again. "I'm taking you home. It's only a short way and there's no reason for you to walk."

"There's no need...I don' mind..." Sarah protested, but noticed that they were on their way up the hill. "Thank you. And for tonight, too."

As Sarah stepped from the Ford in front of her house, she noticed with pride that several neighbors had peered out through curtains to see the source of the unfamiliar rumble. She held her head high and sang out, louder than necessary, "Good evenin', ladies. I had a pleasant evenin'." A sly smile played with her lips as she climbed her steps and stopped to wave goodbye. This was indeed an interesting and promising evening, she thought, as she entered her home.

Chapter 22 – Pride Goeth

[May 1910]

Sarah's knees shook underneath her gray wool skirt, a gift from Mary Rose Markham. Eyes darting around nervously, she determined no one was looking at her any more strangely than they normally gaped at a woman of color dressed like a lady. Despite her terror, she felt good, strong and indecently proud.

It was nearly unheard of, what she was doing, what she had done. Book signings in Nelsonville? And by a colored woman? There was only one bookstore other than Markhams, the newsstand at the end of the block. So far only two customers had meandered far enough back in the store to even notice her, sitting on Mary Rose's tall stool beside a circular rack displaying Sarah's book *Pride Goeth*. Almost as much a source of pride as her first book was the portable circular rack her hero Billy Blake Markham had built just for her.

"Sarah," he had said, "wherever you have an audience, now you can set up shop. Just set up the rack, fill it with books, and you're in business."

The rack held twelve books in a Christmas-tree arrangement but in place of a star stood a handcarved wooden medallion, the letters S and W intertwined. She had wept when Bily Blake explained the symbolism: Sarah Washington at the top. But then, she wept often these days.

It had taken the horrific death of a little girl to break Sarah out of her paralysis of fear, to make her take pencil in hand, work in a frenzy and finally take the finished manuscript and board a train to Philadelphia. Once she arrived in the historic city, the site of five small publishers, two of them black, her courage would advance and retreat. When it retreated, she forced into her mind the image of dear Katie Corbin, Marcia's best friend, lying dead in a plain pine box, her mother collapsed in mindless grief over the coffin. That image, while it made her nauseated, also made her determined. She would set her jaw and strengthen her step, her shoulders proud. Determination would drive her forward from one publisher to another.

Close to despair, Sarah allowed her grief and anguish to show as she entered the last of the five publishers after four others had turned her away. Sarah knew if she didn't succeed here, her book may never reach the eyes of anyone outside her immediate family and friends. All that heartbreak, all that frenzied work day and night for four months would be for naught.

Writing while Jeremiah slept, or after she had tucked little Will in for the night had her exhausted, her eyes sunken and her already slim body looking angular and bony.

Gasping with exhaustion, Sarah stepped up to the door marked "Editor" in this cramped, musty-smelling office. She easily bypassed a middle-aged woman filing her nails in boredom at a desk marked "Receptionist-Clerk." The receptionist-clerk didn't even look up. Sarah rapped at the door, her heart pounding a tattoo.

Surprise and a little annoyance in his eyes, a portly man with white hair sticking up in spikes opened the door. "Huh? Who're you?" he growled.

Finding her voice with effort, she replied, "Sir..uh…forgive me for interruptin'…but I have a book I think you need to read. Everyone needs to read it." She straight-armed the manuscript into his chest, his hand grasping it in a defensive gesture, his eyes wide. "Please, sir," Sarah implored. "You have to take it…before another baby dies."

Annoyance battling with admiration, Piers Meyer, editor-in-chief of Pilgrim Publishing, found the audacity of this woman refreshing. He examined her face more thoroughly, deciding he liked what he saw. With an exaggerated sigh, he backed up a step, gesturing with his available hand for Sarah to enter.

Stunned at his receptiveness, Sarah went the direction he pointed, moving gracefully despite the tumult she was feeling.

Continuing his silent evaluation of the unusually bold colored woman, he pointed her toward the only uncluttered chair in the room. Momentarily unsure of propriety, Sarah stood, glancing at the chair, then at the man, a full head shorter than she was, then back at the chair as her stomach lurched.

Catching on, he shoved a stack of papers aside then perched on the corner of the desk. Sarah let herself down into the worn leather chair. "Sir? Uh…Mr. Meyer…"

"That's who I am. Who might YOU be?"

"Oh, I'm Sarah Washington, sir, and I appreciate…"

"I'm sure you do. Now let's hear about this book, Sarah Washington. What makes you think I 'need' to read this book any more than any of the other two dozen books piled up on this desk?" He lowered his fuzzy white brows in an attempt to look fierce, which Sarah found suddenly amusing. The tension whooshed out of her body and she relaxed back into the chair, realizing she was up to doing mental battle with this man.

"Well, sir, Mr. Meyer, because none of those other books tell the truth, at least not the way it needs to be told. That's why…sir." She met fierce with fierce and locked eyes with her opponent, if that's what he was.

Uttering a snort which passed for a laugh, he leaned back on one arm. "I do believe I'm going to like you, Sarah Washington, and if your writing is anything like your demeanor, I suspect I may like your book too. So tell me, what story absolutely has to be told?"

For the next half hour, Piers Meyer found himself captivated, moved to tears, and totally in agreement: this is the truth. This is the person to tell it. Not since *Little Tom's Cabin* had a portrait of malignant hate and powerful courage screamed so loudly for attention.

Promising an immediate thorough read, Piers Meyer resisted the urge to hand her a contract on the spot, the book unread. Instead, he agreed to write to her within a week, "if your manuscript is suitable for my press," knowing already that it would be.

Excitement kicking in as her realization mounted, Sarah nearly floated out of the editor's office. She tried to decide if she was shocked at her success or if she really knew it all along, just like her friends Jane and Mary Rose had told her. Suddenly it hit her: "By the Lord's grace, I'm gonna be an author…Oh Lordy! I AM an author. Lordy, what have I done?" Similar soliloquies played themselves over as her mind swirled all the way to the trolley stop and the ten-block ride to her rooming house.

* * *

That was in January, cold, gray January. Now, a mere four months later, she was indeed a published author, doing the first book signing ever, and in the town where a grisly crime had driven her to push beyond what she ever dreamed possible. Her first book signing was in April in Philadelphia, Piers Meyer standing beside her proudly, meeting hateful stares is defiant ones. His words and the sign he had prepared proclaimed that Sarah was "the voice of truth, be ye bold enough to read it."

The book *Pride Goeth* was labeled a novel. Nevertheless, it told in no uncertain terms the color line that ran through Athens County, comparing the lives of Sarah's slave grandparents with the name-only freedom experienced by poor blacks in a small town far north of the Mason-Dixon Line. Centered around Katie Corbin's horrific murder just yards from City Hall, it told boldly that the war was not over. The book was well received in forward-thinking Philadelphia, and when released in more conservative Boston, it still moved off the bookshelves.

But Nelsonville? Sarah knew she had taken a dangerous risk. She and Piers had discussed at great length the options available to her; her editor had advised against a book signing in Nelsonville. This was her home, the town her husband worked in and her children attended school in. Even worse, this was the scene of the crime. Little Katie, Marcia's friend, had committed no crime but yet she was found naked, her chubby body bloody and covered with leaves, stone cold dead, staring sightlessly at the sky.

Sarah discussed the book signing with Mary Rose and Jane, who encouraged her to follow her own heart. She prevailed with Piers, insisting that she would be careful but she wouldn't hide from her work.

The murder tortured Sarah. Her mind rolled: someone must have seen Katie. She was found less than 50 yards from a playground in a well-traveled area. Did she scream for help? Sarah knew Katie's scream, like a sticking door hinge, setting one's teeth on edge. When Marcia and Katie got too wrapped up in stickball, Katie's scream would bring all the mothers dashing out their doors, only to find Katie and her friends happily diving for balls, not very ladylike, but certainly safe. Was that why no one came to her aid? Her "Help me!" scream was not different enough from the one they had all learned to tune out?

"Oh, Lordy, that poor, poor baby," Sarah whispered whenever she thought about the last moments of Katie's life. But it was the pain she felt which made her override Piers' counsel. If putting herself out there would spur someone else to be brave and come forward, it was worth the risk.

Immediately after the crime, the black community came together in shock, rage and anguish; this was the second child abduction this year. Even worse, this one had snuffed out the life of a smart, funny child and torn Cora and Clyde Corbin's hearts from their chests. To their credit, most of the white citizens of Nelsonville expressed anger and shock as well.

White merchants, led by Billy Blake Markham, put up a $1000 reward for the capture and conviction of this demon child-killer. But the investigation into Katie's death seemed perfunctory at best.

Marcia woke screaming night after night. Mary Rose Markham had fainted dead away when Sarah's son Paul ran to her house to tell her the chilling news.

Recovering, Mary Rose ran immediately up the hill to Sarah's house to see how she could help Cora.

Cora Corbin had delivered two of Jane Neeley's children and when word reached Jane of Cora's tragedy, she flew into a rage which lasted for hours until Bud took her to Sarah's house to join the growing group who stood vigil outside and inside the Corbins', their tears flowing, their rage fueled less by grief than by their impotence.

Noone believed the police, headed by infamous racist Gene Linbach, would give this grisly crime the attention it deserved. The earlier rape case was still unsolved.

As time passed, the helplessness drove Sarah to do the only thing she could do: write about the crime and the lack of solution. She would put pencil to paper and words to this wordless abomination. As the investigation went on haphazardly, one suspect was dismissed after another, including the man who had abducted little Cassandra and never been convicted.

Late at night by candlelight, Sarah would report Cora's daily trips to the police department where Terry Prentice would greet her with a sad smile and then a head shake, telling Cora he was trying to sit in on the suspect interviews whenever he could, but no one had yet incriminated himself or another. The rape and murder had taken place at 4 in the afternoon, a busy time of day, school out for the day, children playing at the playground beside City Hall on their way home from school, just what Katie had done every school day for years. Yet no one saw her, as a predator grabbed her, dragged her into the bushes, beat her to unconsciousness, raped her viciously and strangled the life out of her.

Each frustrating day, Cora would ask to speak to Chief Linbach, to be told he was out on a case. Each day, Cora would trudge back home with a heavy heart and no news for her husband or her son Lloyd, who had found Katie's battered lifeless body and run home for help after trying unsuccessfully to carry her on his own.

Chapter 23 – Expanding the Kingdom

[November 1910]

When Edward Markham and his family opened his fifth store in late 1910, the one in Columbus, he became the first Ohio merchant to own a "chain." In short, the Markhams made history. F.W. Woolworth, Sears and Roebuck, and Montgomery Ward were all nationwide by then, but no one else, especially no one from small town Ohio, had achieved such merchandising excellence. He, the senior Markham, was often asked his "success secret" by newspaper reporters or by marketing students hoping to match his accomplishment; those inquiring individuals surely expected something terribly sophisticated, something based on rules generated in Harvard Business School. They most certainly didn't expect cracker-barrel wisdom but that's what they got: "To be successful in business? Easy! Listen to your customers and do just a little more than they expect you to do." It worked for the Markham chain. None of the Markhams who worked with the stores ever lost touch with their customers; none stopped listening; none stopped doing a little more than was needed. And the empire continued to thrive.

Some of Edward Markham's wisdom came from one of his retailing heroes, Henry Sands Brooks, who had founded Brooks Brothers nearly one hundred years earlier. His motto had been: "To make and deal only in merchandise of the finest quality, to sell it at a fair profit and to deal with people who seek and appreciate such merchandise." Edward was pleased that this fifth store was carrying men's merchandise so that he could return just a bit to the man who had set such an amazing standard for American haberdashery. He and Billy Blake were both garbed in soft, handsome Brooks Brothers suits this morning, his grey worsted wool and Billy's of soft gabardine, the shade of coffee with cream.

Billy Blake and Mary Rose attended—and worked—the grand opening of E.A. Markham's on South High Street in Columbus, Ohio. Billy, handsome and sophisticated looking but still uncomfortable in his high-collared pin-striped shirt and tie under his sophisticated suit, was nevertheless totally at ease with the throng of people who rushed the entrance the minute the door opened. He beamed and shook hands with one and all, looking much more like a man running for office than a man who just opened a store…but that was the affable nature of Billy Blake Markham which allowed Edward to recognize with pride and a lot of relief that his "kingdom" would be in capable hands once he passed it on to the man destined to succeed him on the throne. With a crowd of adoring customers, Billy Blake Markham, his blue eyes flashing, was clearly in his element. Edward and Mary Rose stood on the other side of the entrance, passing out flyers and warm smiles to all and sweetheart roses to the first one hundred female customers, and directing them to the various departments they requested.

Mary Rose, Edward noted, looked exceptionally lovely in a washed silk periwinkle frock, much dressier than she liked, but very suited to her trim figure. It was ankle length, narrow in the skirt—the new "hobble" style which required a slit up the side to be able to walk, showing cream silk stockings and high-heeled cream leather low boots. The New York fashionable garment gave her more height with its long, slim lines and, with a laced-in ivory eyelet weskit emphasizing her tiny waist, the periwinkle silk reflecting her eyes, she looked like a cover of the brand-new fashion standard, *Vogue Magazine*. Edward thought to himself, as she "worked the crowd," what a marvelous political wife she would make, if Billy Blake had a different calling…an interesting thought, indeed. Her business instincts were as strong as Billy's; she was thriving in this flurry of fashionability and fame.

As the customers began to circulate throughout the store, Edward signaled to Billy Blake that he was now free to circulate as well. Billy Blake's brother Stewart was already at the back of the store, beside the elevator, passing out store directories and offering punch and cookies, looking young and innocent at eighteen, but already possessed of excellent intelligence, business acumen, and poise. He had graduated at the top of his high school class that same June, and although he had been offered several college scholarships, Stewart had decided to hold off beginning his academic career so that he could be there for his dad and older brother for this and the previous opening. Stewart loved this business! He beamed at the customers who came his way, especially at the young ladies, Billy Blake noted with a chuckle, as Stewart flirted shamelessly with a brown-eyed coquette.

"A man of my mettle," the older brother mused, "with an eye for the pretty ones, I see!" Determining that the reception table was in competent hands, Billy nodded to his wife, who was chatting briskly with an elderly matron about hats. "She can handle whatever comes her way," the proud husband thought.

At that moment Billy purposefully shifted his focus to that of a customer seeing the store for the first time, knowing how important first impressions could be…and he began a critical examination of layout, merchandise display, traffic flow, placement of cash registers and wrapping tables. Although he had never been to New York, he and Mary Rose had carefully read the trade journals which discussed newer concepts of display; E.A. Markham's was striving to be a trendsetter, following in New York's footsteps, utilizing the excellent artistic eye of Mary Rose and the sense of balance which Billy Blake had always possessed. All other Markham's stores were attractive but pragmatic, arranged for convenience. With the acquisition of Frederick Hunt, the Markhams' visions were becoming realities.

The first Markham-Hunt collaboration, the renovated Lancaster Markham's, was a trend setter, with its Frank Lloyd Wright influence. It combined modern design with well-established comfort, featuring a covered portico and a pair of "conversation nooks" just to the right and the left of the entrance, an update of Billy's "book nook" in the first and second stores. Fred Hunt had expanded his original vision of a box-like building with a Victorian façade…and had brought the design screaming into the twentieth century, when requested to do so by the bold and creative Markhams. As customers arrived at the Lancaster Markham's for the first time, they stood transfixed by the curves and gentle slopes of the exterior, and when entering, received another jolt with the large mosaic patterns in the floor tile, giving the illusion of anything but right angles. It was shocking, but still very maneuverable…easy on maintenance, as well.

This one? Well, this one had to shine in an already glittering market in the Ohio capital city. This one had to capture the essence of Paris, of Venice, of New York…this one had to be "Elegance" with a capital E. Elegance used lots of gold, black marble, white marble, expanses of glass. Fred had nearly gutted the sturdy brick building on the corner of South High and Mound Streets in Columbus. Only a block from its biggest competitor F. and R. Lazarus, Fred had the idea that the Lazarus Building was ugly and pragmatic; for Markham's, he wanted magnificent and pragmatic, a challenging mix. The creative builder, with Mary Rose and Edward's input, designed full-panel glass windows which, although perfectly rectangular, used gilt design at the top to give the illusion of gentle, arching space…centered around the Roman letter M for Markham's, of course, which had become a trademark. The family had given him carte blanche to add the newest in electrical lighting for those windows, and although the exterior dimension had changed very little, the windows and magnificent gold-framed double entryway door on both streets also had the brightest and most attractive of lighting in the entire city. The final result was eye-popping!

As Billy Blake Markham continued his perusal, his thoughts frequently returned to his builder, Fred Hunt, who had done so much with this cavernous space…and thanked his guardian angel for the decision he and his father had made to hook their wagon to his star!

The first department within the entrance was jewelry and small gifts. What was the purpose here? he asked. To draw the eye to collections, groupings? Yes, that made sense, and that seemed to be what was happening. The valuable, more expensive jewelry, although locked within glass cases, was strikingly displayed on either black or deep purple velvet, and Mary Rose had selected scarves, gloves, even hosiery, to garnish those cases, helping a woman to visualize her entire outfit, and thereby justify her purchase.

Mary Rose had helped Edward and Billy Blake to understand a woman shopper's mindset; a married woman tends to feel guilty at indulging herself, to think of what the children need, what the home needs, even what her husband needs, before considering luxuries for herself. Therefore, the "justification" element was an essential one in creating displays aimed at women. For this reason as well, she had suggested that some displays in the jewelry and cosmetics departments attract male buyers with little reminder signs, such as "Wouldn't she look lovely in these?" or "Have you forgotten how much she does for you?" Men were much more likely to spend money on luxuries…and not feel the need to justify them.

But for the women who did wish a luxury or two, subtle messages were communicated, showing multiple ways, for instance to wear one piece of finery. She had taken an elegant ruby-toned crystal brooch—an expensive one—and shown it pinned to a velvet hat, closing a scarf, on an evening bag, and attached to a string of pearls, in one small but breathtakingly beautiful display case right in the center of an aisle where it was impossible to miss. For this case, Mary Rose had selected a backdrop of deep wine brocade and had surrounded the entire interior perimeter of the case with sprays of well-crafted, artificial lilies-of-the-valley and seed pearls. Billy stopped in front of this case and felt himself pulled into the vibrant elegance, just the sensation he would want for his customers. "I've got to hand it to her, she'd good, that woman of mine," he admitted. "This is wonderfully done. Wonderful balance…"

As he moved on, he frowned at a case which seemed to have no central idea, no theme at all, just women's cosmetics lined up in nice military rows…neat, but unimpressive. "No, this won't do. They look like they are marching off to war, not yearning to go home with beautiful women." He stood in his habitual pose, legs slightly spread, right elbow resting in left palm, the way he stood when smoking a cigar, but without a cigar to hold, his right hand cupped his chin, an odd pose…and he studied the case intently until a theme planted itself in his mind. Only then did he step behind the case, open it, grasp a pretty dressing-table hand mirror for a base, and group items of a scent (lilac, of course, for Mary Rose) together on the mirror: cold cream, dusting powder, astringent, and cologne, for which he located an atomizer as an accessory, one which was attractive with the mirror, and a tiny silver-plated hairbrush…when completed, a boudoir theme, intimate, elegant, and intensely feminine. "Not bad for a man," he congratulated himself, thinking in terms Mary Rose and her best friend Jane, who now thought of themselves as suffragettes, would have enjoyed! Clustering the remaining items behind the display group, he stepped in front, peered critically, and decided it passed, not with the finesse his wife would have provided, perhaps, but certainly much better than before.

He was learning from Mary Rose's instincts, though, and had become much wiser with display. Noticing with satisfaction that two ladies had discovered the display he had just created, he nodded to them with a smile and gestured to Miss Seldon, who was the clerk for the cosmetics area, to offer her assistance to the female shoppers now clustered before the case, noting with pleasure that she was already aware of the potential sales and wearing a warm, sincere smile was on her way to greet them.

The salespeople who graced Markham's Stores were well chosen. They had to understand Edward's philosophy of putting the customer first, and he and Billy had helped to train the Columbus group for several weeks prior to the early-November opening. He wished that Mary Rose's friend Jane Neeley lived in Columbus so that she could work in the store. She had quite a gift with people, Edward had noticed; she had come up with Mary Rose on two Sundays in a row to put special touches on the displays as well. "Lovely little Jane…I wish she were here… but if wishes were horses, then beggers would ride," Edward had said in his special, flowery way, and of course, Jane had another life.

So…fourteen women and three men were now representing Markham's in the Columbus store. Billy Blake felt confident that the forty-year-old widow Blanche Seldon was one of the better employees, one with intelligence and natural charisma, able to read what the customer didn't say as well as what she did say…and lead that customer gently to just the right purchase. She was also gifted at accessorizing, a strategy which raised the dollar sales figure but added to customer satisfaction: "That scarf is brilliant for you, Mrs. Roberts! You need to see the suede gloves we just received! They would be perfect with the scarf…" and so on. Smart sales technique, true, but even better for bringing customers back again and again, looking for her expert guidance. It was a hard technique to teach…one either had it or one didn't. Fortunately, all the Markhams had it, and so did this excellent sales clerk. Edward already had his eye on her for a management position if she continued her excellent standard.

Actually, the eldest Markham son Harry had found the male sales staff, a fact which shocked but pleased both Edward and Billy. Although not interested at all in selling, Harry was becoming a very good judge of character, a possible outgrowth of his study of law, and, no doubt, the hours he had been forced to hang around the store in Caldwell as a teenager. He had taken three days off from Harvard in early October and traveled to Columbus to help Edward interview for sales positions. His recommendations were astute and all three of the men he recommended had indeed been hired and trained: Bob Wiggins now sold luggage and leather goods; Tully Sullivan worked part-time in the shoe department, and Alfred McLaughlin was the assistant manager and part-time bookkeeper…good hires, all. Billy was proud that his brother had found a different way to support the merchandising empire the Markhams were building.

As different as they were, Billy loved and respected his brother Harry-the-Lawyer; Harry also worshipped Billy Blake. Billy often thought with pride that Harry may not be a merchant but he was most certainly a Markham to be proud of, an asset to the family tree…and, it was turning out, to the family business as well. One day, when James Clavenger retired, the Markham clan would have its own family barrister!

The ambience of this newest of Markham's stores was definitely different from all the others, more upscale, more elegant, geared more toward a city crowd than the General Store in Caldwell, more than the Dry Goods store in Nelsonville, for instance. Edward and Billy had talked at great length with their attorneys, with their builder, realizing their architectural and design concept was not only ahead of its time but possibly even out of its element. But with Mary Rose's encouragement, the company had decided to trust the people of Columbus, to open a New York store in Midwestern America, mainly to prove that it could be done, and in Columbus, home of Ohio State University, to prove that Columbus was more than a "cow-town."

Once the building was renovated and stocked, all that remained was to bring in the world! That was a breath-holding time for the Markham group. If people didn't come…it was all in vain. So, using New York advertising mentality, the family had stretched its advertising budget on this one, using large newspaper ads but also some letters directly to other merchants in Columbus and to customers of the Athens, Nelsonville and Lancaster stores who lived closer to Columbus. Direct mail was an expense, indeed, but it seemed so personal—and the one thing Edward would never change, Billy knew gratefully, was the personal nature of his stores, the way the sales staff learned customers' names, the way customers trusted Markham's staff to teach them about fashion and to help them afford lovely new things without destroying the family budget. And as Billy scanned the now-packed aisles of his latest project…he breathed a giant sigh of relief and pride: They came!

* * *

As Billy Blake continued his circuit of the new store, Edward was doing his own research, chatting casually with customers as they shopped, but mentally logging the information he gained: where they lived, what they did for a living, what they liked in a store, and most important of all to the mercantile kingpin, what they would like to see Markham's do in the future.

This "mental research" was one of Edward's specialties, one he believed was his primary reason for success: walk, smile, chat, listen, log and process. He had learned even more than he hoped! They—his Columbus customers—liked the F. and R. Lazarus store up the street for many reasons, but one reason was that they offered services Edward hadn't considered: free delivery, free gift-wrapping, and even a coffee shop where they could rest before another onslaught of shopping. His mind was already churning and the floor plan being examined for a restaurant; he made the decision on the spot to buy out the tiny shoe repair shop next door, if he could, to turn it into a restaurant which could be accessed both from within the housewares department or from South High Street. He could barely wait to get home to begin to formalize the plan! He knew Fred could find a way to make it happen…and in record time.

Now, in his late fifties, Edward Markham had a finger on the pulse of retail. His ability to adapt his business approach to the market was drawing interest from newspaper reporters and other merchants. Although he gave interviews frequently, he continually minimized his marketing genius, attributing his success to listening. Frequently coming under fire from so-called marketing "experts," Edward would smile, nod, demur, and continue to thrive. His sons Billy Blake and Stewart were "apprenticing" every time they watched their father conduct an interview, always leaving the reporter somewhat frustrated at learning no new, brilliant, college-graduate marketing secret; they had already learned a cardinal rule he taught them, that one never makes oneself look better by making one's competition look bad. None of the Markhams ever had anything but praise for the competition: "Oh, you shop at Lazarus? Good for you! Lovely store! Now you have another new 'home away from home'!"

Edward stood back near an outer wall and surveyed his latest project. The white marble flooring was terribly expensive, but added so much class, he decided, and also made the store look much larger and cleaner than did the polished dark oak his other stores had; a good investment, he determined. The archways which divided the four major segments of the lower floor were graceful, adding visual variety but not a true wall, smart for the flow of traffic. Yes, this was an architectural success, Edward declared, and from the looks of the seven first-floor clerks who were all busy ringing purchases or showing items to delighted customers, the grand opening was on its way to being a financial success as well. Nodding to himself immodestly, the patriarch moved off in search of his sons and daughter-in-law who were also taking the pulse of the new business.

The bustle of business generated noise, enough noise to let customers know that others had also found their shopping Mecca, but what could have been a din in the cavernous space the new establishment had been when empty was now muted by fabric swags which graced the archways, by fabric wallpaper in false arch patterns. The interior designer Edward had hired to take over where Fred Hunt left off had indeed been worth every dime. This store looked ritzy yet approachable, the model Edward had been trying to achieve, pricey yet somehow affordable…a feat accomplished partly by Mary Rose's instincts about packaging, creating multiple uses, coordinating.

Edward had to check himself from looking too self-satisfied…but that he was! This store, the fifth star in the Markham crown, was the pinnacle, the apex of his work. Starting with a general store in Caldwell, a store much like its predecessors in the previous century, brought to a coal-mining town, or a railroad town, or the like, a store which was practical, which catered to the needs of the public, this store was nevertheless a very different genre. This was New York, maybe Paris…brought to Ohio! And all by a small-town man who had never been to college, never been to Paris, not even to New York.

At that moment, Mary Rose placed her hand on his arm. "Pleased with yourself, are you?" she purred quietly, one eyebrow raised, "You're practically humming…"

He chuckled at his daughter-in-law's intuitiveness. "You nailed it, missy. Look at them! They love the store! They love the atmosphere! They love your displays! We have something to be proud of, my dear," and he embraced her quickly. "But let's go see how Stewart is holding out…" And they walked together toward the elevator alcove. Glancing down at Mary Rose, he admired how sophisticated she looked today, and how fit and relaxed, in spite of having a baby at home less than seven months old. "Are you tired, dear? You've been on your feet, and on those high heels all morning."

"Dad, I never felt better! You know I could spend hours in the stores…but I imagine the children might not like that idea, nor, for that matter, would Sarah. She has a family of her own…" she answered. It was true: Mary Rose sparkled when she put on her "store face," as she called it. The vivacious young woman leant an air of warmth and hominess to their marketing endeavors, but never let it be thought that she was any less shrewd in a business sense than her husband or father-in-law. Edward knew, although he had never mentioned it to Billy Blake that in a crisis, she, his clever Mary Rose, could carry on with their work without missing a beat. She knew women; she stayed current on fashion. But she also had an amazingly keen sense of numbers, could keep books, cut corners, stretch money better than either of the men could do. Her instincts about design and display had been astute, and she was now the main window-dresser for the Nelsonville store. In fact, her New Year's Eve display had won a designer award for the Nelsonville store, the first ever in the Markham's chain.

When the Columbus store was ready for its pre-opening publicity, she traveled up from Nelsonville to work on windows with Alfred McLaughlin, the manager, who had actually attended art school, but who had found himself deferring frequently to Mary Rose's startling and effective ideas. The two of them had decorated all nine of the massive display windows, five on High Street, the other four on Mound, and the *Columbus Citizen* had done a full-page spread featuring several of the striking, artsy windows…the best kind of publicity, free publicity!

It had been her idea to "fly" merchandise, to have it suspended from strong but invisible cables, utilizing the space within the windows, drawing the eye upward as well as laterally. An amazing woman, Edward knew, with an innovative mind. He could barely imagine what trick she had up her sleeve next! Ever since an ad in *American Woman Magazine* had intrigued her with its asymmetric design, she had been using the "fly" strategy, odd diagonals, unusual juxtapositions of graceful curves and stark angles as well as color combinations and fabric contrast which jolted the eye.

Evening strollers in the downtown Columbus area found themselves mesmerized by Mary Rose's creations, standing for minutes at a time staring at the startling designs and admiring the merchandise. All of this framed, of course, by the Fred Hunt-created gilt-framed show windows. Many of these evening strollers were the early customers today at the grand opening, their appetites whetted for a week by the astonishing brilliance of the windows. This was merchandising at its best, Edward knew: the special Markham touch, Edward and Billy Blake to prospect locations, to negotiate deals, Frederick Hunt to put the Markham visions into realities, Mary Rose to apply her artistry, even Harry to use his astute observations about character, and devilishly clever Stewart to charm and flatter...quite a dynasty, the patriarch thought proudly, a cat-like smile playing about his lips.

Chapter 24 – Fashion Show

[New Years Day 1911]

The room took a collective gasp as she stepped out of the burgundy velvet curtain; the silence held for two seconds, three seconds…then she began to walk, right foot directly in front of left, left in front of right, her head held high, shoulders swaying in opposition to her hips, sensual but regal at the same time. Although her heart pounded like a hammer and sweat slicked her back and chest, no indication of her fear reached the audience. She approached the end of the platform which was arranged in a T-shape, pivoted gracefully to the left and strode confidently to the edge of the T, where she paused briefly, frozen into a pose worthy of a sculpture by Michelangelo, one hip jutted forward, head looking over her right shoulder…and one by one, just a single sound, then two, then more, the stunned audience began to murmur and applaud.

The first sound to reach her ears was a buzz of commentary, just below the level of audible; she was afraid to breathe, unsure of what she was hearing, but when the symphony of applause penetrated her focus, the model took a deep, ragged breath, dropped her head just slightly to make eye contact with Mary Rose Markham and Jane Neeley, standing frozen in the archway at the back of the main entrance, arms linked, who were also not breathing and in danger of oxygen deprivation…and her face broke into a wide, confident smile, dazzling the audience and breaking the tension in the room. Seeing that smile, Jane and Mary Rose applauded wildly, jumping up and down like children, hugging each other and wiping tears.

The model pivoted again, and hips swinging, moved, sleek and cat-like, to the opposite end of the T, her hand throwing the sheer lace cape open to reveal a form-fitting evening gown of caramel satin, low cut in back, off the shoulder, featuring a bodice of ivory closely woven lace, gathered to an x between her breasts and captured with a broach of mother of pearl. The gown was simply cut but of exquisite design…and no one could have shown its classic silhouette better than the stunning beauty Sarah Washington, her skin the shade of café au lait.

The professional make-up artists Mary Rose had hired for this New Year's Fashion Extravaganza had been taken aback initially when they saw this subject, but as they began to work rouge into her high, angular cheekbones, they found themselves excitedly searching their supplies for just the perfect glittery mocha eyeshadow, just the right dark plum shiny lipstick…completing a work of art which nature had already begun, staring in admiration at her in the mirror as they worked.

There was no doubt: Sarah Washington looked magnificent. She glowed in these garments. As shocked reporters scribbled frantically, their excited heads bobbing up to look at the model, down to their tablets, back to the model, they too wore smiles, knowing how newsworthy this fashion debut was. "Trendsetting" was a word many of them applied to this show; "shocking" was another. Not only had Markham's moved into the world-class network of fashion with this, its fifth store, but it had dared to cross a barrier which was only now being attempted in Paris: a fashion model of color! The reporters, just like the other audience members, were stunned, it was true, but as the buzz in the room escalated, those news hounds scanned the faces to see the reactions, and scribbled some more, as shocked by the approval they saw as they were by the model. One by one, they scuttled out the door, incredulous but excited, heading for their offices or the nearest telephone, each hoping to be the first to break this astounding story.

Although five beautiful models showcased Markham's garments today, including one other lovely graceful amateur who worked for Edward as a sales clerk, it was Sarah Washington who brought the house down, a small crescent-shaped headdress set with mother of pearl to match the broach and one very long ostrich plume serving as an exclamation point to her fashion statement. So many tall women tend to wear flat shoes and minimize their height; here was a woman, 5' 10", wearing chocolate patent leather high-heeled shoes, extending her neck to accentuate its elegance…and she was breathtaking.

Proudly, Sarah exited the stage, turning for one last pose at the curtain, savoring the applause. Back of the curtain, as several of the Markham's sales girls who had volunteered to help with the fashion show assisted Sarah and the other models to change their garments for the final entrance, Sarah realized that she was trembling and felt weak, giddy, in fact and slightly nauseated. Sitting for just a moment to regain her composure, one of the young assistants whispered shyly in her ear, "You were beautiful out there. They loved you."

Turning a grateful smile on the timid young lady, Sarah replied, "Gracious me! I didn't realize how nervous I was! Thank you so much for helping me." With that, taking a deep cleansing breath, she regained her feet and slipped out of the evening gown which the young lady placed on a hanger, into a handsome chocolate brown motoring suit with mid-calf-length skirt, the newer, shorter length making it easier to get into and out of automobiles which were the latest rage. Low leather boots looked sporty but still sophisticated; a wide-brimmed hat with very sheer white chiffon scarf which tied under the chin completed this outfit, a very different look from the first. Her make-up refreshed, checking herself in the mirror, Sarah thought, with a small chuckle: "Not bad. Now if I had an automobile..." But she was ecstatic that her employer...and friend...Mary Rose Markham had the courage to face possible disgrace by asking her not only to attend but to actually model in this show. It was a dream come true...

* * *

Newly promoted store manager Blanche Seldon watched the costume change from the corner of her eye as she fussed over the garments being returned to a rolling rack. When Mrs. Markham had begun to plan this show, Blanche had been excited, had believed that the already-successful store would reach an even bigger market with the publicity generated by this event. She knew Lazarus had an edge on the Columbus market, but Markham's was rapidly establishing a toehold, in spite of...or perhaps because of?...the owners' tendency to reach outside of traditional, accepted business practices. But Columbus was a conservative Midwest city. New York, to the residents of Ohio's state capital, was as far away as Paris and just as foreign.

Her skepticism, which she wisely kept to herself, had reached its limit when Mrs. Markham had shown her the line-up of models for this, their first ever New York-style runway fashion show. A colored woman, walking the runway, wearing garments designed for wealthy white matrons? Would this step be the one to break the Markhams' chain of successes? Had they finally gone too far?

Yet Blanche had to admit Sarah Washington was a beautiful, classy colored woman, one who looked like she could fit in with the upper-class colored, the wives of doctors and lawyers, who were slowly but surely finding a place in Columbus society. When Sarah stepped through those curtains, Blanche had held her breath in fear: would this be the loose brick which would topple the fortress? Would the Columbus women be horrified and angry that a colored woman was being held up as a figure to emulate? Blanche nearly fainted as the gasp and its ensuing silence reached her ears.

Peering out through a crack at one end of the curtain, she felt her stomach churn as she saw the wide eyes and open mouths of the women in the first few rows…as those women looked at each other, eyebrows raised, then back at Sarah, time stood still for Blanche. She couldn't tell, by perusing their faces, if their shock was in horror…or in awe. Although it was probably only a few seconds which went by until the first few hints of applause began, it was the longest three seconds in Blanche Seldon's life…and then she heard it, clapping, a buzz of conversation. Releasing her suspended breath in a gush, which rendered her slightly light-headed, she realized that the buzz was one of shock, yes, but even more of surprised approval.

Relief flooded over her, replaced rapidly by exhilaration as she watched the faces turn from shocked to dubious to approving. Watching also the runway, Blanche had the impression that Sarah grew even taller and more imperial as the atmosphere in the room exploded. "Who would have believed it?" Blanche murmured to herself, "Who would ever have believed it?" Then she answered herself: "Well, of course, Mr. and Mrs. Markham would have believed it…I should have known…"

Now, as Sarah dressed for the final act, the outdoors ensemble, Blanche Seldon had to admit that, as usual, the Markhams were right. This was working. Not only working, but making a brave statement. Sighing with a mixture of relief and pride, she stepped toward Sarah, touching her arm lightly, saying, "Mrs. Washington, you were wonderful out there. Congratulations."

"Mrs. Seldon. It was…it was like nothing I ever felt before. But you made it possible, picking beautiful garments…anyone would look good in them…"

"No, it was you. And of course, Mrs. Markham who knew how you would look and handle yourself. Now go out there and show them one more time what stylish Ohioans will be wearing this year. Here, let's open this top button; it looks more relaxed. Do you have the gloves? Yes…all right. Here. Let's just wear one and carry the other. That's good; here you go," as the stage director beckoned to Sarah, Blanche gave her a warm, encouraging smile and a gentle push toward the runway, and then returned to her favorite vantage point, at curtain edge so that she could watch both the runway and the audience.

* * *

Sarah's eyes filled with tears at the praise, but she fought them away and stepped out, as elegant in brown linen as she had been in satin. Her head felt awkward with the large hat, but she peered out beneath the brim with a bemused expression, transferred her leather glove to her left hand, opened the remaining buttons as she did a full turn, revealing a tailored white silk blouse tucked into the waist of the skirt. Applause filled the air; she noticed with amusement that the music was "In My Merry Oldsmobile," appropriate for the outfit, but not easy to walk to! She picked up her stride, a jaunty bounce now, and the room went wild with sound.

Prepared this time for her entrance, the audience had been waiting to see her a second time. The outfit she was styling was an expensive one, and hard to wear, perhaps, unless one was tall and stately, but with the eternal suspension of reality which always accompanies women when they watch magnificent fashions parade before them, every woman in the room was visualizing herself in the rich, stylish motoring suit, oblivious to height, weight, body type. The longing was almost visible as a cloud in the room, longing for the clothing, for the height, for the bearing, the elegance now being displayed. Somehow the model's color had become a non-issue, at least for the moment, to all who gazed in admiration at Sarah Washington...

...all, that is, but for a widely scattered few, a pair of narrowed eyes here, an angrily pinched face there... Wise enough to notice the uniform chord of approval in the room, these scattered few seethed silently, insidiously. As it always is with people who bear a mountain of hatred, those few found one another's eyes in the cheering crowd; thoughts were transmitted, resentment transferred, hostility reinforced. Ugliness of thought and intention persists, in spite of evidence that it is not the common sentiment in a room, and when starved of company, it creeps out into that room and seeks out other minds and hearts equally closed to beauty. Uncanny...a barely perceptible nod of the head, a gesture toward a darker corner near a side entrance and a subtle migration began. Lost in the sound and animation of hundreds of applauding men and women, these movements were not noticeable from the stage, nor from the back entrance where Mary Rose Markham and Jane Neeley stood, beaming and clapping madly, nearly hysterical with joy.

Moving only a few feet at a time, the dissenters reached the intended alcove at nearly the same moment. Few words were exchanged; enmity required little language. As the size of the group grew, so did the anger. Individual thinking became collective thinking. Seeds were sown.

* * *

As she scanned the faces of the crowd, Blanche Seldon could barely contain the pride and thrill she now felt. Having recently received her promotion to women's fashion manager, there was little she wouldn't do for the Markham family, who had trusted her with so much responsibility. It was exciting and gratifying to see that the choices and judgments her employers had made were coming to positive conclusions. She chuckled as she watched her employer and her friend acting like giddy school girls, dancing around each other and laughing as the fashion spectacle drew toward its finale. Mary Rose Markham could be so businesslike and professional at one moment and then downright silly at the next, Blanche thought, with an affectionate smile; that was one of the reasons she was so well-liked by the staff of E.A. Markhams. "Real," they called her, not uppity or snobbish, and her husband was…well, just a love of a man. Blanche was also aware half the young women who worked in the store had a fancy for young Mr. Markham…but he was most definitely taken!

Blanche continued to scan the audience, the row of reporters near the entrance, all looking like cats with a bird in mouth…then her eyes fell on a group of men and women who were clearly not sharing the excitement of the moment…watching them, their incensed faces communicating silently, her joy turned into dismay as she read disturbing emotions on their faces. "What ever is going on back there? Who…oh, my! That doesn't look at all good…" her thoughts whirled. She counted, the best she could see from her limited vantage point, nearly a dozen people, huddled together in conversation, peering from time to time at the stage then back at their associates.

Sarah Washington had just finished her triumphant walk through the curtain to thunderous applause. The other four models were lined up, ready to strut onto the stage for the finale. Blanche took one last look at the unpleasant knot of people, then scurried back to the center of the curtain to give one last tug here, pinch there, so that all five lovelies would look their loveliest for one last moment. As she complimented them, fussed with ruffles, straightened bonnets, and listened for the musical cue she had been given…"Meet Me in St. Louis"…she shook off her worried look and replaced it with a broad smile, which felt frozen. "Let's go, ladies! Look at that crowd! They want to eat you for dinner! Give them one last taste!" Blanche encouraged them, as the musical cue reached the backstage. Off they went, in rapid succession, strutting to the music, pivoting, posing, and giving the audience one last delicious look. The sound in the room was nearly deafening; the louder the applause, the more the models pranced.

Dead-center, Sarah's final position was center stage and a brilliant centerpiece she made! As the planners of this extravaganza had specified, the models reached their final position and froze, looking like beautifully sculpted mannequins. It was hard on the muscles, but the effect of the maneuver was powerful. They held, held, held as the crowd was ushered out, receiving at the door a photographic review of the garments they had seen this afternoon. Only when the doors were closed, with the audience out and Mary Rose, Jane, Edward and Stewart in, did the women relax their pose!

"Relax, ladies! You were nothing short of splendid!" called Billy Blake Markham, applauding them himself. As the women relaxed, working stiffened muscles and chatting among themselves, Edward marched toward the stage. Quieting quickly as the much-revered patriarch of the Markham family approached, the models smiled expectantly.

"First, I would like to say that everyone who stopped to speak with me was more than pleased with what you hard-working women did today. You showed them, not only stylish clothing, but character. You looked proud and strong and intelligent. My daughter-in-law tells me that is the image modern women are striving for today," and the people in the room chuckled, the women nodding in agreement, Mary Rose linking her arm through her father-in-law's.

Edward continued, "Now, go back and get dressed and join me in the Blue Room. I have a surprise: a luncheon catered by Morrison's Café, complete with champagne! And no one is watching weight today!"

As the models left the stage to be assisted with their garments by Blanche Seldon and her hand-picked crew, the four Markhams and Jane Neeley took seats together at the rear of the room, realizing how much energy their tension and excitement had utilized. Edward looked unruffled, but Mary Rose, Billy Blake and Stewart were still finding it hard to sit still.

"Did you see Carol Ann in that evening gown, Dad? I think that was one of the best moments...well, maybe second best..." Mary Rose bubbled. "I am so proud of Sarah! I can hardly stand it! She just took over the room, didn't she?"

"That she did, my dear. You were right. Did you hear that? I said 'You were right,' didn't I? Write that down!" Edward teased.

"No need. I have it memorized! But you were the brave one, you let me hire Sarah. Oh, Billy, she was so scared this morning, I almost cried for her. She was convinced that she wouldn't remember the steps Carol Ann taught her, or would fall or something. Jane walked her through her positions over and over...Jane could have done the show if the clothes would have fit her! So, Dad, did anyone say anything about Sarah?"

"Lots. Lots of things like, 'beautiful,' 'spectacular,' and lots of words like 'wow,' and…well, a few said 'brave' and 'shocking'…do you see me smiling? That's what we were hoping, daughter of mine. Stewart, how did you know that purple dress I thought was ugly would look so good with the right accessories? Oh, and on Maria, of course…" Edward teased, punching Stewart's arm, knowing Stewart had taken quite a fancy to the youngest of the models. Billy Blake snickered as Stewart blushed handsomely.

"Just runs in the family, Dad. Smart, ya know?" the just-turned-nineteen-year-old replied. "So let's go eat!"

"Why not? All that nervous energy made me hungry enough to eat this chair! So, Markhams…and Mrs. Neeley…let's go join our stars in the Blue Room," Edward replied, rising to his feet and pulling Mary Rose and Jane into each arm.

"After you, kind sir," Jane teased. She adored this wooly bear of a man who reminded her of what her father might be like now. His moustache was like Theodore Roosevelt's and he had recently adopted the round, metal-rimmed glasses of the President, but the resemblance stopped there, as Edward Markham was tall, even taller than his two sons, still walking erect and proud. He liked to pretend he was gruff, but no one was fooled for long. The Markham men just couldn't help being charming, Jane mused, as she was treated like part of the family for this very special occasion or for any occasion, for that matter.

As the ecstatic Markham brood joined their tired but equally thrilled employees and models in the Blue Room, another group of individuals were meeting at the coffeeshop just across the street from E.A. Markham's. Talking very quietly, nevertheless, hate was spewing out, building steam and boiling over. Plans were made. Evil was cultivated. The Markhams would regret this latest insult to humanity, all vowed.

Chapter 25 – By the Light of the Silvery Moon

[January 1911]

The moon rose, full and shimmering, in the January sky, lighting the scene with an unearthly glow, light objects appearing green and luminous, dark objects, shadows only. It was eerie, all right, but also strangely hypnotic. The winter air was crisp and biting with brisk wind through the denuded trees along the canal. Billy Blake Markham drove slowly and cautiously along the state route which connected Columbus and Nelsonville, unnerved by the bizarre ghostly appearance of objects along the road and the way moonlight distorted his depth perception. Relieved to see the Nelsonville City Limits sign, he realized he had been holding his breath, which he released in a puff of fog.

Despite the cold, both Mary Rose and Jane had nodded off to sleep, crowded in the seat beside him, the rumble seat out of the question in January. Although he could have used the company to stay awake himself, he let the women sleep. They had worked hard on the inventory in Columbus and it was a long ride back home. As a matter of fact, they had worked hard the whole week since the fashion show, and for that matter, the week before it. On this return journey, the women had chattered for the first hour, oblivious to their male companion, but as drowsiness and fatigue won out, they had drifted off, almost at the same time.

Smiling to himself, Billy Blake recognized how much alike the two were, how they often read each other's thoughts, finished each other's sentences. It was good, he knew, good for Mary Rose, even better for Jane, whose life hadn't been an easy one. Her husband Bud's recent promotion to mine foreman was a blessing, a credit to his hard work and quick intelligence. The salary, though, allowed them to move to a house off the mine property, and to hire some help for the boys. And Bud's sister had come to stay all week, enabling Jane to spend the time away.

Edward had insisted on paying her for her work, which she had objected to initially, but realized she was earning her pay and it would help out with "new home" bills. She loved to travel with Mary Rose—both on store business and to work on their suffrage mission—and now she was able to do so more easily, and with Bud's blessing.

Billy Blake had to give Bud a lot of credit. He hadn't objected in the least when Jane had asked to spend the week in Columbus with the Markhams, staying at the Great Southern Hotel so that they could begin work bright and early. That was a trusting man and a loving one, Billy recognized. "Good man, Bud Neeley…" Billy Blake mumbled.

The silence gave him time to ponder the past week's dizzying occurrences. Only a week had passed since the extravagant and daring fashion show in Columbus which had rocked the central Ohio marketing world. Edward Markham had done it again, the papers declared, had set the pace for boldness in fashion, both with his courageous use of non-traditional architecture and artistic displays of bold garments the likes of which Columbusites had seen only in the pages of *Vogue Magazine*…and with his bringing of a New York fashion show to this Midwestern city. "Was Columbus ready?" the *Citizen* questioned, answering its own query with, "…obviously, judging by the excitement of the crowd attending the Markham's New Year Fashion Extravaganza" and "one source reported nearly being trampled by the sea of animated customers, competitors, and reporters." Its fashion section had devoted three full pages to the new E.A. Markham's store and the fashion show!

Billy Blake and Edward had worked alone, although exhausted, on January 2, the day after the show, in the office on the third floor, waiting like Broadway producers for the newspaper reviews…whooping at full volume when the paper boy brought them their copies and they saw the store's bold exterior gracing the entire first page of the fashion section! Together they opened the paper—and there, covering three of the four-column width was a photograph taken at the foot of the T-shaped stage, that photo snapped just as Sarah Washington struck a confident pose, one hip jutting forward, her hand on the brim of her motoring bonnet. She looked both stunning and professional, father and son agreed, but the caption disturbed them: "Sarah Washington, family servant and would-be author, takes center stage. Is nothing off-limits for the Markhams?" That was disconcerting, to say the least.

It had not been an easy decision, Billy Blake remembered, putting Sarah in the show. For several months, Mary Rose had searched for a way to involve Sarah in the stores, a way to honor Sarah's request to work with them. Ideas had come and been discarded. She had asked only to wait on customers in the Nelsonville Dry Goods store, but that prospect worried both Billy and Mary Rose. Nelsonville wasn't...well, it was a northern town but not nearly as modern in its thinking as cities farther east. Blacks and whites kept a nervous peace, one which dissolved when events in other cities, such as the one in Springfield, Illinois, in 1908, reminded the citizens that with emancipation had come competition, competition for jobs, for housing, even for success in business.

Nelsonville existed—and prospered—primarily because of the demand for coal; black miners worked the mines in an almost equal number to white miners. In the depths of a coal mine, color was irrelevant, skill, training, a willingness to work hard at a back-breaking and dangerous job being the only qualifications.

On the surface, however, relations were strangely different. White men who would find no trouble passing a coal cart to a black man found great difficulty passing hard earned money over a counter to a black banker, or having their hair cut by a black barber...and wouldn't dream of inviting a black man home to dinner or over to play poker in the shed. It just wouldn't occur to them to do so. In some ways, the women seemed even more inconsistent, more biased in their choices. A colored nanny or housekeeper was the preference, and with that choice went trust. Nevertheless, when searching for a fourth for a quilting party or bridge, that same woman who had been entrusted with the white matron's children suddenly became invisible, never an option as a personal associate.

Mary Rose had discovered this uncomfortable and disconcerting discrepancy only recently, in the early fall, when she and Jane had decided, after much deliberation, to invite Sarah to join them as a guest at a lawn party in Mary Rose's expansive back yard, celebrating her favorite season and enjoying the last of Ohio's brilliant days. At first Sarah had declined, offering instead to tend all six of Mary Rose and Jane's children. Mary Rose Markham, however, rarely took no for an answer and her will prevailed.

It was only a week after Mary Rose and Jane had convinced Sarah to join them at a suffrage meeting, and, buoyed by the success of that venture, the two had risked including Sarah in a more social endeavor.

The menacing weather of the previous week had, fortunately, given way to Ohio's magnificent "last gasp"—Indian Summer. He remembered how his wife had described the afternoon. Sarah had dressed carefully and discretely in a plain beige linen dress with small hat, in which she looked lovely, but nervousness jolted her as she stepped off the back step of the Markham's expansive porch to walk toward the refreshment table which had been set up on the back lawn, shaded by a lovely apple tree. Many neighbor women had come into the yard and, seeing Sarah, assumed she was acting as a servant, giving her drink orders, which both embarrassed and infuriated Sarah. Others who recognized her as the author of the scandalous *Pride Goeth* simply snubbed her altogether.

When Mary Rose noticed Sarah's pinched face and asked her what was the trouble, Sarah had initially denied any trouble, but when pressed, explained that she didn't belong there, not as a friend. Although Mary Rose disagreed vehemently, and despite her later efforts to include Sarah in the groups of ladies sitting on the porch discussing their children, or in the croquet game in progress on the lawn, those efforts were to no avail. The white women, while not outwardly rude, made it clear they found it objectionable that a black woman was attending in any role but servant. Conversation simply went silent. On that day, Mary Rose bid goodbye to many a friendly acquaintance, vowing to have no more to do with women of such narrow views.

All this had been reported to Billy when he arrived back at home following the party, finding his wife and Sarah both silently doing dishes and moving about one another in the kitchen, stiffly, wordlessly. Always sensitive to his wife's moods, he deduced quickly that the party had not been a roaring success, but it took Jane, who was straightening up the back yard, to fill him in on what had transpired which was causing the awkwardness between Mary Rose and Sarah.

"She was wonderful, Mary Rose was, Billy; she stood up to those women and told them Sarah was her guest. But it didn't make any difference, after all. The biddies drank their punch, lifted their noses toward Sarah, and left. It was awful." Jane had explained, shaking her head sadly. "I wanted to strike them! You know, Sarah handled it with so much dignity, but I could see she was really hurt. I will never understand what makes people think the way they do...do you understand it?"

"No, not really. I think sometimes people are just afraid of what they don't know. The women my wife knows aren't bad people, but they only know one way, I guess. What a shame. Sarah Washington is worth ten of those narrow-minded wenches. Is Sarah all right, do you think?" Billy queried.

"It depends on what you mean by 'all right.' You saw her, didn't you? Did she seem all right?" At that moment the back door opened and Sarah came onto the porch, her satchel in her hand, her face solemn.

"Mr. Markham, is there anything you need before I go home? There's some sandwiches left in the kitchen, and lots of fruit..." Billy Blake Markham locked her in eye contact and her words stopped.

"Sarah, you have no need to wait on me today. Thank you, though. And Sarah?" He paused, weighing his words. "There will be another party." Her eyes filled with tears which she fought valiantly to hide.

"Not for me. But thank you. Now I do need to get home to Paul and Marcia. I will be here at nine on Monday. Miz Neeley…thank you for including me in your plans."

Jane had been standing silent, but at that, she rushed to Sarah and gave her a hug. "It's Jane, Sarah. Not Mrs. Neeley."

Unsure what to do, Sarah patted the small woman's shoulder, fighting more tears.

"You're a good woman, Jane. I'm glad Miz. Markham…uh, Mary Rose… has you for a friend."

Looking up into Sarah's warm, sad eyes, Jane replied softly, "And you are a good woman and a friend, not to mention the bravest person I know.. She's lucky to have you, too. I will see you next week," and she stepped back with a smile.

Not sure what to say, just nodding, Sarah walked away from them and down the driveway, looking weary but dignified, moving toward the steep hill which led to her home on Beatrice Street.

Looking after her sadly, Billy Blake remarked to Jane, "That was nice of you. I don't know what to do. It seems so unfair, doesn't it?"

"Yes. And that is exactly why Mary Rose and I go to our meetings…for women like Sarah, not just like us." Sighing, she went on, "I wish there was a way to shake people up right now," and she stepped onto the porch and through the back door, leaving Billy Blake standing looking off in space.

After a moment, he moved to his gardening shed and removed a pair of shears. Working with his flowers always helped him think. This time was no exception. An idea had begun to take shape. "Hmmm. Maybe there is a way," he remembered musing, as a plan presented itself.

Striding to the back door, a half-dozen late blooming peonies in hand, and into the kitchen, where Mary Rose and Jane were finishing the clean-up tasks, Billy Blake startled the women with, "I know what we can do! I've got it! Nelsonville might be too provincial to appreciate Sarah, but Columbus shouldn't be!!"

Stopping their tasks and gawking at the quiet man who was speaking in such an uncharacteristically energized manner, they exchanged puzzled looks. "What, Billy? Do about what? What are you talking about?" his wife queried.

"Let's take Sarah to Columbus to work sometimes. Then if that goes well, we can…well, we'll think of something…" Billy Blake stopped, looking thoughtful.

Mary Rose and Jane were still staring at him, but as his words sunk in, they looked at each other, questioning. Both minds were working synchronously, not uncommon for those two. Little by little, all three began to smile and nod.

"I think you are the smartest man in the whole world, my lord and master," cried Mary Rose as she moved to hug him.

"Of course I am! I married you, didn't I?"

"Yes, you did, oh clever one. Now scoot out of here so we can finish up this mess and then gossip! Heaven knows we have enough to gossip about, after the fiasco this afternoon! We'll have some fun after all!" Swatting at him with a dish cloth, Mary Rose shooed her husband to his favorite spot, the back porch, while Jane watched with a laugh.

The mood of doom and gloom was gone. The two friends finished their afternoon replete with giggles and whispers, sounds Billy Blake Markham loved to hear.

Later that night, as he and Mary Rose lay in bed, he had said to her, "My dear, what if we take Sarah to Columbus for the grand opening, and see how she handles herself? We'll have to figure out something for the children, of course, but Mother might help out. Once we get the store opened, if Jeremiah doesn't object, I think she would like that. I really think the bigger city might be more accepting, you know?"

Silently, Mary Rose pondered his words. "You know, I think they would. Columbus has lots of black people, professionals, even, always has…I think you've got something!"

"Okay, let's talk about it at breakfast. You are right about her, you know. She is worth a lot more than those spoiled, empty-headed floozies…" Kissing her forehead, Billy Blake pulled the sheet up and turned out the light.

"Goodnight, you wonderful man. We'll talk…"and she fell instantly asleep. That always amazed Billy Blake, how his wife could fall asleep in the middle of a sentence!

* * *

It was nearly midnight as Billy Blake sleepily pulled his Model T onto Fort Street, the last leg of his journey home. He was exhausted and very glad that Jane was spending the night; another five miles to her new home just south of Nelsonville would have been the straw that broke the proverbial camel's back. Lost in reverie and fatigue, he didn't notice at first, as he turned off Columbus Street onto Fort, that the sky seemed unusually bright for a winter midnight, but as he began up the hill, his attention was drawn to a glow unlike any he had seen before with natural causes. He was suddenly wide awake.

An alarm went off in his head and he reached his left hand over his right arm to shake Mary Rose's shoulder. "Honey. Wake up. Something's not right…wake up!" It took a good shake to pull her back from her slumber world. Finally her eyes opened, as did Jane's.

"What…hmmm? Are we home? What did you say?" she asked, trying to shake off the fog of sleep.

"Look. Look at the sky. Mary, I think that's fire!" His gut wrenched with fear. He was almost certain he was right, the glow was from a fire…and it was coming from the direction they were traveling.

Fully awake now, Mary Rose's eyes were wide and her face blanched with fear. "Oh, my god, Billy! The children! Oh my god…hurry!" She gripped his arm in terror.

Jane grasped her other hand, frozen in fear as well. Her boys were with the Markham children, and all of them were in the house with Sarah. Jane closed her eyes and gripped the gold cross she always wore since her marriage to Bud, his wedding gift to her. "Please, God, please…"escaped her lips, her hand clutching Mary Rose's with a force which would have surprised both of them, had their attention been anywhere but on the ominous glow ahead, which now was obviously filled with sparks and black smoke.

Tears sprung unbidden to Mary Rose's eyes; her breathing was shallow. "Billy, is it our house? Go faster…" But he was already pushing the car to its limit on a steep hill. Just a few seconds and they would crest the hill…hearts pounded in unison.

The first thing the terrified trio saw when reaching the top of Fort Street hill was a blaze reaching high into the night…but the house, in smoky shadows, was standing intact. Confused, Mary shrieked, "What's burning, Billy? It's not the house…what IS that?"

Unable to answer her, he was forced to pull the car to the side of the road fifty yards from the driveway…because the crowd of curious and horrified onlookers was so thick he couldn't travel any farther. Before the car had reached a full stop, Mary Rose and Jane were out and running toward the house, fighting their way through the throng of horrified but fascinated neighbors, ignoring Billy Blake's shouted pleas to wait for him. The sound of the inferno was deafening, crackling and roaring; Mary Rose and Jane's desperate voices, calling for Sarah and for their children, were lost in the din.

Closer and closer they clawed their way toward the house, tears of fear and fury blinding them. As they reached the edge of the lawn, both of them stopped to get their bearings and began to frantically search the crowd for children, for Sarah. Mary Rose shouted to Jane, "The house looks all right! Let's cut through this way," grabbing her hand and pushing yet another crowd out of their way as they fought their way up the gentle slope of the lawn.

Peering back over her shoulder, Jane cried, aghast, "Oh, mother of God, Mary…it's a cross. They're burning a cross…look! That's what it is…oh, those devils!"

Mary Rose paused briefly, her mouth agape, looking the way Jane was pointing. "Ooohhh! Who did this? Why?" and with a gasp and a brisk head shake, "…come on. Let's find the children…" Pulling Jane with her, she rushed toward the back of the house, toward the porch.

As the two terrified mothers cleared the hill and leaped for the porch, through the crackling came the sound which they had prayed to hear: "Momma! Momma! We're here, Momma!" Just past the back porch, huddled together near Billy Blake's gardening shed were six children, one in the arms of Sarah Washington, who had been protecting them from the ashes and flying sparks with her own body. The five older children broke loose now and charged to Mary Rose and Jane as Sarah, cradling Will, sank to the ground, sobbing and keening in terror. Within seconds, Billy Blake's long legs brought him to the frozen tableau of children, mothers and caregiver, all locked together in an embrace and wailing in relief from pent-up terror and in sorrow and confusion.

As Billy Blake did a silent role-call and found all present and accounted for, the rage in him grew to unbearable proportions. "Attack a man's family and you attack his soul," Edward had always said. Disbelief mixed with anger; he extended his arms to encompass as many of his loved ones as he could, as his tears mixed with theirs, his agony met theirs. But the fury grew unchecked.

The fire raged on, despite feeble efforts of the fire department to extinguish it. The burning cross was more than ten feet high, a specter no one was likely to forget, one which would haunt dreams for years to come. Looking over his shoulder toward the fire, his eyes fell upon the dark side of the house, the side edged by the driveway. Something was there, darker than the house, reflected for a second at a time as the wind shifted, carrying flames and their unnatural light to creep into the darkness. His face contorted as he read, painted in huge black letters on the white wood shingles: "Nigger lovers." Letters fashioned in a childlike hand…but spawned of an evil no child could fathom.

As he gaped incredulously at the words which defiled his home, he saw from the corner of his eye one pair of sorrow-filled brown eyes watching him. Sarah had raised her head from the huddle comprised of women and children, followed his eyes and seen what he had discovered. Now she looked at him silently, years—or centuries—of grief mirrored in her eyes. He met those eyes, read in them responsibility, culpability. "No," he mouthed to her. She just nodded slowly, her face in the darkness revealing agony.

One by one, the combined family members released their hold on one another and regrouped, mother and children, weeping still but more calm than a minute earlier. Mary Rose was the first to notice the silent communication taking place between her husband and Sarah. "What, Billy?" she asked, then followed his eyes to the acrimonious message on the wall. The pain on Sarah's face suddenly made sense and was almost more than Mary Rose could bear. "No, Sarah! You didn't do this. No!" and she reached her hand toward Sarah.

Sarah's head fell forward, her shame a burden too heavy to withstand. "They came because of me…" she choked out. "I saw them building it…and I couldn't do anything…the children…" She began to rock back and forth in the ageless posture of unbearable grief, tears coursing down her cheeks.

"When, Sarah? Who did you see?" Billy Blake asked, his hand on her shoulder.

"Don't know…they wore…hoods. They came because of me…I should've known…"

Nine pairs of eyes watched her in silence, grieving at her grief, the smallest children frightened to see their mothers and their caregiver broken, weeping. "The picture in the paper…the one of me…it was wrapped around a brick…they threw it through the window in the sunroom. That THING was already burning…I thought the house would burn…the children were sleeping but…I didn't want to scare 'em but…" she shuddered, took a ragged breath, coughed. "I couldn't think…get 'em out, was all…blankets to keep 'em warm…the house didn't burn…thank the Lord…" She stopped talking, sunk to the cold ground, oblivious to the freezing temperature.

Mary Rose broke the silence. "Sarah. You are a hero. The children are safe. You didn't know this would happen…none of us did. The children are safe. You are safe…" Weeping, she stepped toward the woman huddled on the ground, opened her cloak, took it off and wrapped it around Sarah's shoulders.

The gesture restored reality. As Sarah regained her composure and rose, shaky but in control, the four adults rapidly assessed the safety of the home.

Determining that no embers smoldered, no sparks had taken hold, Billy herded the group to the back porch. "Wait here, out of the wind. I'll be right back," he ordered.

The homeowner strode past the defilement and stepped back into the glow of the fire, which was being battled now by the fire hoses. The flames had subsided; one arm of the cross loomed dark and charred but was no longer burning. Billy Blake sought out the fire chief, Clarence Johnson, finding him back by his truck, assessing the situation. Startled to see the home owner, the chief called, "Oh, Mr. Markham, you're here! Is everyone all right? Mrs. Markham and the children?"

"Yes, they are fine…physically. Johnson, is it safe to take the children inside? They're so cold…but the fire…is the house safe?" turning worried eyes toward the roof of the porch.

"Yessir. We wetted down the roof, the walls closest to the fire. I just inspected the perimeter for hot spots. The damage is minimal, mostly smoke…" He stopped, eyeing the cross which now smoldered, the tendrils of smoke making it look even more sinister. "We'll get this…thing out of here once it is cool enough, but there'll have to be an investigation, you know…this sort of thing hasn't happened in Nelsonville…"

"You do that, investigate all you will," Billy Blake spat out. "Take a look at the north side of the house for your investigation, too. For now, I'm taking my family and friends inside." Billy Blake Markham turned on his heels and bypassed the smoldering symbol, glaring at it as he passed. Circling the south side of the house, he visually inspected, seeing nothing out of order.

Seeing him come from the south side, Mary Rose stepped off the porch to meet him. "What did he say, Billy? I saw you talking to Clarence. Did he know who did this?"

"No. Nothing. Come on, Johnson says it's safe to take the children inside where it's warm…" His anger made it difficult to breathe. His thoughts swirled as he led his flock back into his embattled home.

Chapter 26 – Three Stand Tall

[January 1911]

Smoke filtered through the cracks around the door and through the broken window, but not enough to make the house unsafe. As Billy Blake Markham shepherded his traumatized group into the front room, he noticed, with a look of agony, that the smoldering abomination was still visible through the front windows, no longer aflame but still menacing. Pulling the curtains closed, he caught his wife's eye, asking silently what to do next. His mind had gone blank.

Picking up his cue, Mary Rose spoke softly. "Sit down, everyone, rest. Sarah, will you help me get water for everyone? Billy, we'll be right back." She pulled at Sarah's arm, hoping to restore her from her nearly catatonic state. Meeting Sarah's eyes, Mary Rose willed her back. Wordlessly, Sarah moved, trance like, the direction she was being pulled. A child or two still sniffled, but Jane had somehow gathered all of them into her lap and her arms and was rocking, rocking and humming tunelessly, hypnotically. It seemed to be working; eyelids began to droop, heads lay back against her, but still she moved, as if transfixed.

Just inside the door to the kitchen was a comfortable breakfast nook which the family used more than the dining room. It was warm and intimate, allowing Billy Blake and his family, while breakfasting, to peer out at his garden and at the bird feeders he had hung nearby. Mary Rose led Sarah there, walking her to the first bench and gently pushing her down to the bench, sliding in next to her. Out of sight of the children now, what little control Sarah had maintained melted away and she began to tremble violently, silent sobs racking her shoulders.

Putting both arms around Sarah's shoulders and locking her hands together, Mary Rose held tight, resisting Sarah's attempts to turn away. Whispering in her ear, "It's over. It's okay. Everyone's okay." Mary Rose let her own tears flow as well. How long they sat that way, neither could say, but it must have been several minutes before Mary Rose noticed that the trembling had stopped. Pulling back to look at Sarah's face, she saw grief and a haunted agony, which broke her heart over again.

Mary Rose realized Sarah was speaking: "It's because of me. They did it because of me. I should've expected it…because of me…" Sarah's voice was lifeless, monotone.

"No! Not because of you! They did it because they are stupid and cruel and wrong-headed! You did nothing wrong…THEY did. And we're all right…the children are all right…you protected them…it's all right…"

Shaking her head sadly, Sarah moaned, "No, it'll never be all right. Th' children…they could've…oooohhhh…Lord have mercy…" and her tears began again, her eyes shutting in an attempt to block out what was indelibly printed on her brain.

"Look at me, Sarah," Mary Rose implored. "Look at me, please." She released her grip of Sarah's shoulders and used one hand to gently turn her in the seat, then to raise her chin. "We all knew what we were risking. Billy Blake knew. Jane knew. None of us were willing to be beaten by hatred left over from who knows when. You are the bravest woman I have ever known, Sarah Washington. Brave and strong. The children have you to thank for their safety. You would have willingly given your life to protect them…wouldn't you?" She forced eye contact. "Wouldn't you, Sarah?"

Sighing and nodding, Sarah rasped out, "Of course. But they wouldn't have been in danger except for me…"

"No! That's not true, Sarah. People who do things like this put everyone's children in danger every day. I am so blessed, Sarah. I have a wonderful family…and you are part of it. My children have another woman, someone besides me, to show them right and wrong, how to stand tall and not back down to ignorance and stupidity. How to be a woman, be a man. Don't you dare let this break you! Don't you dare!"

Hearing, but doubtful, Sarah nodded, her eyes shutting over the horrific specter which still tortured her. "Yessum…if you say…" Sarah replied without conviction.

"I do say. I know I speak for Jane, too. We are proud of the things we have done together, the three of us. WE started this, not you, and we wouldn't change it, even now. Yes, it's been scary, dangerous. But it's right, Sarah. It's the way things are supposed to be. You know that."

Sarah nodded slowly, thoughtfully. "Yes…" she said again. Mary Rose later swore she could feel Sarah's spirit re-entering her body at that exact moment, as the agonized look turned to simple grief, now tempered with acceptance. "What about that water we were bringing the children? D'ya think they forgot?" A tiny smile fought to break through.

Together the two women prepared a tray of water, juice, and glasses and another of cookies and fruit; each carrying one, they walked back into the parlor…where everyone but Billy Blake now slept. Seeing them, he put his finger to his lips, motioned to them to stop in the dining room, and rose to meet them. "Jane just dropped off herself. She has all six children on top of her…how she can sleep under that…"

"She's amazing, that's how," Mary Rose responded gently.

Billy Blake spoke softly: "Sarah, Chief Johnson told me a minute ago that Jeremiah was here."

She looked up, worry showing in her tired face. "Oh, my, he must be frantic!"

"Well, not any more. He saw the flames from your house and was afraid for you and the children, so he ran down the hill looking for you. The chief assured him you were fine and so were the children. He told Johnson that he would wait at your house with your children. He seemed lost at what to tell the kids, but he asked Clarence to let you know that he was taking care of your family and would try to prepare them to listen when you get home."

"Should I go, I wonder…the little ones might wake and need me…oh, I don't know…"

Sarah seemed incapable of making the smallest decision, she was so traumatized from the incident. Billy Blake pondered a moment, then said, "Stay, Sarah. Jeremiah is a good man and he can handle it, now that he knows you are safe. You need to rest more than anything else. Stay tonight and I will take you home in the morning."

Acquiescing, Sarah's fatigue seemed about to render her senseless, but she insisted on helping Mary Rose with the food. The three adults shared a light meal in weighted silence, seated at the round dining room table, surprised that they were hungry.

Outside, the last of the horrified neighbors trailed back inside their homes, leaving the Markhams in peace. Slightly refreshed but all suffering from the exhaustion which follows on the heels of terror, Sarah, Mary Rose and Billy Blake carried the sleeping children upstairs to tuck them into bed, covered Jane with a quilt, and agreed that Sarah should sleep as well. She curled up on the sofa and was immediately asleep. Billy covered her with one of Mary Rose's afghans before turning out the light.

As Billy Blake and his solemn wife crept into their bed, silence fell over the house at last.

* * *

Dawn crept through the front windows of the Markhams' home, tiny fingers of pink and buttery yellow, caressing the cheeks and shoulders of six sleeping children and four exhausted adults. Outside, it sought to bathe the grisly reminder of terror and hate with cleansing light.

A few early rising spectators had returned, their morbid curiosity insatiable. Police Captain Terry Prentice and Fire Chief Johnson huddled together yet again, shaking their heads in dismay and confusion. Their five-hour investigation had revealed absolutely no concrete evidence. Prentice was thankful Chief Linbach was away on family business or he would have suspected a sinister involvement. The name Wilton Smith sprang easily to both men's lips, but they both realized that that was too simple; this wasn't the work of just one man. This crime was bold, even for Smith; Fort Street was a heavily traveled thoroughfare in Nelsonville. Prentice had a hunch that this was the work of outsiders.

Terry Prentice wasn't surprised that there had been violence as a result of the Markhams' bold step. Chief Linbach had slammed the *Tribune* down on his desk three days earlier, opened to a photograph, picked up from the *Columbus Citizen*, of Sarah Washington walking the stage in Columbus. His face had contorted in hate and disgust. "Hell and damnation, will those Markhams never be satisfied? They'll have every nigger in Ohio wanting to be teachers and lawyers, even mayor and governor…we'll have a nigger uprising, you mark my words! They'll never stay in their place now!"

Stomping out of his office in a rage, Linbach had left Terry Prentice and Officer Jerry Matheny exchanging disgusted and worried looks. It occurred to Prentice again that his boss might have some involvement with the Klan…but no solid evidence had ever connected him.

Linbach was shrewd…no scandal was tied to his name, although the community knew how he felt, knew his heart was cold.

As Prentice poked through the rubble at the foot of what remained of a ten-foot high cross, his mind raced through recent events, whispered innuendo, personal hunches.

Markham had brought him the brick and its wrapping. No surprise there, he realized. He needed to talk more with Mr. Markham, he knew; there might have been threats or warnings which the Markhams had chosen not to report. This was a tragic situation, no doubt, made just bearable by the fact that no one was injured, the house was still standing.

As he continued to examine the rubble, the front door of the Fort Street home opened and Billy Blake Markham, rumpled and groggy, stepped toward them. Surprised to see him this early, Prentice strode his way. "Good morning, Mr. Markham. I didn't expect to see you so early. Did you get any sleep at all? How are the others?"

"Everyone is still out. Terry, who did this to us?"

"I wish I had an answer for that, sir. No one saw anything…you know how that goes."

"Oh, they saw," Billy Blake hissed. "They're afraid, obviously. I would be too, I guess, in their place. Maybe someone will come forward and tell what they saw…or maybe not…there is no way someone could build a ten-foot cross and light a bonfire on a public street and no one see it." Billy Blake shook his head, ran his fingers through his tousled hair in frustration. "The Klan, of course…you may never catch them…"

Sighing deeply, Prentice replied, "That's what I'm afraid of, Mr. Markham. We know a few of the members, Smith, Clooney, that Wilson guy…the ones everybody knows about, but the others? Who knows what evil is buried beneath the smiles of bankers, businessmen? And they're bold and getting bolder. The Grand Dragon sends out letters to the newspaper, and no one can figure out who HE is."

"Your boss, maybe…" Billy Blake replied bitterly.

"Uh…I wouldn't know, sir," Terry Prentice responded, his eyes averted.

"Well, keep me informed, please. I know you will. How soon can I start to clean up this…thing? I don't want my family to look at it any longer than they have to."

"We should be finished pretty soon. Is Mrs. Washington okay, sir? She was so brave with the children last night, but it was obvious she was terrified. Almost couldn't talk…I tried to talk to her, to reassure her, but she just turned away and sheltered the children. Poor woman…" Prentice said.

"She took it hardest, of course. My wife talked to her, but she blames herself."

"Of course. Well, give her my best, and of course, Mrs. Markham and Mrs. Neeley too…we'll be out of your way soon."

"That's okay, Terry. Do what you've got to do." Billy Blake turned and started back to the house. Before he reached the porch, however, he heard the sound of a horse and buggy approaching from the south. Turning, he saw Bud Neeley pulling over to the side, his face incredulous and blanched as he stared at the remains of the charred cross.

Hurrying out to meet him, Billy Blake spoke first. "She's fine, Bud. They all are. It's just the yard…they're all asleep, but they're fine, I promise you."

"Who...would do... such a hateful thing?" Bud stammered in rage and shock.

"We don't know. But you need to know Jane and the children were never really in any danger. When we got home last night, it was burning like crazy but Sarah had the children all out behind the shed, safe, in case the house caught. It was pretty awful...but everyone's okay. Jane was amazing. She had all six of the children hanging on her, crying, even Ronnie and Frankie, and somehow she got them all settled down and to sleep. Come on in. The others are still sleeping, but I'm sure you want to see for yourself that your family's safe." Billy Blake headed back toward the house, Bud at his side, fuming silently, his heart lurching erratically.

Before they reached the porch, however, the door opened and Mary Rose, Jane and Sarah, all looking disheveled and exhausted but composed, stepped onto the front porch to see what was left of the spectacle. Seeing Jane, Bud bolted toward her, just as she leaped into his arms, fresh tears starting. They stood silently, locked in an embrace, weeping quietly, looking first at each other, then at the rubble, then at nothing, just holding on, eyes closed. He murmured, "My darlin', it's okay, darlin'...you're okay..."

The others turned away, giving Bud and Jane some privacy. Just as Billy Blake reached the women on the porch, he saw Jeremiah literally charging down the hill, his long legs extended, toward them all.

"Sarah! Sarah!" Jeremiah's voice called, as he raced the remaining half block toward her. Rushing past Bud and Jane, her fatigue vanishing, Sarah met him at the edge of the yard and flew into his waiting arms. He held her at arm's length and examined her closely for injury, then, satisfied, pulled her back into a tight embrace, rocking her gently.

"I'm okay, baby. I'm okay," she crooned as he rocked her back and forth in his muscular arms. "Everyone's okay."

"I was so scared, Sarah, but I know'd you could take care of ever'body. I wanted to stay and help, but the children...they was scared, an' they couldn' stay alone..."

"I know, I know. Are they all right? Did you tell them what happened? Where are they now? Who's with them?" Sarah questioned, concern clouding her face.

"Miz Gordon saw the fire and come over las'night. I as't her to come back this mornin' so I could come here. She's with Paul and Marcia. They're scared but okay. I told'em you'd tell'em all about it when I brought you home." Locking her back in his arms, Jeremiah just held on tight, smoothing her hair with his strong hand. "I was afraid o' somethin' like this…I knew somethin'…" but she shushed him with a kiss.

His jaw set in a grimace, his hazel eyes filled with emotion, Jeremiah looked into his wife's intelligent, grief-filled eyes, eyes which were imploring him to understand. Suddenly, he did. He felt her passion, her vision infuse him with energy, with determination. He spoke with an intensity which surprised even himself: "Yes. We are right. You are right. You have to write it, and keep tellin' it until everyone hears. We have t'do this, Sarah…stand tall. Stand for what we know is right. Or they'll crush us all…" He raised her chin, put his arm around her shoulder and walked with her back toward where the Markhams and Neeleys waited, declaring, "And that's not gonna happen."

Shaking hands with Bud and Billy Blake, Jeremiah met their eyes with dignity. They read his message. Bud, his arm around Jane, said softly, "This isn't going to stop our women, ye know. We have to be as strong as they are, help them fight for what's right. It's not just their fight. It's everyone's fight…or the Lord help us all."

"It is indeed. They have shown us how to stand up and never back down. I, for one, think we are blessed with three powerful, brave wives," Billy Blake proclaimed, reaching out for Mary Rose. "I think the world had better watch out!" And he gave her his signature wink.

On the charred front lawn they stood, in proud, defiant silence, three men, three women, peering at the remnants of last night's terror, the morning sun gilding their faces.

Epilogue – Ghosts of Boomtown

Nelsonville, Ohio: It is now a sleepy, quaint, rambling town of fewer than 5000 souls, settled delicately into the foothills of the Appalachians. A two-lane state highway bisects it. The highway went through over fifty years ago but still displays the backs of homes and retail establishments as if the bisection happened yesterday. One often wonders when the residents of those homes would catch on to the fact that their homes' backsides were now exposed. Those who know well the history of this southeastern Ohio town know, however, that the houses once faced the canals which were the lifeblood of Ohio commerce in an earlier century. They also know that many ghosts reside in the town, ghosts of miners, of settlers, of factory workers, canal boat operators, and soldiers...friendly ghosts. Ghosts of runaway slaves, their pursuers, those who aided them...mournful ghosts. Ghosts who molded the history of the town...and continue to watch over it.

A half-century ago in Nelsonville, going to the swimming pool on the other side of the highway meant going down "to the canal" in a local vernacular. The expression is hard to understand without knowing the rich but troubled history of this quaint, homey town. Myers Street, or perhaps North Street, traverses the route once taken by giant coal barges. Segments of crumbled wall, built of the strange yellowish block created in the Hocking Valley, back by the railroad tracks, are the only remaining remnants of the once-mighty Hocking Valley Canal. Canal Street, the local street which carries the United States highway through the town, was built along the site of the old canal. The canal once carried coal, iron, and salt from the mines to their destinations, either north to the Great Lakes, or south to the Ohio River.

Just before the turn of the last century, the budding railroad caused the demise of the canal systems. Trains could move greater quantities of coal, salt, and clay much more rapidly than the canals. For a very long time, the Hocking Valley Railway, affiliated with the Chesapeake and Ohio, was a strong, unifying force for a coal-mining boom town. Now it is but one locomotive which takes the sightseer on a 13-mile scenic track through the breathtaking rolling hills into the past. Other cars sit idle and rusty on abandoned track a quarter mile south of the scenic railroad site, adjacent to apartments, an anachronism and a curiosity for children and nothing more.

The train station looks just the way it did in 1920, history preserved for future generations. It allows passengers, while purchasing tickets for the scenic trek, to examine photos and memorabilia of a long-gone era, an era when Nelsonville was the hub of prosperity and glamour. All aboard the Hocking Valley Scenic Railroad. This tourist adventure into the past is not only educational and enjoyable, but also symbolic: Nelsonville itself seems to be just one scenic trek into the past.

The heart of the town, a picturesque public square, complete with Civil War monument, is warm and welcoming, with a huge iron fountain which still works—sometimes. Nearby, several ornate metal benches allow friends to chat while watching the local children skateboard in the street, or during various holidays, to enjoy high school choirs and elementary pageants. It was once the setting for a Hollywood movie—many years ago, but the locals still refer to those exciting film-making days as if they happened yesterday. Residents of Nelsonville are into nostalgia; they don't have much choice.

In a necklace encircling the square stand a few dozen buildings solidly built in the mid- to late-1800s, all in good repair and fully utilized, the First National Bank built in the 1880s and still operating in its original location, for instance. One such pearl is Stuart's Opera House. A sturdy brick structure of three floors, it was built in 1879, closed in 1924, but recently refurbished. Theater groups use it often and well in an effort to return it to its glory days in the Roaring '20s and earlier, when coal mining brought wealth and excitement to Nelsonville.

Nelsonville was, in 1907 or so, the center of not only Athens County commerce but of much of southeastern Ohio commerce as well. Elegant and yet comfortable, the Opera House today stages plays on the upper floor where a theater-goer is awe-struck by the acoustics and by the richness of the wood flooring, much of it left unencumbered by rugs or furnishings The floor gleams as it must have when Elsie James, the queen of Vaudeville, performed to a packed house.

The theater seating, while not original, does nonetheless further develop the image that one has somehow stepped into a time warp. Lighting is simple but effective, electric, of course, but with the ambience of gas light romance. Cherry red drapery and gold cording hint at the opulence of the nineteenth century and several exquisite antiques—a ruby velvet arm chair, a roll top desk, an intricately carved upright piano, among others—complete the upper floor.

Below, entry level, a bar area, all turn-of-the-century wood and brass, is used for refreshments which theater patrons may enjoy in one of the five or six period armchair groupings scattered throughout the lobby. It is an enticing experience, spending time in the reconstructed past of Stuart's. It is difficult not to feel the presence of some of those performers and their appreciative audiences of over a century ago. Ghosts, yes, but agreeable ones…

Another gem in the necklace is the Dew Hotel which also dates back to before the Civil War. It too has had a rebirth in the past decade. One imagines elegant carriages with graceful steeds pausing in front of the entrance while brocade-garbed, bejeweled ladies and their waistcoated escorts disembarked. It was grand once; it deteriorated into a claptrap through the 1960s and was saved, just barely, from the wrecking ball only by its placement, along with Stuart's Opera House, on the Historical Register in the 1970s and also by the valiant efforts of local citizens. The good people of Nelsonville have always fought valiantly for their town; they have needed to fight, fight for Nelsonville's very survival.

A large covered balcony graces the second level of the Dew House, large enough, perhaps, for thirty or more couples to waltz, in pleasant weather, to the strains of "The Blue Danube" wafting from the lobby. During the Christmas season today, festivals brighten the ambience of sleepy Nelsonville. Many use the covered entrance to the Dew for large kettles of wassail and homemade soup, their aromas floating in the air, pulling visitors by the nose, and thrusting them back 150 years.

Presidents Harding, McKinley, and Theodore Roosevelt campaigned vigorously in Nelsonville. During their time, it was a flourishing center of activity, drawing families from surrounding towns to attend plays and operas at Stuart's or to listen to Teddy's gruff but mesmerizing speeches from the balcony of the Dew. There was good money in coal mining then and the ripple effect allowed merchants to thrive.

Unfortunately, the fortune from coal didn't extend to the men from whose agonizing labor the profits were made. Their lives were bleak, their families often living in dire poverty. Families of miners in the southeastern Ohio towns like Nelsonville became known as "patch families." Tiny vegetable "patch" gardens supplemented the very limited income of the miners, providing just enough food to survive. In earlier days of coal mining, the men and boys were not even paid in cash, but rather in chits or scripts to the "company store," a term made famous by Tennessee Ernie Ford in his sad and true ballad "Sixteen Tons." What an injustice, profiting from the hard work of those miners and then requiring them to buy what little they could afford from the company store, thereby exploiting them yet a second time…

In the twentieth century, coal companies ceased the practice of paying by chit, but miners still had little choice but to purchase their needs from those company stores, as transportation into nearby towns was often difficult. Those employed by the businesses which encircled the mines, however, found excellent selection in the stores of Nelsonville. Stores such as Markham's prospered. But when the coal industry was no longer a viable one, Nelsonville took its first of many serious hits, reducing the majority of the citizens to worse than poverty. Those who could do so left for other areas which still needed miners; many worked piecemeal at other industries. Most just shuffled from place to place, hoping for better, finding worse.

Much of this fascinating town is fashioned from the product of another local industry, brick and strange-looking brownish red block. Where there is good coal in the hills, there is good clay, and southeastern Ohio is known for the best clay for bricks and paving blocks. Many of the block factories stand silent now, giant kilns providing forts for local urchins who conveniently ignore the "No Trespassing" signs. These remnants of the past are indeed tempting, their igloo appearance inviting further exploration. In many of the outlying areas surrounding Nelsonville, in Haydenville, for instance, the kilns are accompanied by rows of identical block housing, a few occupied yet, the majority derelict. These were "company homes," residences for the workers who stoked the furnaces, prepared the clay, molded the blocks in a once-prosperous industry. These strips of meager homes are much like the coal industry, now. While not totally extinct, both are breathing dying gasps, a factory here, a mine there.

A new plaque at Diamond, a tiny village on the northwest edge of Nelsonville, proclaims proudly that one is now entering the original home of "Star Bricks." These odd, incredibly sturdy bricks can be found seventy-five miles away in the German Village area of Columbus to this day. They rattle one's bones as an automobile travels over them. Nelsonville and Athens have as many brick streets as they have asphalt. At one time, most of the brick streets in Ohio were made from bricks crafted at Diamond or Haydenville.

Haydenville, site of one of the area's largest brick factories, is five or so miles from Nelsonville, and is fashioned almost exclusively of rows and rows of brown Nelsonville block homes, so identical to the eye that one can barely imagine coming home after a Friday night in a local bar and actually finding one's own home! These bricks bear the imprint of a star and the words "Nelsonville

Block" and are holding up to wear very well. Another thriving, proud industry which supported families—not in wealth, certainly, but a sustenance—has now dried up to one last factory—how many blows does this lovely, nurturing town have to endure?

One more blow, evidently. November of 2001 was the last time the assembly line in downtown Nelsonville produced Rocky Boots. Rocky Boots are worn around the world and are known as some of the finest footgear hunters and laborers can possibly find. An outgrowth of the Brooks Shoe Factory which dates back to the 1940s, Rocky Boots provided jobs for hundreds until the exodus of American-made products to Korea, Taiwan, Mexico, forced Rocky Boots to begin outsourcing, just to survive.

It is hard to imagine Nelsonville without the shoe factory; there was always a shoe factory! A significant percentage of the blue-collar workers from Nelsonville have worked on the assembly line at Brooks-turned-Rocky Boots. The patriarch of the remaining Brookses and CEO of Rocky Boots, Michael Brooks, is a proud third generation resident of Nelsonville. Brooks protested in the 1990s, "If it can't be made in Nelsonville, Rocky Boots won't make it," then had to eat his words only a year or so later.

The number of hard-working souls employed dropped suddenly from several hundred to just 72; those faithfully laboring, proud craftsmen and -women hung on valiantly, but in November of 2001, the dreaded announcement came: Rocky Boots was shutting down the line. Tearful workers hugged each other, shook their heads, looked around, not wanting to pick up that last check and go home—never to return.

Once again, Nelsonville must shoulder the grief of its residents, who hold their heads high. Like the few surviving miners, they know they did their jobs with dedication and skill, but the world no longer requires those skills. Those skills served them so well in this place at this time, but few of those workers have the types of social skills and additional job skills which would make them employable outside Nelsonville. So what to do now?

Looking ahead in Nelsonville? Who knows? Looking back…they came to Nelsonville by horse, by train, on foot, in droves, in families, alone…but they came. The Markhams came to Nelsonville to develop a marketing empire amid the excitement and prosperity of its boom days. They lived, loved, raised their family and died there; their remains rest in Greenlawn Cemetery.

The Neeleys followed the coal mines from Pennsylvania through Perry and Vinton Counties and finally to Nelsonville. They struggled and their lives were fraught with woes…but they too died there, buried nearby in Keeton Cemetery.

Sarah and Jeremiah Washington came, first generation freed blacks, to this northern town to find a home. They found that home but they also found racial hatred, more disguised than what their parents, freed slaves, endured, but nonetheless enough to make "land of the free" a debatable description. Nonetheless, they stayed. They lived, they loved, they raised their family…and they endured.